BROKEN CROWN

USA TODAY BESTSELLING AUTHOR

T.K. LEIGH

BROKEN CROWN

Published by Carpe Per Diem, Inc

Cover Design: Cat Head Media, Inc.

Cover assets:

© 2023 willeecole

Used under license from Deposit Photos.

BOOKS BY T.K. LEIGH

ROMANTIC SUSPENSE
The Temptation Series
Temptation
Persuasion
Provocation
Obsession

The Broken Crown Trilogy
Royal Creed
Fallen Knight
Broken Crown

The Inferno Saga
Part One: Spark
Part Two: Smoke
Part Three: Flame
Part Four: Burn

The Possession Duet
Possession
Atonement

The Beautiful Mess Series
A Beautiful Mess
A Tragic Wreck
Gorgeous Chaos

The Deception Duet
Chasing the Dragon
Slaying the Dragon

Beautiful Mess World Standalones
Heart of Light
Heart of Marley
Vanished

CONTEMPORARY ROMANCE
The Dating Games Series
Dating Games
Wicked Games
Mind Games
Dangerous Games
Royal Games
Tangled Games

The Redemption Duet
Commitment
Redemption

The Book Boyfriend Chronicles
The Other Side of Someday
Writing Mr. Right

For more information on any of these titles and upcoming
releases, please visit T.K.'s website:
www.tkleighauthor.com

For a free eBook, sign up for T.K.'s newsletter.

https://www.tkleighauthor.com/newsletter-signup

Or scan the code below

PART I

Doubt

"Doubt is an uncomfortable condition,
but certainty is a ridiculous one."
~ Voltaire

CHAPTER ONE

Esme

I tap my fingernails against the armrest in the back seat of the SUV, staring out of the window, the city alive with tourists and locals enjoying one of the first nice spring days. People sit at sidewalk cafés. Or pose for photos. Or hop on a boat for a tour of the canals. It's the type of day I'd typically spend outdoors, basking in the sun on my face as I celebrate the end of winter.

Not today, though.

Sadly, my father has other plans.

What those plans are, I have no idea.

Which is why there's currently a heavy knot of dread weighing down my stomach.

It's taking every ounce of resolve I possess not to fidget with the hem of my skirt or chew my nails down to the quick. Every few seconds, I steal a glance at Archie in the front seat. As always, his expression gives nothing away, including why my father ordered me to the palace for an unscheduled meeting.

On a Saturday.

Whatever he needs to speak to me about must be important.

Which only makes my unease grow.

My mind goes through all the possible reasons my father might want to see me.

One stands out amongst them all.

My surprise visitor last night.

I bite back the infectious smile threatening to form on my mouth from the memory of Creed practically barging into my apartment. I've pinched myself countless times since he left early this morning, wondering if I imagined it all.

But my sore muscles and the ache between my legs is evidence I didn't. That Creed and I have finally found our way back to each other. I didn't think this would ever happen. Thought he'd carry the guilt of Adam's death for the rest of his life.

It was because of that guilt I kept the truth from him.

But last night, I realized by doing so, I'd added to his burden. If Creed knew Adam's final act on earth was one of selfless love for his brother, maybe he'd realize he deserved the happiness Adam was willing to sacrifice everything for him to experience.

And that's exactly what happened.

The second I revealed what happened that night all those years ago, every single wall Creed had erected around his heart came crashing down, the chains shackling him to a life of regret and shame freeing him.

Freeing us.

But now I worry we weren't as discreet as I thought.

Creed had assured me he was careful, using the back

service entrance to the grounds of Gladwell Palace so the guard stationed at the front gates wouldn't see him. He even parked in the staff lot and walked to my apartment.

Did someone see him anyway?

Did we already screw ourselves before we've had a chance to be together?

God, I hope not.

After what seems like an eternity, Archie finally pulls the SUV through the imposing gates of Lamberside Palace and continues toward the private entrance leading to my father's personal residence.

The instant the SUV comes to a stop, a man in the standard butler uniform of a red jacket and dark pants opens my door and bows.

"Your Highness." Oliver, the head butler, extends his arm, helping me out of the car. "This way, please. His Majesty is expecting you."

I draw in a deep breath to suppress the nervous butterflies swimming in my stomach, sending up one more prayer that this has nothing to do with Creed.

While it wouldn't be the end of the world for me if someone learned about us, completing his military service is important to Creed. The one thing I've learned about Creed Lawson is that he's a proud and honorable man. If he's going to walk away from his career to be with me, he needs to do so with honor.

Something that won't be possible if anyone learned we were together last night.

And in New York.

The corridors are distressingly quiet as I follow Oliver toward my father's personal residence, although there's nothing personal about my surroundings, even in the residential wing. It's maintained with the same precision as the rest of the palace, everything more akin to a museum than a home.

I felt this way when I first moved here after my grandfather's death.

I still feel the same way now.

"He's in his study. You may go ahead."

I give Oliver a small smile, then continue down the long corridor, pausing outside a set of ornate double wooden doors before knocking.

"Come in." My father's deep voice reverberates into the hallway.

I hesitate, analyzing his tone for anything that might give me a clue as to my reason for being here.

As always, it's impassive.

Smoothing a hand down my dress, I open the door and slip inside his study.

"Your Majesty," I greet with a slight curtsy.

Standing from the couch, he offers me the same respect and gives me a subtle bow of his head. Then he walks toward me and wraps me in a hug, pressing a soft kiss to my cheek.

"How are you, Esme?"

"I'm well." I force a nervous smile, praying he can't pick up on my anxiety.

Or my guilt.

"Good."

A protracted silence passes as he gazes at me, a flicker of something in his blue eyes I can't quite explain. Then he clears his throat, dropping his hold on me.

"You're probably wondering why I asked you here, especially on a Saturday."

"The thought has crossed my mind."

"Unfortunately, something was brought to my attention

last night. Something that pertains to you." He makes his way to the couch and sits on one end, gesturing for me to join him.

I hold my head high as I walk on shaky legs toward him and lower myself onto the opposite end, keeping my spine straight, my legs crossed at the ankles as I angle them toward him.

"And what's that?"

"It's Callie Sloane."

I briefly close my eyes, but mask any hint of the overwhelming relief filling me that this has nothing to do with Creed.

"What about Callie Sloane?"

"Human remains were found in the trunk of a car pulled from Sufford Lake last night. The identification number was filed off, but the make and model match the vehicle that was registered to Callie Sloane."

"And the remains?"

"Forensics pulled DNA from the bones. It matched the DNA on file for Callie."

"So it's her."

He nods subtly. "Or what's left of her after being submerged in over a hundred feet of water for the past ten years. Luckily, Sufford Lake is notoriously chilly, so it helped to preserve quite a bit of evidence."

"Were they able to determine the cause of death?"

"Their investigation is still in the preliminary stages, but based on striations found in the bones of her rib cage, it's believed she was stabbed in the lower abdomen."

"Just like Gianna Vale." I give him a knowing look.

"When the Chief of Royal Police informed me of the discovery, I thought the same thing. But he said Callie wasn't stabbed to death, as was the case with Gianna."

I tilt my head. "Then how was she killed?"

"The hyoid, the U-shaped bone in the neck, was fractured, which leads them to believe she died as a result of strangulation."

"Strangulation? Do they know who's responsible?"

"They have a lead. Strangulation is often attributed to domestic violence cases."

"Jameson Gates?"

"Jameson Gates?" he repeats, clearly taken aback by my suggestion, brows knitting together in confusion. "Why would you suggest that?"

"Because he secretly dated her. Plus, Hayes Barlow once accused him of this very thing."

Years ago, I never would have considered Jameson capable of something like this. Would have thought it just as absurd as my father does. Probably even more so.

Lately, I'm no longer sure.

Every time I see him, I can't shake this strange feeling in my gut that he's not who he claims to be. That he's hiding something. That he has a dark side.

And maybe Callie was the unfortunate victim of that dark side.

"I assure you, Jameson Gates is not involved in Callie Sloane's death."

"You just said it yourself. Death by strangulation usually implies a domestic relationship."

"Regardless of the ridiculousness of the suggestion, there's not a single shred of other evidence tying Mr. Gates to Callie's disappearance. But there *is* a connection to Hayes Barlow."

"Hayes Barlow?" I shoot back incredulously.

He nods gravely. "At the time of Callie's disappearance, he owned a house on Sufford Lake."

"Sufford Lake is quite large," I argue. "Not to mention, if he was involved in her death, why would he bring attention to her disappearance?"

"All I can tell you is what the people trained in this sort of thing relayed to me. Based on witness statements from those familiar with both parties, there's evidence that Hayes Barlow was infatuated with Callie Sloane. The reason she'd wanted to keep her relationship with Jameson Gates a secret wasn't because of who he was, but because she feared how Hayes would react. Unfortunately, he found out, so Callie broke things off with Jameson to protect him from Hayes. Maybe even protect herself from him, too. As you may recall, Hayes Barlow was notorious for being a bit of a hothead, especially on the track."

"But that still doesn't explain why he'd go to the extremes he did to get the police to investigate her disappearance. Why would he do that if he killed her?"

He holds up his hands defensively. "All I know is what the investigators told me. It's possible he reported her disappearance to cover his tracks. When no one took it seriously, he was upset he wasn't getting the attention he thought he deserved. It's not too much of a stretch to think he could have killed Callie, especially after what he did to Adam." His eyes gloss over. "What he almost did to you."

Anyone else would bask in the obvious affection and worry in their father's voice.

But lately, I've been questioning everything.

Like whether Hayes Barlow is really responsible for Adam's death.

And who the man I'm certain I saw behind the wheel of the car chasing us could be.

And why I'm positive that man is the same one who pointed a gun at me a few months ago.

"What if Hayes Barlow didn't kill Adam? What if it was someone else?"

"Esme…." He squeezes my hand. "While I'm the first to admit the proof of his involvement in Callie Sloane's death isn't all that strong, at least not yet, I think we can both agree it's hard to argue he wasn't involved in what happened to Adam, not with all the evidence retrieved from Barlow's residence. Evidence directly tying him to the crime."

"All that evidence could have been planted. He could have been set up. Plus…" I trail off, unsure if I'm ready to go down this road with my father. Is it even worth it, considering Hayes is dead?

But if there's even a slight chance someone else is responsible, that person needs to answer for what he's done. Adam deserves as much.

"What is it?" He peers at me with interest and compassion.

I may not have always had the best relationship with my father, but since my return to Belmont and my brother's MS diagnosis, he's been better. He's taken a genuine interest in our needs and wishes.

He's been a father again.

"I've been having these…dreams."

"Dreams?"

"They started after the goodwill trip."

"I see." He briefly averts his gaze, a pained look crossing his expression. "And what do you see in these dreams?"

"I see that man pointing a gun at me."

"Charles Thacker?"

I part my lips, but snap them closed.

"Let me guess. You don't think he did it, either."

My lack of response is the only answer he needs.

"Esme…," he exhales yet again. "A man matching the

general description you gave was seen fleeing the scene and getting into a car. That exact car was found just a few kilometers away with Thacker's unresponsive body in it. He'd taken his life."

"The description I gave was of a man in a dark coat, dark beanie, and dark scarf. All I could see of him were his eyes and nose. Hell, half the palace staff would probably match that description if dressed accordingly." I bite my lower lip. "I saw him."

"I'm aware."

"No." I wave him off. "In my dreams, the man who pointed the gun at me is the same man who ran Adam off the road. Who poured gasoline all over the car." I swallow hard. "Who lit it on fire. And it wasn't Hayes Barlow. I don't... I don't think he did it." I quickly shake my head. "Actually, I *know* he didn't do it. Hayes Barlow had blue eyes. The man in my dreams has dark eyes with flecks of gold."

I meet my father's gaze, begging him to believe me, despite the mountains of evidence to the contrary. For a second, I can see the wheels turning in his head, as if he's giving my theory serious consideration. Then his shoulders fall and he expels a long breath.

"I can't imagine how difficult it must have been for you to lose your chief protection officer in such a traumatic way. For you to nearly die along with him. Then to almost lose your life again just a few months ago. But I assure you..." He brushes his thumb along my knuckles. "Charles Thacker was responsible for what happened during the goodwill trip. He was notorious for his outspoken and extreme anti-monarchist stance. He was found dead of a gunshot wound from the same type of weapon he pointed at you. As for Hayes Barlow, I don't think I need to remind you about the copious amount of physical evidence found at his house tying him to Adam's death."

"What if it was all planted by someone to make it seem like he's responsible?"

On a long sigh, my father pulls himself to his feet. I stand, as well, allowing him to take my hand in his. "That would take a hell of a lot of planning. I understand this may not be what you want to hear. That maybe you're looking for some sort of meaning behind all the horrible things you've endured. I often look for meaning behind it, too. But the truth remains. Hayes Barlow was a troubled man who saw everything he worked hard for go up in smoke and took it out on Adam. And Charles Thacker viewed you as a representation of everything he disagreed with about this country. The two incidents aren't connected. These dreams are just your brain playing tricks on you. Nothing more. Okay?"

I can't deny that my father has a point. My argument in favor of Hayes' innocence is solely based on what I see in my dreams. Not on reality. I may not be a lawyer, but I doubt any court of law would acquit anyone based on a dream.

Maybe my dad's right. Maybe I *am* just looking for meaning behind it all.

"Okay," I say, unsure if I'm saying it because I actually agree with him.

Or because I'm scared what it might mean if these incidents *are* connected.

CHAPTER TWO

Creed

I draw in deep breath after deep breath, doing everything in my power to hold my weapon steady when it feels like my world's spinning around me.

This can't be. I thought this man was dead. Everyone said he was. Medical professionals and forensic experts claimed that based on the extreme amount of blood found on his boat — blood containing his DNA — it was impossible he was still alive.

Despite that, my eyes tell me Hayes Barlow is very much alive.

And he's standing in my brother's office as if he belongs here.

This is the last thing I expected when I walked into my house this morning after leaving Esme.

Hell, it's the last thing I expected…ever. Especially after my father called to inform me about the discovery of Callie Sloane's body and that Hayes Barlow is the prime suspect.

But when I came upstairs and saw the door to my brother's office cracked open even though this room is off-limits, I knew something was wrong.

I never could have anticipated coming face-to-face with my brother's killer, though.

"I told you," I growl, flexing my grip on my weapon as I step closer, studying every inch of him.

Hayes has aged in the past ten years. His once dark hair now sports a light dusting of gray. He's no longer clean shaven, facial hair dotting his jawline, making him barely resemble the clean-cut race car driver that was once a favorite in the European circuit. He also seems bulkier, like he's spent the last decade working out daily. Regardless of his changed appearance, there's no mistaking those blue eyes. Ones I'd hoped never to see again after learning he killed my brother.

"You have two seconds to tell me what the fuck you're doing here before I put a bullet in your head." I clench my jaw, moving even closer, my finger itching to pull the trigger.

Put an end to this man, for once and for all.

Several tense seconds pass as I wait for his response, the room like a vacuum of sound. I no longer hear the hum of cars driving along the street. Or children playing. Or our neighbor mowing his lawn. All I can hear is my heart pounding like a jackhammer against my ribcage.

And the rage bubbling inside me.

Finally, Hayes relaxes his posture in defeat. "I need your help," he admits in a resigned voice.

"Help?" I scoff, incredulous. "You break into my home—"

"Adam's home," he interjects.

"Don't," I bark, erasing the last few feet between us, my weapon mere inches from his head. "Don't you dare say his name, you bastard. You don't deserve to speak it. Not after what you did."

"I didn't kill him," he seethes through a tight jaw, frustration and despair covering his expression. "I'd never…" He shakes his head, taking a minute to collect his thoughts before focusing his gaze on mine. "He was trying to help me. Help Callie. After I told him everything I knew about her disappearance, he said he'd look into it. But then the man with the scar followed me—"

"Man with the scar?" I scrunch my brow, unsure why I'm even entertaining his story.

"Callie mentioned seeing the same man following her in the days before her disappearance. I didn't think anything of it. Until I saw him myself after I'd accused Jameson Gates of murder. When I told Adam, he insisted I disappear. Told me he had a gut feeling about something and it was too dangerous for me to stay. That if I wanted to help Callie, I needed to leave. So that's what I did. He set me up with a new identity and everything." He pinches his eyes closed. "I should have known they'd kill him, too."

I lower my gun as I process his version of events. I shouldn't believe him. No rational part of me should buy this story.

But I *did* find copies of a new ID hidden in this office a few months ago. If Adam thought Hayes' life was in danger, I have no doubt he would have done whatever he could to help him. To protect him. It's who he was.

"And your boat?" I lift my weapon once more, but I don't aim it directly at his head. More at his arm. "Your blood was found on it. According to forensics, no one could have lost that much blood and survived."

He smiles shyly. "As Mark Twain said, 'The reports of my death are greatly exaggerated.'"

When I simply glare, unamused by his remark, he expels a long sigh.

"Truthfully, I had nothing to do with that."

"You expect me to believe you had nothing to do with faking your own death?"

He holds up his hands. "I don't expect you to believe anything. I *hope* you believe me, but I know how all of this must sound. If I were in your shoes, I'd be just as skeptical. Trust me when I say I don't have the skills to fake my own death. I wouldn't even know how to go about doing that. I was more than happy to stay hidden. Which is what I've spent the past ten years doing."

"Then why come out of hiding now? If someone went through the trouble of making the world think you were dead, why not reap the benefits of that?"

His jaw clenches, the vein in his neck throbbing. "It was one thing for the world to think I was responsible for killing your brother. For nearly killing the princess, too." He swallows hard, his voice heavy with anguish when he speaks again. "I can't stand aside and let them accuse me of harming Callie. I…"

He closes his eyes in an attempt to get his emotions under control. Then he returns his determined gaze to mine.

"She's why I came out of hiding. Why I'm risking everything. I need to get her the justice she deserves. But to do that, I need help." He gives me a hopeful look. "*Your* help."

"You can't be—"

"Believe me. If there was anyone else I could trust to do the right thing, I'd ask them. But I have no one. So I'm begging you to do the right thing and help me."

"The right thing would be to turn you into the police." I lift my gun. "Or put a bullet in your head. You deserve it for what you've done."

His mouth warps into a crooked smile. It's not conniving so much as it is resigned. "I think we both know you already would have done that if you didn't have doubts of your own. You don't strike me as the type of guy who'd break the rules without good cause."

I part my lips, but I have no response to his assessment.

The truth is, I *have* questioned Hayes Barlow's involvement in Adam's death. But that's only because of Esme's dreams.

As I've reminded myself, it was just a dream. There's a mountain of physical evidence tying Hayes to my brother's murder.

Even if there wasn't, even if his story *was* convincing, I can't help him. It's bad enough I haven't already called the police. The last thing I need right now is to jeopardize my future. Agreeing to help Hayes Barlow clear his name would do just that.

"You need to leave," I tell him in an even voice. "Now."

He doesn't move right away, as if waiting for me to change my mind.

When several protracted seconds pass and I don't relent, he releases a long sigh. Then he shuffles away from the window. But as he passes the desk, he pauses, grabbing a pen. I tighten my hold on my weapon, not taking any chances.

Finding a sticky note, he scribbles on it. I nearly berate him for making any changes to this room that's been kept the same since the day my brother died, but I'm curious about what he's writing.

Once he finishes, he places the pen in the exact place he found it, as if he knows this room has been frozen in the past. Then he walks toward me and presses the sticky note to my shirt.

"In case you change your mind." His eyes meet mine one last time before he disappears into the hallway.

I don't move for several seconds, listening as his footsteps retreat. It's not until I hear the front door close that I relax, returning my weapon to its holster and peeling off the sticky note, my gaze skating over his barely legible scrawl.

I want to believe he's guilty. That he's responsible for my brother's death.

And now Callie Sloane's murder.

But if he is, why would he give me his address?

CHAPTER THREE

Esme

A sea of photographers and reporters swarm outside the Monarch Hotel when Archie pulls up in front of it, the night sky illuminated by the constant flash from the cameras. This is the last place I want to be right now.

After the news of Callie Sloane's death, it feels wrong to carry on with our lives as if nothing has changed.

I didn't even know her, but the news of her passing hit me hard.

Because I know, deep in my soul, that Jameson Gates had something to do with it. That Hayes Barlow is just being used as a scapegoat yet again.

But how do I make everyone see that? The mere notion of Jameson Gates being involved in something as gruesome as murder is preposterous. The man devotes so much of his time to charity.

Still, I can't shake the feeling in my gut he played a part.

"Ready, ma'am?"

At the sound of Archie's voice, I snap out of my thoughts, shifting my gaze forward and meeting his eyes. "Yes. Thank you, Archie."

"Of course." He slips out of the SUV and hurries to open my door, extending his hand toward me.

The instant I step onto the sidewalk, the sky lights up with all the flashes from the cameras, my irises burning. I do my best to ignore them, pretend they're not there, focus on something else instead. Months ago, I never would have been able to make it more than a few feet without having a panic attack. I've been better lately. I still have moments when I have to remind myself I'm safe. But the panic attacks are becoming fewer and less debilitating.

My lips stretch tight across my face in a forced smile as I continue toward the hotel for tonight's society event masked as a fundraiser. Reporters yell questions at me, most of them about Callie Sloane's remains being found and Hayes Barlow's supposed involvement in her death. But as I've been trained, I keep my mouth shut and do what's expected of me.

I smile.

I wave.

I play the part of the beloved princess who has her shit together.

Until a face in the crowd stops me cold.

It's Hayes Barlow. He's aged, grown a beard and facial hair, but there's no mistaking his blue eyes. The despair in them that night over a decade ago as he accused Jameson Gates of killing someone he cared about is permanently imprinted in my mind.

But Hayes Barlow has been dead for nearly ten years. How could it be him?

I squint, certain my brain must be playing a trick on me. But as I attempt to get a closer look, he's no longer there.

In his place is someone else.

Who just so happens to have a gun aimed at me.

There are no screams. No panicked cries as people try to get out of the way. Which tells me this isn't real.

That I'm dreaming yet again.

But unlike all the other times I've relived this traumatic experience in my dreams, I'm not immediately tackled to the ground. Instead, I stare at the man for several long moments.

For months, his face was foggy, none of his features all that clear. But tonight, I can see each detail with alarming clarity — angry lips, clef in his chin, and a prominent scar along his right jawline.

With a malevolent sneer, he applies pressure to the trigger, but I still don't move, daring him to shoot me.

When he pulls the trigger, I don't feel anything. Or hear anything.

I look behind me, thinking he must be a bad shot if he missed at this close of a range. But the crowd of reporters is gone, along with the line of cars waiting to let their occupants off.

I'm somehow in the back seat of the SUV with Callie Sloane, her empty eyes wide, mouth agape, the color drained from her face. I glance at the front seat, expecting to see Adam.

Instead, Creed is slumped over the wheel.

It doesn't matter that I know nothing about this is real and I'll soon wake up. I gasp for air, hyperventilating at the sight of his lifeless body. I frantically try to help him, but I can't move, my arms restrained. I look down to see my wrists are bound to the arms of a chair. Which makes no sense, since I'm in a car.

At least I was.

Not anymore.

Suddenly, I'm transported to my bedroom, death lingering in the air as I observe Creed kneeling beside me, his wrists bound together in an agonizing grip. Then the man with a menacing scar appears before us, his gun glinting in the light as he presses it against Creed's temple.

But he shows no fear. Instead, the only thing I see in his dark eyes is his love for me and his assurance that everything will be okay.

With an ominous chuckle, the man with the scar pulls the trigger, the deafening shot startling me awake.

I jolt upright in bed, panting and clutching tightly to my chest as if that will help contain the terror consuming me. I swing my gaze toward the window, expecting to see Creed's lifeless body on the floor, blood pooling around him. Instead, there's nothing.

My hands shake uncontrollably as I peel the duvet off my body, my skin slick with sweat. My legs feel like jelly beneath me, but I still manage to lurch myself forward toward the bathroom. I totter in the darkness for a few moments before the sensors awaken, casting an eerie florescent light in the room.

I squint against the brightness, then turn on the faucet and splash water on my face, exhaling a long sigh.

"It was just a dream," I remind myself as I place my hands on the ledge of the vanity for support, every inch of me still jittery. "Just my subconscious twisting around a traumatic event."

Even I don't believe myself. If these dreams are simply me reliving these traumatic events, why was I tied to a chair? Why was Creed also restrained and kneeling on the floor? And who's the guy with the scar?

Sucking in a breath as if it may be my last one, I close my eyes, hoping to ground myself in reality.

And therein lies the problem.

The dream felt real. More real than any of my previous night terrors. I doubt anything will ever convince me otherwise.

CHAPTER FOUR

Creed

I stare at the ceiling, watching the shadows of tree branches, listening to the occasional hoot of a lone owl or a car driving in the distance. Other than that, the world is peaceful at nearly four in the morning.

Except my mind is definitely not at peace.

How can it be when the only thing I've thought about all day is my surprise run-in with Hayes Barlow?

I've tried to erase it from my memory, pretend it never happened.

But that's easier said than done, especially when I showed up at the football pitch for AJ's match and saw the look on Rory's face, a dead giveaway that my father had already shared the news about Callie Sloane's remains being found.

It felt like a huge deception to sit there and keep Hayes' surprise appearance from her. I justified my actions by convincing myself that the truth would do more harm than good. Rory seemed to have a hard enough time with the reminder of the man who'd taken Adam from her.

But did he?

As much as I refused to admit it earlier, I've had my own doubts regarding Hayes' involvement in Adam's death, even if that doubt has only recently surfaced because of Esme's dreams.

I've told myself repeatedly what she saw in her dreams wasn't real. That Hayes Barlow targeted Adam because he lost his sponsorships. That Charles Thacker, a known anti-monarchist, tried to kill Esme because of everything she represented.

That these two events are completely unrelated.

But if Hayes Barlow is responsible, why didn't he exhibit a single sign he was lying?

I've been through hundreds of hours of training on how to keep a poker face in the most intense types of interrogations. Hayes Barlow has no military background, let alone any special ops experience.

Yet there wasn't a single twitch of his facial features. Not a single swipe of his tongue along his lips. Not a single umm or like. The entire time, he maintained unwavering eye contact, begging me to listen to him. To believe him. To help him.

But even if I do believe him, I can't help him.

It's bad enough I know he's alive and haven't turned him in.

I can't do anything to jeopardize my future. Not when I'm so close to having what I've wanted for so long.

To finally having Esme.

I need to focus on clearing these final few hurdles, namely telling Rory I'm moving out and informing my father I'll be retiring from the guard at the end of August. I can't get distracted by a sob story told by a man I have no reason to believe or trust.

While I'd hoped to get a good night's sleep, considering I spent most of Friday night making up for lost time with Esme, it's proving to be impossible with the way my mind keeps replaying my conversation with Hayes. So instead of fighting it, I slip out of bed and pull on a t-shirt and shorts before padding down the stairs and into the kitchen, powering on the one-cup brewer. Once it finishes, I grab the steaming mug and head into the living room, lowering myself onto the sofa and flicking on the TV to catch up on the news.

Not surprising, today's big story is still Callie Sloane's remains being uncovered in the trunk of her car at Sufford Lake.

Or, more accurately, Hayes Barlow's involvement in her death.

No one seemed to care about her when she disappeared, but now that Hayes has been blamed for her murder, people are coming out in droves with a story about his obsession with her. That he was notorious for having a temper, especially during races. That he took a particular interest in Callie from the second she joined the team. That he completely lost it whenever a guy would look at Callie the wrong way, even going so far as to fire them from his crew.

Then again, I can't help but wonder if all these people are just upset that Hayes fired them because they were sexually harassing the only woman on the team. Part of me thinks it might be the latter.

"You're up early."

I snap my eyes away from the screen as Rory strolls toward me in a tank top, hoodie, and a pair of wine-glass-patterned pajama bottoms AJ got for her this past Christmas.

"I couldn't sleep." I offer her a small smile. "What are you doing up?"

"Couldn't sleep, either." She sits beside me on the couch. As her eyes land on the screen, her expression falls.

"Sorry." I reach for the remote, about to turn it off, but she darts out her hand and clutches my wrist, stopping me.

"It's okay." She releases me, pulling her sweatshirt closer to her petite frame. "It's better than seeing all the footage of the car fire being played on a loop, like they've been doing. After all, the public loves a juicy murder." She runs her hands along her pajama pants. "I learned that when Adam died."

I take a sip of my coffee, recalling those days all too well. I'm surprised I didn't end up in jail for assaulting a reporter. Then again, I was pretty numb from everything. After a few weeks, those vultures moved on to the next hot story.

Just like they will with Callie.

She'll be forgotten by most.

Except by those who will feel her absence every day for the rest of their lives.

"Do you think he did it, though?"

"Excuse me?" I jerk my head toward her.

"Hayes. Do you think he did it?"

I blink, taken aback by her question.

I may have spent all day questioning his involvement, but that's because he broke into this house, into Adam's office, and begged me to believe he had nothing to do with it. To help clear his name.

"What makes you say that?"

She pinches her lips together and shakes her head, her eyes focused on the screen as file photos of Hayes Barlow from his racing days appear before cutting to a famous clip of him kicking cans over in the pit after losing a race he was favored to win.

"They keep playing that one clip over and over," she remarks. "All day, whenever I turn on the news, I either see that, the fire, or him lashing out at a reporter for asking about his mum's terminal cancer after she'd just been diagnosed. I don't know." She heaves out another long sigh, then lifts her eyes to mine. "With Adam, there were heaps of evidence connecting him to the crime. It seems like the only piece of evidence tying Hayes to Callie's death is the fact that he had a temper.

"Don't get me wrong," she adds quickly. "I'm not trying to claim he's some sort of honorable man. I just hate all this trial by media going on in the world. When did we become so dumb as a society that we'll just blindly believe someone could commit horrible crimes, all because they were known to lose their temper? We all have bad days. We all get upset. Is that enough reason to condemn someone?"

I shouldn't be surprised by Rory's statement. She's always been incredibly sympathetic, regardless of any alleged crimes someone may have committed. That's just who she is.

It's one of the reasons Adam fell in love with her all those years ago.

"I'm sure there's more going on behind the scenes we don't know," I assure her. "I have to trust the police wouldn't make these kinds of accusations without the sufficient standard of proof. Her car *was* found a short distance away from where Hayes had a lake house."

Rory tilts her head, her gaze sweeping over my face. Did she hear how forced and robotic my response sounded? I sure as hell did.

"I guess you're right." She pinches the bridge of her

nose, heaving out a long sigh. "I'm sorry. I don't know what's gotten into me lately." She pushes to her feet.

"You have nothing to apologize for." I stand and run my hands down her arms. "When I heard about it, I questioned things, too. I think it's a normal response, considering Hayes' connection to our lives."

"Thanks, Creed." Her gaze meets mine. "I don't know what I'd do without you. I don't know what *AJ* would do without you."

I paste a smile onto my face, her words like a knife to my chest.

There's no question in my mind I need to get my own place and move on with my life. But the reminder of how much my nephew needs me forces the guilt I've saddled myself with for ages to bubble back to the surface.

"Do you…want to come upstairs?" She touches her hand to my bicep, a glimmer of something in her green eyes.

It's not desire. There's never been anything remotely resembling desire or passion between us, not like there is between Esme and me. With Rory, it's more like a tiny ray of hope that I'll help numb the sorrow, even if for only a short while.

"I, uh…" I step away from her, roughing a hand through my hair. "I'm not so sure that's a good idea."

She doesn't say anything right away. Just stares at me. Finally, she nods. "You're right. AJ might wake up early."

I part my lips, on the brink of telling her that's not the reason. That we need to stop this unhealthy arrangement.

That I'm moving out.

But four in the morning on the day after she learned the man who killed the love of her life could be responsible for another death isn't the ideal time.

"Yeah." I swipe my mug off the coffee table and head

into the kitchen, rinsing it in the sink. "I'm going to head to the gym. Talk later?"

She wraps her arms around herself. "Right. Of course. Have a good workout."

I give her one last smile, then head upstairs to change.

I didn't plan on hitting the gym before five on a Sunday morning, but it's better than staying here.

CHAPTER FIVE

Esme

A chill clings to the air as I walk along the empty palace grounds toward the athletic center, a slight chill in the air. I hadn't planned on coming here today, but after a fitful night filled with troubling dreams, I figured a distraction would be good.

Since I can't use Creed as a distraction right now, working out is the next best thing. It's often the one part of my day when I can turn off everything else, focus all my attention on what I'm doing, whether that's cardio, lifting weights, or even working the punching bag.

Right now, I'm desperate to focus on something other than witnessing Creed die in my dream.

I swipe my access card outside the large building that houses the state-of-the-art training and fitness center reserved for palace employees. I could work out at the gym in my apartment, but I needed to get out of there. Go somewhere to clear my head and forget what I saw. Get away from the negative energy filling that place.

Not surprisingly, the fitness center is empty at five on a Sunday morning, as I expected it would be. I head past the rows of treadmills and elliptical machines toward a line of punching bags in the far corner. Dropping my bag to the floor, I unzip it and grab my mitts and earbuds, popping them into my ears. Once my mitts are secure on my hands, I do a few easy jabs and kicks, slowly warming up. After several minutes, I lose myself in the music and routine, tuning out everything else as my punches and kicks become harder and more intense.

It's surprisingly therapeutic.

Kick after kick, punch after punch, I do everything to chase away my demons. To push the man with the scar from my memory. To forget seeing Creed get shot in my apartment while I remained bound, unable to help him. But no matter how hard I kick or punch, I can't erase the memory of Creed's eyes staring back at me as the life drained from them.

So I kick even harder.

Punch even more brutally.

Sweat even more profusely.

Still, nothing works.

When a deep voice cuts through my trance, I panic, not sure what's real and what's my subconscious trying to mess with me. I whirl around, about to defend myself against whoever it is, even if it's merely a figment of my imagination.

A strong hand wraps around my forearm, preventing me from delivering any sort of blow, and I snap out of my trance. My eyes widen as they fall on Creed's face, a hint of a smile on his lips.

But it disappears in an instant, brows drawing together in concern.

"What's wrong?"

"Wrong?" I pant, unsure what he's referring to.

But the second the word leaves my mouth, I hear it. There's a quiver in my voice. My eyes are burning, my cheeks wet.

"Sorry." I turn from him, yanking off my gloves and wiping my cheeks with my arm, removing my earbuds. "I don't know what came over me. I guess I went somewhere else for a minute."

"Hey." He touches a hand to my shoulder, forcing me to face him. He envelopes me in his embrace, and I draw in a shaky breath, finding instant comfort in his warmth and familiarity. His arms remind me he's still alive. That should be enough to settle my emotions.

Instead, it only makes me cry harder.

"You don't have to hide from me, Esme." He brings his fingers to my chin and tilts my head, our eyes meeting. "The news of Callie Sloane got to you, didn't it?"

I part my lips, on the verge of telling him she's been the furthest thing from my mind since I woke up, as horrible as that sounds.

But I'm not sure I can tell him the real reason. Not sure I can relive this particular dream right now.

"Yeah." I force a smile, mindful to keep my gaze trained on his. "I didn't even know her, but no one deserves to die like she did."

"She certainly didn't," he agrees, not making a single move to drop his hold on me. And I don't want him to, either. I want to stay in his arms.

It's the only place I've felt even a modicum of peace over the past few months.

But it's too risky. I can't let Creed jeopardize his future for me. We have a plan. We need to stick to it.

I push out of his hold and grab a towel from my bag, wiping away the rest of my tears. After taking another minute to compose myself, I face him, clearing my throat.

"What brings you here? I didn't think anyone actually came here this early, especially on the weekend."

He shrugs, dropping his gym bag onto the floor. "Couldn't sleep."

I don't have to ask why. I can only imagine what memories the news of Callie Sloane's body dug up for Creed.

"How's Rory handling everything? And AJ?"

He runs his long fingers through his hair, the gesture causing his shirt to lift up and reveal a sliver of that delicious little V.

My pulse kicks up, and I bite on my lower lip. It doesn't matter I spent the other night naked with him. That I could probably draw every inch of his body from memory. He still makes my heart beat a little faster, my breathing to become a little more uneven.

I hope he always will.

"As good as can be expected." His response forces me to snap my gaze back to him. "It wouldn't be so bad if the news would stop showing all the archive footage of the car fire whenever reporting on Barlow's past criminal behavior."

"I've been avoiding the news all day," I say, then blow out a laugh. "Who am I kidding? I avoid the news *every* day."

"Probably a smart idea."

A comfortable silence passes as we stare at each other, drinking each other in. All the tension and uncertainty that plagued me when I first arrived here less than an hour ago has vanished.

And I doubt it has anything to do with my workout.

"Well, I didn't mean to interrupt you. I'll give you some privacy." He flashes me a smile, then turns, slinging his bag onto his shoulder and walking toward the door.

He only makes it a few steps before I call out, "Creed, wait."

He pauses, glancing back at me with a single brow raised.

"You don't have to leave on my account. I get we're trying to be smart about this. But we can still work out together. In fact, I wouldn't mind some extra self-defense lessons, all things considered."

He doesn't immediately respond. Just stares at me, gaze searching mine. I can physically feel his indecision, torn between wanting to use this as an opportunity to spend time with me and keeping his distance, as we promised we would, considering how everything blew up in our faces last time.

"I don't want to clam up again," I continue. "I want to be prepared the next time—"

"It not your job to be prepared."

He advances toward me, stopping a breath away. His body is so close, I can feel the warmth radiating off him. Can smell his addictive scent. Can taste his lips on mine.

"It's my job. I mean, *our* job," he corrects. "The royal guard. It's why we're always close by. To protect you."

"And I'm eternally grateful for everything the guard does. I don't expect to ever have the ability to react as quickly as you do. But I'd feel better if I had more training than the once or twice a year simulated hostage situation. Please."

I expect for him to tell me to ask Archie about setting up some lessons, since he's my chief protection officer. It's what he should do.

But Creed and I have never been good about doing what we should, at least where the other is concerned. I've always been completely powerless to deny him.

And based on the indecision and longing swirling in his orbs, I know he's just as powerless to deny me.

"You're right," he says finally.

"I am?"

"Like you said…" He drops his bag back onto the floor. "Some extra training is probably a good idea, all things considered. They should have made it a priority after…well, everything." He swallows hard, his eyes flickering with remorse before his expression turns playful. "But don't think I'm going to take it easy on you just because I've seen you naked." He winks, his lips curving up into a sly smile that has my heart beating faster. It's just a smile, but it still makes my insides melt, butterflies flapping their wings in my stomach.

"Don't worry about me." I waggle my brows. "I can take it."

"We'll see about that…" He leans toward me, the heat of his breath on my neck causing a delicious tremor to slither through me. "Princess."

I close my eyes, taking a moment to compose myself.

It doesn't matter how many times I've heard Creed Lawson call me princess. It still completely unravels me.

But in the best way possible.

"Let's start with a review of basic pressure points, since they're the quickest and easiest way to disable your opponent long enough to escape."

And like that, sensual Creed turns into the trained protection officer he typically is.

Truth be told, it's kind of hot watching him run me through different scenarios, making me do the same thing over and over until I get it right, not letting me give up until I do.

With each new skill he teaches me, my confidence increases, the anxiety plaguing me all night evaporating.

"One last exercise before we call it a day," Creed announces what feels like only a few minutes later, although the clock on the wall tells me we've been at it for over an hour.

"I'm not tired," I tell him. "I can keep going."

"And I love that about you." Treating me to a lascivious grin, he takes a long sip from his water bottle.

He even makes that look sexy, especially in his gym shorts and t-shirt that clings to his chest and biceps.

"But you need to rest, too. So get on the mat. On your back."

"My back?" I arch a brow.

"You may not always be on your feet. Your opponent may get the better of you and knock you to the ground. It's just as important to know what to do in that situation."

I take one last sip of my water and do as instructed, lowering myself onto my back. He joins me, kneeling by my side.

"Keep in mind that fighting from the ground is extremely difficult. You're not going to be able to do any of these things right away, which is why I want to start teaching you some of these skills today. But keep practicing, and they could save your life someday."

"Got it."

"Good. Now I need you to spread your legs a little."

I resist the urge to make a joke, knowing how important this is. Once I follow his directions, he straddles one of my legs, then wraps his hands around my neck. It's not harsh, but it's not light either.

"You're going to trap my leg in place by hooking yours across it from behind."

I do as he asks, but it still doesn't feel sturdy or like I have the upper hand. He does.

"Can't I just try to knee you in the junk?"

"That's not a guarantee. This is. A split second after you've trapped my legs, you'll want to roll your hips to the side, reach for my face, and kind of push me in the same direction as your hips."

I follow his directions, and to my surprise, the force of my hips at the same time as I push his head away helps me regain control, securing him in a scissor-lock.

"Good." He taps my leg and I release my hold on him, allowing him to untangle from me. "Now let's try to put it all together. And quickly. The longer it takes, the more opportunity you give your attacker. Ready?" He gets back into position, straddling one of my legs, and I nod. "And, go."

When he returns his hands to my neck, I waste no time in hooking my leg across the back of his, then flip him over.

"Don't stop holding my head out of the way," he instructs when I loosen my grip. "You'll need to keep up your strength until you're ready for the next step."

"And what's that?" I grit out.

He releases his grip on me. "You'll find out next time."

"Next time?" I collapse onto the mat, enjoying the reprieve. Despite all my insistence that I'm not tired, my muscles are pretty spent.

Probably because I was still sore from the hours of calisthenics the other night.

"Yeah." He joins me, his own labored breathing mixing with mine.

I like knowing I made him work just as hard as he made me. Although, he certainly makes all this stuff look easy. Still, I'm glad we're doing this.

"Unless—"

"I like the idea of a next time." I roll onto my side,

resisting the temptation to hook my leg across his waist like I do whenever we share a bed.

He adjusts his body so he's facing me, our chests heaving in time with each other. "So do I." His lips curve into a small smile, making me want to cup his cheek and trace the lines of his face. It's torture for him to be so close, for his kiss to be within reach, yet still feel miles away.

"How did they do it?" I muse, partly to myself, partly to Creed.

"Who?"

"Nickie Ferrante and Terry McKay."

"I'm not sure who—"

"The main characters from *An Affair to Remember*."

"Ah." Realization crosses his expression. "Of course."

"How did they do it?" I ask again as emotion wells in my throat. "How did they make it six months? It's only been twenty-four hours and I'm ready to lose my bloody mind here, Creed."

"I know." He smiles, but it doesn't reach his eyes. "I think they knew going into it that it wouldn't be easy. That there would be days when it hurt so damn much they didn't know how the hell they'd survive another day, let alone months."

I swallow hard through the lump in my throat, his words describing exactly how I feel right now.

Then his expression softens. "But I also think they knew if they could just make it a few more months, they'd be free to be together without any sort of guilt or regret hanging over them. They'd both be in the right place to start their lives together." He slowly inches closer, his lips tempting me with their proximity. "Then it would finally happen, and all the waiting and anguish and torment would be worth it."

"What would happen?" I murmur breathlessly.

"The first kiss of the rest of their lives."

I whimper, the heat of his breath dancing on my mouth causing a rush of desire to trickle down my back.

"And because they waited, because they made sure to get rid of all obstacles facing them, they were free to enjoy that first kiss."

I sense him shift away and reluctantly open my eyes, watching as he pushes himself to his feet. He extends his hand, and I place mine in it, allowing him to pull me up. To my surprise, he yanks my body against his.

"I absolutely intend on enjoying the first kiss of the rest of our lives. And I'm not going to do anything that could jeopardize it." He curves closer. "Even if I'm ready to lose all bloody control right now." He releases me, bending down to sling his bag over his shoulder. "I know you'll be worth it." He gives me a sly wink. "You always are."

Then he turns, not looking back as he makes his way out of the gym, leaving me a pile of mush that has nothing to do with the strenuous workout he put me through.

One thing is certain. These next five months may just kill me.

CHAPTER SIX

Esme

"You didn't hear a word I said, did you?"

Marius' annoyed voice cuts through the memory of my morning with Creed, and I snap my eyes away from the busy sidewalks, pretending I hadn't just been somewhere else.

Or fantasizing about someone else.

All day, I haven't been able to get Creed out of my mind. How much our impromptu morning workout left me wanting more.

But it's selfish of me to want more right now. Just like all those years ago, Creed would bear most of the risk. I can't ask him to do that. Instead, I'll have to be content with spending whatever time I can with him.

It still doesn't make me burn for him any less, my body desperate for some sort of release.

I have a feeling my vibrator will be getting quite the workout over the next five months.

"Sorry." I bring my teacup to my lips, the sun warming my face as we sit in my favorite café enjoying afternoon tea. "I went somewhere else for a second." I flash a smile, then take a sip of my tea before lowering the cup back to its saucer.

The entire time, my two friends stare at me, their analytical stares studying me with intense scrutiny.

"Okay, spill." Marius leans back into his chair, resting his calf over his other knee, an air of relaxation about him as he settles in for whatever conversation he thinks we're about to have.

"Spill what exactly?" I arch a brow, looking back and forth between Harriet and Marius.

"Oh, come on, Ezzy." Harriet rolls her eyes. "You don't think Marius invited you to tea out of the goodness of his heart, do you?" She winks at him. "You should know by now there's always an ulterior motive with him."

Marius straightens, playfully shoving Harriet. "I don't *always* have an ulterior motive."

"So you didn't say anything about dragging Ezzy out for tea today so you could get the inside scoop about that little sidewalk scene Friday night?" She crosses her arms in front of her chest.

"Marius?" I give him an admonishing look, feigning indignation. "Is this true?"

"I may have said something to that effect," he admits. "But that's not the only reason I wanted to see you today. I adore you." He sips on his tea. "But I'm also dying to know what you and Creed talked about. Things looked pretty…intense."

"That's putting it mildly," Harriet mutters.

I peer into the distance, trying to collect my thoughts.

Friday night seems like it was a lifetime ago now, instead of two days. So much has happened since then.

So much has *changed* since then.

"I took your advice, Mari," I say nonchalantly.

"You did?" His eyes practically bulge out of their sockets.

"What advice is that?" Harriet gives us a quizzical look.

"To tell Creed the truth about the night Adam died," Marius explains. "How he was taking Ezzy to see Creed to make things right."

"And you told him?" Harriet raises a hopeful brow.

"I did," I say with an infectious grin. "Well, not right away. I told him I loved him, but—"

"Well, it's about damn time!" Marius slams his hand on the table, drawing the attention of several other patrons, including Archie.

I give my chief protection officer a reassuring smile before returning my attention to Marius.

"But it still didn't matter," I continue in a soft voice, not wanting anyone eavesdropping in on our conversation. Granted, we're at a fairly secluded table, but I can't take any chances. It's one thing to tell Harriet and Marius. They're the most trustworthy people I know.

But no one else can know the truth.

"He made his decision, and it wasn't me." I smile sadly, the memory of him pushing me away causing my throat to close up. "He still deserved the truth, though. So I told him Adam wasn't taking me to my mother's grave the night he died. You should have seen the anguish on his expression. It was so heart-wrenching that I couldn't get out the rest of what I needed to say. So I walked away. Thought that was the end of it. Until he showed up at my apartment—"

"He went to your apartment?" Marius presses.

"When?" Harriet asks.

"Friday night. Well, I guess it was technically Saturday morning because it was after midnight."

"What did he want?"

"The truth about where Adam was taking me. And that's when I realized something."

"What's that?" Marius asks.

"I spent the past ten years keeping the truth from Creed because I didn't want to burden him with any more guilt. But by keeping the truth from him, I burdened him with guilt, anyway. If he'd known Adam's last act on earth was one of love for his brother, maybe Creed wouldn't feel this intense need to make things right between them. Wouldn't continue sacrificing his happiness. So I told him the truth. That his brother gave me a choice of where to go and that I chose Creed. That I'll always choose him."

"Good for you." Harriet reaches across the table and squeezes my hand, her support unwavering, as always. "Then what happened?"

Pulling my hand away, I draw in a deep breath, lifting my tea cup to my lips again. "And then…"

"Yes?" Harriet leans closer, her rapt attention glued to my every move.

I smile over my tea cup. "We made love."

"It's about damn time," she exhales, sinking back into her chair. "The sexual tension between the two of you at Anders' party the other night was bloody intense. I'm glad you finally worked some of that off."

"Did we ever."

My friends burst out laughing, and I join them, feeling surprisingly at ease, despite the unsettling dream I had last night.

But just like this morning at the gym, just like the night I begged Creed to stay with me after nearly getting shot, he seems to chase my nightmares away.

I hope he always will.

"So…," Marius begins, and I can already sense where this conversation is headed, "how is this going to work? Last I checked, he's still in the royal guard."

"He is." My expression falls. "Which is why we've agreed to keep our distance."

"Wait. You're *not* together?" Harriet furrows her brow.

"Truth be told, I'm not sure what we are. But he's up for retirement in August."

"He's retiring?" Marius' eyes widen.

I nod. "He is."

"Just so you can be together?"

"I like to think I'm not his sole reason for retiring. That he gets something out of it, too."

"Yeah. Unlimited pussy."

Marius' remark causes us to erupt in laughter once more, the sound carrying through the air. I can't remember the last time I've felt this happy. This carefree. Creed and I still have a few hurdles to overcome, but we're finally on the right path.

"In all seriousness, I'm happy for you," Marius says. "For both of you. After all the shite you've been through these past several years, you both deserve to be happy. I'm thrilled you've found that happiness with each other." He gives me a heartfelt smile that soon turns devious. "I think first born naming rights is fair payment."

"Fair payment?" I snip back. "Payment for what?"

"Oh, how soon you forget the important role I played in you and Creed getting together in the first place. We were sitting in this very café, at this very table, no less, discussing your need to be deflowered when I suggested Creed Lawson do the honors. After you propositioned me first, you hussy."

I chew on my bottom lip, but nothing can reel in the smile that crawls across my mouth from the memory of that day. Of thinking my friends were crazy for even suggesting I ask Creed to take my virginity because he was too honorable.

But there was nothing honorable about the way he fucked me when he finally succumbed to his desires. The things that man made me feel should be illegal.

And he still brings out the same feelings inside me, all these years later.

"I suppose I do have you to thank."

Harriet clears her throat, drawing my attention her way.

"You, too, Harri."

"Thank you very much," she says with an air of authority.

"Precisely why I think you should name your first son Marius," he comments.

"And your first daughter Harriet," she adds.

It feels odd to be discussing the prospect of having Creed's children when I never really gave children much thought. I knew I'd eventually have them. I don't exactly have a choice in the matter, especially since the lack of heirs is one of the arguments in favor of the referendum to turn the monarch into a ceremonial role.

When Tristan and I were together, he often brought up having a family. I didn't completely shoot down the idea, but I wasn't exactly warm to it, either. For some reason, I couldn't picture myself having Tristan Hughes' children.

But I *can* picture myself having kids with Creed. The mere idea of Creed as a father has my ovaries on the brink of combusting. There's no doubt in my mind he'd be an amazing father. Would read to our baby. Change diapers. Sing songs.

I want that. More than I've wanted anything in my life.

"I'll see what I can do."

CHAPTER SEVEN

Creed

I pull the SUV to a stop in front of Anderson's estate and kill the engine. Before I have a chance to reach for the handle, my door swings open. Anderson stands just outside with a brilliant smile on his face.

His hair is disheveled, a stark contrast to the well-groomed look he normally has to maintain. To further the point, he's wearing a pair of board shorts and a t-shirt, flip-flops on his feet.

"What are you doing?" I ask as I step onto the cobble-stone driveway.

"Opening your door. What does it look like, you wanker? Now come on." He turns, heading toward the oversized garage that holds his collection of cars.

"Where are you going?" I jog after him, catching up as he punches a code into the keypad and opens the door.

When we step inside, several overhead lights flicker on,

illuminating a row of perfectly maintained vintage cars. A boyish expression builds on his face, as if they're the only things that bring him joy.

Before he met Nora, I'd probably say that was the case. He collected sports cars because of what they represented — freedom. The ability to escape the real world, even if for only a few hours.

It makes me wonder what he wants to escape from today.

"I think the Jag. The weather's beautiful. Don't you think?" He walks toward a safe on the wall and places his thumb over the scanner. After a few seconds, it beeps, and Anderson opens the door, grabbing a set of keys. "Here. Catch." He tosses them my way.

I react quickly and grab them but don't make a move toward the baby blue 1965 Jaguar Roadster. It takes all my resolve not to hop into the impressive vehicle and tear out of here, like Anderson and I once did as teenagers.

But we're not teenagers anymore.

Things are different now.

"What's going on?" I ask.

"We're going for a drive."

I scrunch my brows. "I thought you wanted to go to the marina. Take out your sailboat."

"We have to get there somehow. We'll take the Jag," he says nonchalantly, as if it's normal for us to take this car out for a drive together.

If we were just friends, it would be normal. But we're not. I'm his chief protection officer first and foremost.

At least for now.

Until I sign my discharge papers, my duty to him and the crown will remain my priority.

"Anders…," I begin, but he cuts me off.

"I didn't ask you to come sailing with me today as my chief protection officer, Creed. I did so as a friend. We used to take these cars out all the time and you didn't say shite about it."

"That was before I was your chief protection officer. Before I was in charge of keeping you safe."

"But I don't want you to be my chief protection officer today. It's why I told you that if you wore anything other than a t-shirt and shorts, I'd fire you." He offers me a sad smile. "I'd forgotten what it's like to have you as a friend. But at my birthday party the other night, you weren't my chief protection officer. I'd like more of that. So let's go for a drive in this bloody awesome car and go out on the water. Consider it your birthday present to me." He flashes me a conniving smile.

"I thought my birthday present to you was taking the night off so I could go to the party Esme threw for you."

Just saying her name causes my skin to heat, my lips tingling with the memory of her kisses. It took every ounce of willpower I possessed not to kiss her this morning. God, I wanted to.

But I also knew I wouldn't be satisfied with just a kiss. I'd want more.

Wanting more is precisely what got us into trouble last time.

I won't risk that again.

"Consider it a bonus gift." He winks, then hops into the passenger seat with an expectant expression on his face.

I don't move at first, just look at the keys in my hand.

Most people think Anderson has everything he could ever want. He's constantly surrounded by people, most of them celebrities in their own right. But it's all very fake.

None of those people actually care about him on a personal level. All they do care about is his social standing and how they can use him to increase theirs.

He may be surrounded by people, but I know how lonely he is.

Or how lonely he was before Nora.

In a world where most of your relationships lack any sort of substance, you search for something that is real. I'd like to think our friendship has always been real, despite my father telling me I can't be his friend when I'm essentially the hired help.

But Anderson's never treated me that way. If he wants to spend the day with a friend, it's the least I can give him, especially after the year he's had.

And maybe a day out on the water is the perfect time to tell him about my plan to retire.

"Okay," I finally say as I hop into the car. "I'm not your chief protection officer today."

"Thanks, mate."

"You bet."

I insert the keys into the ignition and the engine roars to life. When I feel the vibration of the motor humming beneath me, I no longer care whether this is a good idea. Not with how beautiful and powerful this car is.

"Let's go for a drive." Anderson flashes a mischievous grin.

I dampen the clutch and shift into first, edging toward the closed garage door. Once it senses the car, it slides open, the bright sun streaming in.

I lower my sunglasses over my eyes and rev the engine a few times.

"God, I love that sound," Anderson exhales.

"Me, too."

As we drive through the city streets, most people we pass gawk over the car while remaining oblivious to the fact that the next king of this country is in the front seat. For the first time in a while, I don't focus on the fact that he's the future king. We're just two people who've known each other our entire lives enjoying the first warm spring day.

I can't remember the last time I allowed myself to live in the moment. Not be weighed down by my obligations to Rory, my father, or the crown.

It's liberating to finally live for myself.

The engine roars beneath me as I continue out of the city and toward the marina, taking a few detours for no other reason than to enjoy the power of this car, the machine hugging the corners and turns with ease.

When I pull up to the marina gate, both Anderson's and my faces are windburned, our hair a mess. But the guard out front still recognizes us, waving me in without issue.

The smell of salt water fills the air as I drive along the various docks containing boats of different sizes. Some are long and narrow, others wide and sleek. All have ostentatious names befitting their owners — members of the royal family — painted prominently on their sides in gold letters.

Except for a sailboat docked at the last slip. While it's a beautiful vessel, next to the yachts and super yachts, it's quite ordinary.

But it's something Anderson can man without needing a crew of fifteen or twenty. Which is why he wanted it. For a taste of freedom and independence, regardless of how short-lived it may be.

"Ready to take her out?" Anderson asks once I park the car, leaving it with one of the royal valets.

"Absolutely."

We climb onto the boat and busy ourselves with getting her ready to cast off. I don't know as much as he does about sailing, so I follow his orders and we eventually make it into open water, where we're able to kill the motor and let the wind do most of the work.

"Remember that night we got wasted?" Anderson asks as we relax by the helm and have a few drinks — him a sparkling water, me a beer. The winds are calm, the water tranquil, allowing us to float at a leisurely pace.

"Which night is that? If memory serves, there's been quite a few of them."

"That there were." His eyes shine with a nostalgic gleam. "But there was one in particular that stands out. It was a few nights before I left to go to university in the States."

"Ah..." A smile tugs on my mouth. "I remember that. You snuck out of the palace wearing a ghastly disguise and we spent all night getting absolutely wrecked at some dive bar."

"And when we woke up the next morning, some octogenarian was standing over us with a cricket bat, about to beat us to a bloody pulp after she found us sleeping in her late husband's dinghy."

I burst out laughing, my heart warming in my chest from how ridiculous and immature we once were.

How carefree we once were.

"That's when you tried to tell her who you were," I say through my chuckles. "To which she said…"

"'If you're the Crown Prince, I'm the Queen of fucking England,'" he says in his best imitation of the old woman.

Our laughter increases even more as we continue reminiscing. Now that I think about it, it was one of the last times we shared as friends. A few days later, he left for Harvard, and I enlisted in the military.

"Thankfully, your brother came and vouched for me. Never told my father or anyone else about it, either."

I nod, my laughter waning. But not out of remorse or regret, as once was the case whenever my brother came up in conversation. Now that I know the truth, it's helped me look at things through a different lens.

It's helped me see *my brother* through a different lens.

We may have had our fair share of disagreements, but when it mattered, he was always there for me.

Like he was there for Anderson the morning he was almost pummeled to death by an old woman in a floral house coat.

"Speaking of my brother," I begin, clearing my throat. "There's something I'd like to talk to you about. Although I'm not sure if I'm doing so as your friend or your CPO."

"Okay…" Anderson draws out, curious eyes focusing on me. "What is it? Is something wrong?"

"Actually, no. The opposite, really." I lick my lips, briefly staring out over the horizon, nothing but blue ocean visible for miles. "Over the past few days, I've done a lot of thinking."

"About what?"

"Well, my living arrangement for starters," I answer, figuring I'd ease into the conversation with something I'm certain he'll support unequivocally. "Living with Rory, and everything that goes along with that."

"It's about damn time." He takes a sip of his sparkling water. "I've been telling you for years it's unhealthy. I understand you made your brother a promise to always be there for them, but I doubt he meant for you to sacrifice living your own life in order to keep it." He leans closer, dropping his voice. "And I *really* doubt he meant for you to let Rory fuck you while calling you by your brother's name."

I cringe at his statement, but it's true.

An arrangement born out of guilt and regret festered into something incredibly detrimental for far too long. Unfortunately, I enabled it. Didn't put a stop to it, even though I knew it was wrong.

No more.

"I see that now, and I'm done with it."

"So you're moving out? That's your big news?"

"No. I mean, yes. I *am* moving out, although I still need to tell her, but that's not what I want to talk to you about."

"Then——"

"I'm retiring from the guard."

Anderson doesn't immediately respond. Just stares at me in stunned silence, the only sound that of the white canvas sail inflating and deflating in time with the waves lapping against the hull, a few seagulls squawking in the distance.

"It's probably not what you want to hear, especially with the upcoming referendum vote, but I'm eligible in August so——"

"It's about bloody time, you dolt!" he exclaims, flinging his arms around me, squeezing tightly.

"You're not upset?"

"Upset?" He meets my eyes. "Why the bloody hell would I be upset about that?"

"Because now you'll have to get used to a new CPO."

"Who cares about that?" He waves me off, grabbing a grape off the platter of fruit and cheese. He pops one into his mouth. "You're damn good at your job. Which means all the guys on your team are damn good at their jobs. I have no doubt whoever you decide should replace you will be more than capable of stepping into your shoes."

"Any member of the team will do everything in their power to keep you safe from any and all threats."

"Exactly. I'm happy for you, Creed." He squeezes my shoulder and smiles, not a single hint of disappointment in his expression. Then he drops his hold on me. "Have you told your father?"

"Not yet. I just made this decision yesterday, more or less. I'd been thinking about it for a while, but I don't know…" I exhale, relaxing further into the seat cushion. "It's time I start living for myself. Making my own choices. Charting my own course. To hell with the expectations my father's placed on my shoulders all my life."

"Good for you." He lifts his bottle of sparkling water toward me. "To charting your own course."

"Thanks, mate." I clink my bottle against his.

"So what do you think you'll do once you're free?"

"Truthfully, I'm not even sure. I never thought I'd retire from the guard at only thirty-six and have the rest of my life to make my own choices. Considering this is the only life I've ever known, it's petrifying. At the same time, it's also liberating. I can do whatever I want. Whatever makes me happy."

I take another sip of my beer, thinking about what I *will* do. I could go work for my friend's private security company. But is that something I want to do?

"And Esme?"

His question catches me off guard, and I cough, beer shooting out of my nose. "What about Esme?" I ask once my coughing subsides.

"You'll no longer be in the royal guard, Creed. Meaning in just a few months, there won't be anything standing in your way." He rolls his eyes. "Not like that stopped you two before," he adds under his breath. "But come August, you'll be free to be with her."

"I'm aware," I respond as I bring my bottle back to my lips and take a long sip, hoping he can't read too much into my expression. That my big motivating factor for finally taking this leap and making these changes *is* Esme.

"I'm not going to tell you how to live your life," he says with a long sigh, stretching his legs out in front of him. "Lord knows, you've had enough people doing that for you."

"You've got that right."

"I just think that if you're finally ready to make these positive changes in your professional and family life that maybe you're ready to make a positive change in your love life, as well." He pauses as a knowing smirk crosses his mouth. "Unless you already have."

"What do you—"

"It's okay." He winks. "You don't have to tell me anything. It's probably better if you don't, considering she *is* my sister. Just know that whatever you two are, whatever you will be, you'll always have my support."

I meet his gaze. "Thanks, mate."

"I adore you both. And I want you both to be happy. I'm thrilled you're finally able to find that happiness in each other?" His voice raises at the end as he arches a brow in question.

Instead of insisting that we're not technically together, I flash him a smile. "We certainly have."

"Good."

"It really is."

I relax back into the cushion, allowing the sun to warm my face. Everything feels so…perfect. So right. Especially after spending the morning with Esme at the gym. Knowing we'll have more mornings like that will make the next few months easier to endure.

Still, I'm trying not to get my hopes up. Not yet anyway.

In my experience, for every up, there's an even bigger down.

And I can't shake the feeling that when things do turn down, it'll be with so much force that everything will shatter into pieces.

CHAPTER EIGHT

Esme

The bottom of my gown swishes with my steps as I make my way up the grand staircase of the National Opera House, all eyes on me. I hate to admit it, but this sort of thing was much easier with Tristan at my side. He had an uncanny ability to make me forget where I was.

And who I was.

But that wasn't reason enough to stay with him. Not when I didn't love him like he deserved.

Regardless, I'd give anything to have someone at my side during public events these days, especially with the fate of the monarchy making headlines every day. This life can be extremely isolating. The only thing that makes it suck a little less is knowing this strange sort of purgatory I find myself in won't last forever. Hell, it's already been a month since Creed showed up at my apartment and everything changed for us. I only hope the next few months go by just as quickly.

"Your Highness." The men standing guard outside the

royal box greet me with a bow before opening the double doors.

I draw in a breath, preparing to face my grandmother, something I avoid doing as much as possible, then walk in, putting on the mask I must wear in order to survive this life.

As expected, everyone bows or curtsies as I enter, apart from my father and grandmother, who don't have to. Instead, I curtsy at them first. My father, at least, returns the gesture with a small bow of his head. My grandmother doesn't, though, her judgmental eyes looking upon me with disapproval. No doubt she's making a mental list of everything about my appearance she finds offensive.

I look around the space for Anderson, but he's not here yet, leaving me to deal with all these people myself. My gaze falls on a waiter carrying champagne, and I exhale in relief, stepping toward him. But before I reach him, someone grabs the last two flutes, much to my disappointment.

Until the tuxedo-clad man turns around and walks in my direction, extending one toward me.

"I assume you're looking for this?" Jameson says with a sly smile, but it doesn't reach his eyes like it usually does. Instead, there's a sadness about him.

I wonder if it has to do with Callie Sloane.

Or if he's just pretending to be affected about what happened to her.

"Thank you." I take the flute from him.

"Of course. I know how much you love these public events." He winks, his voice oozing with sarcasm.

"Oh, it's the absolute highlight of my life. Donning an uncomfortable gown, only to sit for hours on end so the who's who of Belmont society can see me supporting the arts. Don't get me wrong. I'm happy to support the arts, especially arts education for little ones. I just think there's a better, less ostentatious way to do it."

"Particularly if that way involves yoga pants instead. Am I right?" He tilts his glass toward me.

"You absolutely are." I clink my flute against his and take a long sip, savoring in the effervescent liquid.

Silence descends on us, neither of us knowing how to act around the other. At least *I* don't know how to act around him, considering my suspicions. So I decide to use this opportunity to do some digging. See if my instincts are correct.

"I, uh… I'm sorry about Callie," I say softly so no one can overhear.

While most people here were probably aware of his history with her, I don't want to assume anything. For the most part, his relationship with Callie was kept under wraps. Instead, both Jameson's and the palace publicists claimed the only reason Hayes Barlow accused Jameson of being responsible for her disappearance was because he founded a charity that helps bring home missing women.

"It's been…difficult," he admits, his expression pained. "She'd been missing for ten years, so the chances of her being found alive after all this time were practically nonexistent. But it's still hard. Especially after the police accused Hayes Barlow." He rolls his eyes, his skepticism obvious.

"You don't think he did it?"

He leans toward me, gaze unwavering. "I don't."

His response takes me by surprise. If Jameson were involved in her disappearance or death, wouldn't he fully support the police's conclusion that Hayes was responsible, thus releasing Jameson from any culpability?

But that's not what he's doing.

Instead, he's raising his own doubts.

"What makes you say that?" I press, unable to stop myself.

He glances over his shoulder, body stiffening when he sees Silas Archer.

Which only increases my confusion. I thought they were close.

Maybe I misread that, too.

Jameson touches my elbow and pulls me farther away from everyone. But he still keeps his voice low. "Because Hayes wasn't like that. And him being obsessed with her?" His tone is heavy with disbelief. "I don't buy it." He rakes his gaze over me. "And I get the feeling you don't, either."

"When I learned she was strangled to death, which is typically associated with a domestic murder—"

"You thought I might have something to do with it."

I give him a tight-lipped smile, neither agreeing nor disagreeing.

"Believe me…" He straightens, running his hand through his perfectly groomed blond hair. "I tried to get the police to arrest me."

"You did?"

"I didn't kill her, but if the police are going to stick with this theory that it was a domestic incident, I should at least be considered a person of interest. So I went to the Chief of Royal Police. Told him all about my relationship with her. How we were together until a few weeks before her disappearance." He smiles sadly. "I may not have killed her, but I still feel responsible. Figured if they'd arrest me, maybe I could be at peace and the nightmares would stop."

"Nightmares?" I ask, studying his features for any hint of deception. Any clue this is an act.

For several months, I spent nearly every day with him. Got to know him fairly well. Learned when he was being who he had to be in public or when he was being his authentic self.

And right now, there's no doubt in my mind he's being the real Jameson.

That he's telling the truth.

Maybe my father's right. Maybe the idea that Jameson Gates could be involved in something like this is preposterous.

He donates billions of his own money to charity. More than that, he donates his time, too, often volunteering when there's a shortage, much like myself.

This is a man who once went out of his way to save a dying kitten he saw get hit by a car. He could have just left the poor thing, but he went above and beyond, spending thousands to ensure the tiny creature received the best medical care possible, then made sure he found someone reliable and trustworthy to adopt him.

He couldn't even stomach watching that poor kitten suffer.

There's no way he's capable of doing anything to cause a human to suffer.

Right?

"They're of Callie," he answers finally. "She's calling out to me for help, but I can't get to her. I wake up gasping for air, like I'm drowning in the car with her."

"I know what that's like," I admit before I can stop myself. "Ever since I was nearly shot, I keep having these horrible nightmares about it, too. But this isn't about me." I quickly shake my head. "My apologies."

"It's okay." He laughs under his breath. "It's actually refreshing to hear someone else has gone through something similar. That it's normal. My father tries to tell me to get over it. That 'only pussies need therapy because some whore you banged was killed.'" He rolls his eyes, his gruff voice mimicking his father's almost perfectly. "'Take some sleeping pills and move on.'"

"Parents are really good at fucking up their kids, aren't they? Even when we're adults."

"Too right." He treats me to a warm smile, then clears his throat. Any of the anguish that was present seconds ago has vanished. In its place is the Jameson Gates the world knows and loves. "Well, I suppose I should let you make the rounds. Thanks for the chat. It was surprisingly reassuring."

"Of course."

"Ma'am." He bows toward me.

"Mr. Gates."

He holds my gaze for another second, then retreats, purposefully ignoring the harsh glare coming from Silas Archer as he makes his way through the crowd. Has there always been a strange tension between them? Did I just ignore it because I wanted to blame someone for what happened to Adam, and Jameson seemed a likely target?

"What was that about?"

Anderson's voice snaps me out of my thoughts and I look to my right as he approaches.

"It seemed...intense."

I bring my flute back to my lips. "Just catching up." I take a long sip of champagne, hoping my brother doesn't pry.

It's one thing to tell him about my own nightmares. It's another to tell him about Jameson's.

These types of dreams are incredibly personal. Sharing them is like splitting open your soul, your biggest fears, and allowing the world to see them.

"You sure?" Anderson narrows his gaze on me, forever playing the part of the protective older brother.

"Of course, I'm sure." I roll my eyes, hooking my arm in

his elbow and walking with him through the reception area. "Thanks for being my date tonight," I joke in an effort to change the subject.

"It would be better if you had an actual date," our grandmother snips out, seeming to appear out of nowhere. Her razor sharp eyes pin me with a disappointed stare before she turns her ire on Anderson. "You, as well. I sent you both suggestions for possible escorts." She looks between me and my brother. "Apparently, you chose not to take them."

"I have a girlfriend," Anderson reminds her.

"In America." She grimaces, as if the word leaves a sour taste in her mouth.

"For now. She's agreed to start splitting her time between the States and here with me."

"Really?" I turn my wide eyes on Anderson. "Nora's moving here?"

He beams, excitement oozing from every inch of him. "I asked her this past week when I was in New York helping her get settled into our new apartment. We agreed it was time to take the next step. Next time I go see her, she'll be returning with me."

"We'll see about that," my grandmother remarks under her breath as she retreats, not even trying to hide her animosity toward a woman she's never met.

In her mind, she doesn't have to. Not only did Anderson choose someone who's not from Belmont, but she's also poor, at least according to our grandmother's standards. As if my brother doesn't have enough to worry about with his MS treatment, now he has to stress about how Nora will adapt to this life.

And how our grandmother will treat her.

"Don't worry about her." I give his arm a squeeze. "I'll do everything I can to make the transition as smooth as possible." I hesitate. "Although it might require more alcohol than this country currently has on hand."

He playfully nudges me. "I knew I could depend on you."

"Always, dear brother."

"It's my understanding that come August, you'll have a plus one, as well, won't you?" he whispers.

I inhale a sharp breath. "What are you—"

"Creed told me he's retiring once he's eligible."

"I don't see what that has to do with anything." I take a long sip of my champagne.

"You don't need to pretend around me, Ezzy. I know. Truth be told, it was pretty fucking obvious."

"Because he's retiring?"

"He's also been less moody. And you haven't been shooting daggers at each other whenever you're in the same room. Pretty sure I actually noticed him crack a smile when we arrived and he saw you."

I glance over my shoulder to where Creed's standing guard. While he's trained to look everywhere other than at Anderson, or me for that matter, he briefly breaks protocol, his eyes meeting mine.

It only lasts a few seconds, but with that stolen moment, he tells me everything I need to know. That he loves me. That he hates not being on my arm.

That one day, he'll never leave my side.

"I'm happy for you," Anderson whispers, pulling my attention back to him. "For both of you."

"Thanks, Anders."

"Anything for you."

The lights flicker, signaling the performance is about to begin. Anderson offers me his elbow, and I set my empty glass down on a nearby table before looping my arm through his, an attendant leading us from the reception room and into the seating area of the royal box.

As with everything in our lives, this is a performance as well. I plaster a smile on my face, waving politely to the other attendees as the lights dim.

I start to sit, but as I do, my eyes sweep over one of the boxes on the opposite side of the theater. I instantly freeze, my legs unable to move. It feels like all the oxygen has been sucked out of the air, my world spinning around me.

I've spent the past month convincing myself he's not real. That he's just a figment of my imagination. The result of a traumatic experience.

But how can he be a figment of my imagination when the man with a scar is in this theater?

And he's looking directly at me.

CHAPTER NINE

Creed

Something's wrong. I can feel it in my bones. On the outside, nothing looks amiss. It's just another night at the opera, the who's who of Belmont society here to watch the opening performance of *L'Orfeo*.

But I can't shake the feeling in my gut that something's off.

When I notice Esme seize up, unable to move, I *know* something's off.

Anderson glances my way, his fear-filled eyes begging for help. I hurry toward them and wrap my arm around Esme's waist, quickly escorting her out of the box before any of the other patrons notice what's going on.

It only takes me a matter of seconds to get her into the private reception room just outside the royal box. But it may as well have been hours with the panic gripping me as I watch her struggle to breathe, her lungs wheezing, muscles taut.

"What's going on?" Anderson asks as I help her onto a divan, his voice laced with alarm.

"What's wrong with her?" his father presses, the two of them inches away from her, which isn't helping matters.

The last thing anyone needs when suffering through any sort of panic attack is to have people hovering over them. Not when the anxiety makes you feel like the walls are closing in on you.

I face them, my expression calm. "I need you to give her some space." Sensing movement, I look past them as my father, Archie, and a few other guards file into the room along with Jameson Gates. I lower my voice. "She's having a panic attack."

"Panic attack?" Esme's father repeats. "Why?"

"There doesn't have to be a reason," I tell him. "Now, if you two can give her some space, I'd like to help her through it."

"Of course," Anderson replies quickly, taking several steps back, pulling his father along with him.

I kneel in front of Esme, her breathing still labored, hand clutching her chest. "I'm going to lay you on your back. Okay?"

She nods. It's probably all she can do right now.

"Okay." I splay my hand on her lower back as I carefully lay her down, folding her hands over her stomach. "I just want you to focus on my voice and nothing else. We're going to breathe together. Inhale through the nose for five seconds, then out through your mouth for five. Think you can do that?"

She nods again, her eyes locking with mine.

"Good." I squeeze her hand.

I can feel my father's displeasure from across the room, seemingly incensed that I'd be brazen enough touch her. But this isn't an affectionate touch. I need her to feel grounded. To come back from whatever caused her to seize up like this.

"Now close your eyes and inhale through your nose."

She follows my instructions, and I watch her chest rise as I count to five.

"And exhale."

She parts her lips, a combination of surprise and relief covering her expression as the breath leaves her.

Truthfully, I'm relieved, too.

For a minute, I wasn't sure she'd ever breathe again. Wasn't sure I would. I've been in her shoes before. I know how it feels when you think your surroundings are getting closer and closer, about to crush you to pieces.

"Good. You're doing great."

I squeeze her hand again, absentmindedly caressing her knuckles with my thumb. It's second nature whenever I hold her hand. I know I shouldn't, that it might only draw attention our way, and not the good kind. But Esme needs comfort right now.

"Let's do it again. Inhale through the nose for five."

Her chest rises with her breath again, and I walk her through a few more breathing exercises, not stopping until she's able to breathe comfortably on her own, her pulse no longer racing.

"Do you want to try sitting up?"

She opens her eyes and looks my way, giving me a small smile. It's not as bright as her normal one, but I'll take it.

"Yes."

"Okay." I hook an arm around her waist and slowly help her into a sitting position. But I don't take my eyes off her. Or my hand, keeping hers firmly enclosed in mine. "How do you feel?"

"A little dizzy."

"Just keep taking deep breaths."

She follows my suggestion, her chest rising then falling.

"Can you tell us what happened?" Esme's father asks after several moments, approaching and handing her a bottle of water.

I reluctantly release her hand and give her space, ignoring my father's glare as I join him and the other members of the royal guard.

"I…" She shakes her head.

"Was it a flashback?" Anderson presses.

"Not a flashback," she responds, her voice strong and determined. A complete change from the uncertainty that filled it seconds ago. With her gaze focused on me, she confesses, "I saw him."

"Who?" her father asks.

She briefly closes her eyes and inhales a steadying breath. "The man who shot me. Or at least tried to. He was here. Tonight. In one of the boxes on the opposite side of the theater. By stage left."

"Esme…," he sighs, joining her on the divan and taking her hand in his. "I told you." He drops his voice to barely louder than a whisper, as if embarrassed about what people might think if they learned she's been having nightmares. "I can appreciate how traumatizing that experience was for you—"

"I'm not imagining it." She shoots to her feet, but the sudden movement unsteadies her.

In a heartbeat, Anderson is beside her, supporting her, much like he has all his life.

Once she has her balance, she gives him a small nod, and he releases her. But that doesn't make the concern in his expression disappear.

In mine, either.

"He was here." She points to the ground, resolute and steadfast. "He was real."

"How can you be sure?" Her father stands and moves toward her.

"Because I saw him."

"As you said."

"No." She vehemently shakes her head. "Not just tonight. But in my dreams. His face has been getting clearer and clearer every time. He has a scar along his right jawline. And he was here."

I inhale a sharp breath, my body going ramrod straight.

Did I hear her correctly? Did she say she's been seeing a man with a scar in her dreams? That he's the one who pulled a gun on her and killed Adam?

I want to believe it's all a coincidence. That lots of people probably have scars along their right jawline. That the man she's been seeing in her dreams isn't the same one who Hayes Barlow mentioned when he broke into my house.

Because if it is, then maybe Hayes Barlow *is* telling the truth.

Although, a part of me thinks he's been telling the truth all along, but I didn't want to admit it because it would mean Adam's killer has been roaming the streets for the past decade and I've done nothing about it.

"I know how it sounds." Esme looks around the room, practically begging someone, *anyone*, to believe her. "But he was here. He could still be here. And *he's* the one who tried to kill me a few months ago. Not Charles Thacker."

"With all due respect, ma'am..." My father steps forward, his posture stiff, expression even. "All the physical evidence uncovered in the aftermath of the attempt on your life points to Charles Thacker."

"And the evidence is wrong. Just like it was when Adam died. This man killed Adam, too."

"There's nothing—"

"Shouldn't we do a quick sweep?" I suggest.

Silence falls over the room, all eyes zeroing in on me, particularly from all the other guard members who must think I have a death wish for questioning my father's authority. As the senior ranking member of the royal guard in attendance, this is his operation. He calls the shots.

And I just questioned them.

"I don't see—"

"Would that set your mind at ease?" Esme's father directs at her. "That way, we can solve this matter for once and for all?"

"It would." She shifts her gaze toward mine. "Thank you."

I give her a small smile. I may not know what to believe right now, but I know one thing for certain. I'll always do everything I can to make Esme happy.

To make her feel safe.

"Major-General."

My father snaps his gaze toward the king.

"Please do a sweep of the building, but be discreet. We don't want to cause any unnecessary alarm."

"Certainly, sir." He bows, then turns his indignant expression toward me. "You're with me."

"Of course, sir."

CHAPTER TEN

Esme

"Why didn't you tell me?" Anderson asks the second Creed, his father, and several other guard members leave to search for this mysterious man with a scar.

"Tell you what?" I meet his eyes as he sits on the divan beside me.

"That you're still having those dreams?" he whispers.

"It's not a big deal," I respond in an attempt to downplay them.

"It obviously is, Esme. Especially if they're affecting you like this." He takes my hand in his. "You scared me out there."

"I guess now we're even." I give him a knowing look, reminding him of the scare he gave me before he started more aggressive treatment for his MS. Thankfully, he hasn't had another incident like that in a while. There are days he's more tired than usual, but his body hasn't given out or suffered from momentary vision loss.

"I guess so." A small smile tugs on his lips before his expression falls. "But seriously, Ezzy. You should have told me."

With a deep sigh, I sink back into the divan and take a sip of water. "I didn't think it was a big deal. It's just a dream."

I look toward where my father's having a quiet conversation with my grandmother. It's obvious by her scowl that she thinks this entire situation is ridiculous.

She's probably not alone.

The only one who doesn't look at me like I've lost my mind is Jameson Gates. Instead, when his eyes find mine, there's only sympathy and understanding within.

"But when I saw that man with the scar tonight," I continue, leaning toward my brother and dropping my voice to a barely audible level, "I just… I don't know what came over me. It felt like I was stuck in my nightmare. I couldn't breathe. Couldn't think."

I contemplate telling him my dreams have changed, too. That I don't just see this man point a gun at me, then light the SUV on fire with Adam and me inside. That now I see him shoot Creed in my bedroom. I can only imagine how that would go over, especially with my father. It would most likely confirm his theory that it's simply my subconscious playing tricks on me.

Most of the time, I'm inclined to believe it.

But I know what I saw tonight.

And I saw the man from my dreams.

The man who tried to kill me.

The man who killed Adam.

The man who I fear might kill Creed, if my dreams are a predictor of the future, as crazy as that sounds.

"Are you sure you *really* saw him, though?" Anderson asks

as delicately as possible. "I was standing right beside you. The lighting in the theater was dimmed. The only faces I could make out were those in our box."

"I know what I saw, Anders," I seethe through a tight jaw. "I may have only stared into those eyes for a split second before he pulled a gun on me, but that split second replays in my mind every moment of every day. And the man I saw tonight had the same eyes. And the same scar I've seen in my dreams. I'm sure of it."

"Have you seen this man before you started having these dreams?" His expression exhibits all the compassion I've come to expect from my brother and closest friend. But I still sense his disbelief.

"When he tried to kill me," I snip back. "Before that, when he set the SUV on fire and killed Adam."

"Esme…" He narrows his gaze on me. "I'm on your side here. I just want you to be absolutely certain you've seen this man somewhere other than in your dreams."

I know what he's getting at. The man who attempted to kill me was wearing a dark beanie and had a scarf covering the lower half of his face. When Adam and I were being chased, I'd only managed to look behind us for mere seconds before we were hit. Not nearly long enough to get a good look at the person driving.

The only reason I think this man with a scar is responsible is because I see him in my dreams.

The sound of the door opening cuts through, and Major-General Lawson enters the reception area, Creed and the other guard members following close behind. His tall stature is an imposing presence in the room, just as Creed's is. They share many of the same features, but whereas Creed's hair is longer and he sports a bit of scruff along his jawline, his father keeps his head clean-shaven with no facial hair.

"Sir." He bows toward my father. "We've completed the search, as requested."

I don't mistake the hint of venom in his voice and the icy look he gives Creed.

"What did you find?" My dad moves toward him.

"We did a discreet sweep of the audience, as well as searched all backstage areas for a man matching the description the Princess Royal provided." He briefly glances my way. "I regret to inform you, we couldn't find him, nor do any of the ushers, staff, or performers recall seeing anyone with a scar. If it were any other kind of description, I'd be inclined to keep looking, but considering he reportedly has a prominent…abnormality, I think we can all agree that if a man with a long scar along his jawline had been here, someone would recall seeing him."

"I agree." My father extends his hand toward him, and they shake. "Thank you, Major-General."

"Of course, sir."

My father turns in my direction, beaming a bright smile. "See, dear? It was nothing. Just your brain playing tricks on you."

I part my lips to argue to the contrary, but before I can, he continues, "Captain Walsh?"

Archie steps forward. "Yes, sir?"

"Can you please take Esme home? She's had a trying evening and needs her rest."

I shake my head, bolting to my feet. "Dad, I don't need—"

He holds up his hand. "Take the night off. You've been working very hard. Not getting enough sleep can cause your mind to play tricks on you. Make you think you saw something that isn't real." He turns to head back into the royal box.

"It *is* real," I insist, following him. "He was here. He—"

He whirls around before I can utter another syllable. "*Go. Home.*" His voice thunders through the reception area. "It's not a request."

I wouldn't be surprised if they heard him in the theater. Or, at the very least, in the royal box.

He draws a deep breath as he pinches the bridge of his nose, then turns his attention to Archie. "See to it that she goes directly home."

"Yes, sir." Archie nods, giving me an apologetic smile. I don't blame him, though. It's not like he can disobey a direct order from the king. Not unless he wants to risk losing his job.

"Good." My father looks at Anderson. "Let's get back to our seats. People will be wondering where we've been. It's best we not give them any more fuel for the fire, so to speak."

Anderson hesitates, obviously torn between his loyalty to me and his obligation to the crown.

The story of our lives.

"Go," I tell him. "I'll be fine. I could use a night off."

"Are you sure?"

I force a smile. "I'm sure."

"Okay." He leans down and presses a kiss to my temple. "I'll stop by in the morning to check on you."

"Thank you."

He holds my gaze for another beat, then follows my father back into the theater, Creed and his father trailing closely behind.

Before he closes the door, Creed's eyes find mine. I can feel his indecision all the way across the room. It's like he wants to believe me, but the logical part of his brain won't let him.

And Creed Lawson has always been a sensible, rational man.

Could they be right? Could it just be my brain playing tricks on me?

It would be a much easier explanation. Lack of sleep and increased stress can cause the brain to behave differently. In all likelihood, that's all this was.

Then why did it feel so real?

CHAPTER ELEVEN

Creed

I shouldn't be here. If anyone were to check the security footage and saw me lingering outside the front door of Esme's apartment after letting myself into the building with the code I'm only supposed to use when escorting her to and from official events, I would be summoned before the board of misconduct.

Or discharged.

But I couldn't just go home and forget about tonight.

I tried.

All I did was toss and turn, the rational part of my brain at war with the part that knows this can't be a coincidence. What are the chances Hayes Barlow would mention a guy with a scar, then Esme would bring up seeing a man with a scar along his right jawline mere weeks later?

I'm not a statistician, but I have a feeling the chances are pretty slim.

Regardless, I hated the idea of Esme thinking she was alone.

I saw how people looked at her earlier.

I saw how her own brother looked at her. He wanted to believe her, but he had his reservations.

I'd probably have reservations myself had Hayes Barlow not broken into my house last month.

Now it's all I can think about.

Mindful not to look directly into any of the security cameras, as if that's going to help matters, I punch my code into the keypad. But before I can finish, the door swings open. Esme stands less than a foot away in a robe, her hair a disheveled mess on the top of her head, eyes drooping from lack of sleep.

But she's never looked so damn beautiful.

"Creed, what are you doing here?"

I cup her cheeks as I push her inside her apartment, closing the door behind me.

"I needed to see you."

I rest my forehead against hers, our breaths intermingling. It feels like it's been ages since I've been this close to her. Even during our training sessions, I've been careful to keep my distance.

But tonight, I need this nearness. This connection.

She's the only thing anchoring me to the ground when I'm no longer sure which way is up.

"But what if you get caught? We agreed that we'd—"

"I know. But some things are more important. *You're* more important." I curve my lips into a smirk as I lock eyes with her. "But if you don't want me here, I can go. I—"

"Don't you dare," she interrupts, flinging her arms around me.

I inhale a calming breath as I envelope her in my

embrace, surrounding myself in her scent. In the feel of her. It's a double-edged sword, my being here. Allowing myself to hold her like this.

It'll make me want more of this.

And I can't have that. Not yet. Not after what happened the last time we were careless.

But like I told her. Some things are more important than the potential risk of getting caught. She doesn't deserve to be alone right now.

Maybe I don't want to be alone, either.

Maybe I need her just as much as I'd like to think she needs me.

"I'm so glad you're here," she whispers into my chest, running her hands up and down my back.

"I'm glad I'm here, too." I tip back her chin, my eyes sweeping over her face, fixating on her lips.

The lips I've longed to taste since the last time I left this apartment a month ago.

The lips I've deprived myself of since then.

The lips I'd give anything to feel now, if for no other reason than to feel something other than the uncertainty plaguing me.

As much as I want to, I can't bring myself to cross that line. Not here. Not now. Not when I have absolutely no control when it comes to Esme. She's like a drug. If I allow myself one hit, I'll keep coming back for more and more until it completely consumes my life.

I refuse to do that when I'm so close to finally having everything I've always wanted.

When I'm so close to finally having Esme.

Instead of slamming my mouth to hers and having a hit from my favorite drug, I brush a soft kiss to her forehead, and grab her hand.

"Come on."

She doesn't say a word, just allows me to lead her through her apartment to her private suite. Her eyes remain locked on mine as I help her under the covers and sit on the edge of her bed, bending down to kiss her forehead once more. I push a few wayward strands of hair behind her ear, relishing in her soft skin against mine, admiring how damn beautiful she is.

I could watch her all night. I want to. But that's a recipe for disaster. I'd rationalized coming over here by telling myself I just wanted to make sure Esme was okay, and then I'd go.

But I can't find the strength to pull myself away from her right now. Not when I still see the fear swirling in her deep green eyes like a tumultuous storm. As if she's petrified of what she might see when she falls asleep. As if a demon is lurking in the shadows, waiting to attack her in her dreams.

And I know he is.

The man with the scar is waiting for her.

Her own personal Freddy Krueger.

Despite the risk, I toe off my shoes, then shrug out of my jacket and t-shirt, draping them over the reading chair in the corner. My pants and socks join them before I skirt around to the opposite side of the bed and slide under the covers beside her.

When I wrap her in my arms and pull her body against mine, my front to her back, she sighs, melting into me. I pepper kisses along her shoulder blades, refusing to act on my growing arousal. Instead, I just hold her, offering her some sort of comfort in a world I sense she's questioning more and more with every passing day.

Just like I am.

I didn't want to believe Hayes Barlow. Wanted to forget

everything he told me, write him off as a desperate man with a history of lying and manipulation trying to clear his name.

That went up in flames the second Esme mentioned seeing a man with a scar in her dreams.

Then seeing that same man at the theater tonight.

The practical side of me says I shouldn't put much stock into it. They're only dreams. Not a single other person in that theater tonight claimed to have seen a man with a scar along his right jawline, a distinguishing feature someone was bound to notice.

I try to tell myself it's because he's not real.

I don't *want* him to be real.

But as I watch Esme struggle and writhe through another night terror, this one far worse than any I've seen before, I know I need to do something to help set her mind at ease. Need to do something to stop these dreams from tormenting her. Need to get her the answers she's desperate for.

Need to get myself the answers *I'm* desperate for, too.

CHAPTER TWELVE

Esme

"Pardon the interruption, ma'am." My butler steps into my den the following afternoon, the sun cascading through the mahogany-framed windows. I snap my head in his direction, an expectant brow raised.

I've spent all day lounging on the couch, something I don't do much of these days.

What else am I supposed to do now that all my public appearances for the rest of the weekend have been canceled?

My father's orders.

He thinks I'm overtired and that's why I conjured up this man with a scar. Hell, he probably thinks that's the reason I started having these dreams in the first place.

But I know he's real. And I plan on proving it.

That's why I've spent the last several hours with my sketch pad, attempting to draw the face of the man who torments me. After seeing him nightly for the past month, it shouldn't be this difficult.

But I'm struggling to get it just right. To capture the wildness in his eyes. The pure malevolence in his expression. The fear the sight of him evokes in me.

"Master Jameson Gates is here to see you. I can send him away if you're not up to having visitors."

A few weeks ago, I would have been suspicious if Jameson dropped by unexpectedly.

But we turned a corner last night. He seemed so vulnerable. So…lost.

Much like I feel right now.

While I appreciate the risk Creed took by staying with me last night, he never told me he believed me. It meant a lot that he stood up to his father and suggested the guards sweep the premises, but I noticed the uncertainty in his expression. The only person who looked at me with anything remotely close to understanding was Jameson Gates.

Right now, that's what I need.

"Of course. You may let him in."

"Certainly, ma'am. Should I have tea prepared?"

"Please."

My butler gives a curt nod and retreats. I close my sketch pad and place it on the coffee table, then stand as Jameson enters.

"Your Highness." He bows toward me.

"Mr. Gates."

"I apologize for disturbing you. I just…" His voice trails off, his brows drawing together as he runs a hand through his hair. He pinches his lips together, that same vulnerability from last night shining through.

Like it occasionally did during our fake courtship. It was in those rare moments I saw the real Jameson Gates.

And that was the Jameson Gates I liked.

"I wanted to make sure you're okay." He steps closer. "I was worried about you. Still am."

"I'm hanging in there." I force a smile.

"Good."

"Would you like to sit?" I gesture at the couch. "I have some tea on its way."

"You didn't have to go to the trouble," Jameson remarks as he follows me toward the sofa, unbuttoning his suit jacket before lowering himself onto it.

"I didn't. My staff did. I usually give them the weekends off, but after last night, my father insisted they be on hand today."

"He doesn't want you to be alone. That's all. He cares about you, Esme. You can tell. He's not the same man he was…before."

"I know," I say with a sigh. "I just… I wish he believed me."

"I believe you."

I roll my eyes. "You're only saying that to be nice."

"No, Esme." His expression becomes grave. "I believe you." He leans toward me and parts his lips, but before he can say anything, my butler returns.

"Sorry for the interruption, ma'am." He walks across the room and sets a silver tray down on the coffee table in front of us. "Would you like me to serve you and Master Gates?"

"That's not necessary." I wave him off. Partly because I'm perfectly capable of pouring my own tea. Partly because I'm anxious to know what Jameson was about to confess.

My butler bows, then retreats, closing the door behind him.

I reach for the tea pot, but Jameson beats me to it, pouring some into my cup before his own.

"Still take it with honey?" He lifts the jar.

I nod.

A smile curves his mouth, and he adds the perfect amount to my tea before adding some to his own. I lift my cup and take a sip.

Once he's had a chance to drink his own tea, I face him. "Why do you believe me?"

He sets his teacup down on its saucer and angles toward me. "This man with a scar you see in your dreams..."

"Yes?"

"The scar goes along his right jawline, correct? Then hooks up toward his upper lip?"

I inhale a sharp breath, my pulse increasing as my brain works on overdrive.

He wouldn't know the exact curve of that scar unless he's seen this man himself.

"Exactly like that," I finally respond.

He briefly closes his eyes, expelling a long sigh, as if wishing I hadn't said that.

"Callie mentioned seeing a guy matching that description in the week or so before she ended things. Claimed he'd been following her."

"She did?" My gaze widens, mind reeling with this revelation. I'm not sure what I thought Jameson was going to tell me, but it wasn't this. "Do you think this man with a scar is responsible for what happened to her?"

"It's a damn good possibility."

"But who is he? And why?"

"I believe he might somehow be connected to Silas Archer."

"Silas Archer? I thought you two were close." I take another sip of my tea, hoping this is my chance to get more information out of him. He seems to be in quite a sharing mood. "From what I've seen since I've been back, you spend quite a bit of time with him."

"You know what they say, don't you?"

"What's that?"

"Keep your friends close…" He arches a single brow.

"And your enemies closer," I finish.

"Precisely."

"So that's what you've been doing? Keeping your enemy close?"

He gives a small shrug of his shoulders. "Archer's my father's friend. After Callie disappeared, and you were nearly killed when Adam was taking you somewhere other than the King's Day gala where I was to propose, I don't know…" He narrows his gaze on me. "It's a bit suspicious, don't you think? Hell, I wouldn't be surprised to learn he had something to do with Gianna's death, too. If I remember correctly, you were suspicious about it yourself."

I square my shoulders. "I was."

Although, I'd initially been suspicious of Jameson.

All because of his strange behavior during that last meeting before I left for Paris.

Hell, most of my distrust of Jameson Gates is because of that last meeting and his supposed friendship with Silas Archer.

Maybe I'd been wrong about all of it. There's only one way to know for certain, though.

"You looked at her during that meeting."

He tilts his head. "What meeting?"

"When I essentially broke up with you."

"I'm not sure I'd call it that, considering we were only together by force to begin with. A breaking implies some sort of connectedness. We never had that. It was more of a… contract termination."

I laugh slightly. "I suppose you're right."

He takes a sip of tea before returning it to its saucer, resting his forearms on his thighs. "So I looked at Gianna?"

"It struck me as odd. I didn't think you spoke to her much, but that day, when I all but threatened Archer I'd publicly accuse him of Callie's disappearance if they forced us to continue with that sham of a relationship, you looked at Gianna, almost as if for her approval. Why?"

"I wish I could tell you, Esme." He exhales deeply. "Unfortunately, it was so long ago. After the scare of you almost dying, and Adam *actually* dying, I can't remember much. Or attempt to rationalize any of my behavior. Those weeks are a blur. I'm not saying I *didn't* look at her. Just that I don't know why. After growing up in a world where I never really got to make a decision of my own, it wouldn't surprise me if I looked toward someone for approval." He narrows his gaze. "You know how that can be."

"I do." I chew on my bottom lip, toiling over everything Jameson has shared with me today. And yesterday.

All along, I tried to blame Jameson Gates for being involved in something simply because he looked at Gianna.

Maybe he was just a pawn, and I should have been looking at Silas Archer with more scrutiny. He *had* raised his suspicions about Archer when he told Adam about his secret relationship with Callie.

"Why would Archer want us to marry so badly that he was willing to kill over it? Assuming that's your theory."

"It's the most rational one. And the only reason I can come up with is money."

"Money?"

"There's no doubt in my mind my father was willing to pay him a small fortune once we were married. Again. It's all speculation. There's no smoking gun."

"What should we do?"

"We?" He arches a brow.

"If he killed Callie and Adam, or at least hired some man with a scar to do his dirty work, he deserves to pay. Callie deserves justice. So does Adam."

"And I'd give anything to get Callie the justice she deserves. To make this bastard pay before…" He trails off, pinching his eyes shut.

"Before what?" I slide closer, placing my hand over his and squeezing. He returns his red-rimmed eyes to mine, offering me an appreciative smile.

"Unfortunately, Archer's well-connected," he responds, ignoring my question.

"So am I. As are you."

"But he's one thing neither one of us is. That we'll never be."

"And that is?"

"Dangerous, Esme. Silas Archer is *extremely* dangerous. And calculating. And manipulative. It's why he's been able to get away with all of this for so long. Why he's been able to frame other people for his crimes. But everyone eventually makes a mistake. And I plan on being there when Archer does. Then I plan on making him pay."

There's a harshness to those final words, causing a chill to trickle along my spine, a hint of trepidation washing over me. But I quickly push down any feeling of unease. This man just revealed his deepest vulnerabilities and secrets. Every single explanation he gave me makes perfect sense.

Hell, I probably would have come to the same conclusion if I hadn't been so insistent on finding something wrong with Jameson.

"Well, I should be off," he says after several long

moments. "Let you get back to binge-watching true crime documentaries."

With a wink, he stands from the couch and buttons his jacket. But it doesn't fit his body like it should, the shoulders and waist loose. As I scan the rest of his frame, I notice his pants appear ill-fitting, as well, his belt the only thing keeping them secure.

Physical proof of how much this has been affecting him.

"Thanks for stopping by." I pull myself to my feet. "And for…sharing."

"I hadn't planned on it, if I'm being honest. I just wanted to check on you, especially after you mentioned seeing the man with a scar. I guess…" He trails off, shaking his head. "I guess I just needed you to know that I believe you. And to tell you to be careful. Can you promise me that? That you'll be careful? That you won't go poking around in this?"

"I…"

"Please, Esme…" His voice is choked with emotion as he clutches my biceps. "I've already lost Callie to this. And nearly lost you…twice. I don't want the third time to be the charm. Promise you won't do anything to put yourself at risk. Okay?"

I tilt my head, studying him. Why would a man who's essentially been little more than a stranger this past decade feel so strongly about this? Does he have some ulterior motive here?

It's sad that I've been around selfish, narcissistic people so long that whenever someone does have altruistic motives, I immediately question it.

"Okay," I finally say. "I won't dig around."

His shoulders fall out of relief. "Thank you."

"Of course." I hold his gaze for another beat, then he releases me, bowing slightly.

"Your Highness."

"Mr. Gates."

He turns and makes his way across the room, opening the door and stepping into the hallway. Giving me one last smile, he closes the door behind him, disappearing from view.

I fall onto the couch and bury my head in my hands.

I don't know what to believe, who to trust.

All I do know is this man with a scar is real.

And I need to find out who he is. Why he's haunting me.

Regardless of any promises I may have made to Jameson Gates.

CHAPTER THIRTEEN

Creed

The tires of my car crunch against the uneven dirt road, kicking up a cloud of dust in its wake. I squint through the haze, spotting an isolated house among the endless acres of farmland. Never in a million years would I have anticipated Hayes Barlow hiding out in a place like this.

Then again, I didn't exactly picture myself paying him a visit to begin with.

But I need answers and he may be the only person who can help.

I'd hoped I could get those answers without resorting to this. Over the past week, I've spent every free hour going through all the security footage from the opera, as well as doing detailed background checks on everyone in attendance, along with their known acquaintances, in the hopes of tracking down this man with a scar.

Unfortunately, it's only left me with more questions than answers.

And I need answers.

Esme needs answers.

After witnessing her succumb to one of the worst night terrors I've ever seen, one where even my voice calling out to her did nothing to bring her back, I knew I had to do something to get her these answers.

Even if it means asking for help from the one man I swore I'd never speak to again.

I steer my car past a wooden gate and onto the long driveway, stopping beneath a tall maple tree. Shutting off the engine, I step out and study the two-story farmhouse — white clapboard siding, wraparound porch, and black shutters. The scent of freshly mowed grass surrounds me, a stark contrast to the city air. I look out over the expanse of land, every square inch growing various crops.

"Captain Lawson."

I snap my eyes back to the house as Hayes steps onto the porch, the screen door slamming shut behind him. His white t-shirt clings to his body, damp with sweat, and dust covers his jeans and work boots, presumably from working in the fields all day. He looks weathered. Worn out. More so than he did a few weeks ago. It's obvious the news about Callie Sloane's death still wears on him.

"The man with a scar," I begin, dispensing with pleasantries. "What did you tell my brother about him?"

He crosses his arms in front of his chest and leans against the porch railing. "Am I to assume you've had some time to think about out last conversation?"

I glower at him, not willing to give him any more information than necessary. The last thing I plan on telling him is that the Princess Royal has been seeing this man with a scar in her dreams and is convinced that's who killed Adam and tried to kill her a few months ago.

"I'm just trying to do my due diligence here. If by some chance you're not responsible for killing my brother, I need to make sure the person who is can be brought to justice."

He pushes off the porch. "Come on." He waves for me to follow as he walks toward the door. "This isn't exactly the type of conversation we can have out here."

I hesitate. I still don't fully trust this guy. Don't know what game he's playing.

He opens the screen door and glances over his shoulder. When he sees I haven't moved, he allows the door to shut and turns back toward me, lifting his shirt to reveal his torso and waist.

"I'm not armed, if that's what you're worried about." He does a slow circle, allowing me to scan the rest of his frame. When he faces me again, he asks, "We good?"

"Fine. But I'm keeping my weapon on me."

"Your brother said the same thing to me." He chuckles, then steps into his house, holding the door for me.

As I follow him inside, I scan my surroundings, remaining alert for any potential dangers. But I doubt I'll find any. The place is surprisingly homey. A soft brown couch and matching love seat are nestled against one wall of the living room, a dining table just beyond it. It's not particularly spacious, but I doubt he ever entertains anyone.

That would be too risky.

Instead, he's made a life out here where his closest neighbor is easily several miles away.

"Would you like some tea?" He heads toward the sink and turns on the faucet, running his hands under it. "Or perhaps something a bit stronger?"

"That depends on what you're about to share with me."

He turns off the water and dries his hands on a dish towel. "Something stronger it is." Removing two glasses from a cabinet, he pours a few fingers of a deep amber liquid into each one and brings them to the table, placing them on the surface.

"It's that bad?" I pull out one of the chairs and sit down.

"I'll let you decide for yourself." He lowers himself across from me, bringing his glass to his lips.

I leave mine on the table for now, wanting to keep a clear head. "What did you tell my brother about the man with the scar?"

"Just that I noticed him following me a few days after I… assaulted Jameson Gates." He rolls his eyes. "Which was a load of crap to begin with."

"You'd mentioned that Callie had claimed to see a man with a scar following her in the days before she disappeared, too. Correct?"

Hayes nods. "As did Jack, at least according to Callie."

I furrow my brow. "Who's Jack?"

"Callie's brother."

"Callie has a brother?" I open my notebook and make a few notes.

"Had," he corrects.

"Right. Sorry." I meet his eyes, trying to sound apologetic. "Do you know where I can find him?"

He takes another long sip from his drink, then glances at the ceiling. "Last I checked, he's not too far from you in Oak Lawn."

"Oak Lawn? Isn't that—"

"A cemetery."

"He's dead?"

"Died about six months before Callie disappeared. In a car accident." He gives me a knowing look, an insinuation in his expression.

"What happened?"

"I don't know the details. Only what the authorities claimed. Although, based on my experience, that may not be all that reliable. Even so, they said he was traveling at a high rate of speed and lost control of his vehicle when rounding a bend, which forced him to swerve off the road, down an embankment, and crash into a tree. The impact caused the car to catch on fire, according to the police."

"So he died in a car fire?"

Hayes nods. "Sound familiar?"

"Just because Callie's brother died in a car wreck doesn't mean anything. People die in car accidents all the time."

"You're right." He pushes back from the table, the sudden movement causing me to reach for my weapon.

"Easy." He lifts both hands. "I'm just getting something out of the closet. A newspaper."

I slide my hand away from the holstered pistol at my side, but keep my eyes fixed on him as he strides toward a door tucked in the corner of the kitchen. He opens it and retrieves a small box, rifling through it before pulling out a faded yellow newspaper.

"People do die in car accidents all the time." He returns to the table, handing me the paper.

I study it, not immediately sure what I'm looking at, apart from it being the front page of the national newspaper the day of the avalanche that killed Esme's aunt, uncle, and four of her cousins, propelling her and her brother from sixth and seventh in line to second and third.

Now first and second.

"What does the avalanche have to do—"

"This." He turns the paper over and points to a tiny article on the bottom of the last page, a footnote of an event compared to the big headline.

I read the article and learn that a man by the name of

Warren Clark, a well-known and hated paparazzo died in a car accident a few miles away from the avalanche, although it was completely unrelated to that tragic event.

"I don't see what this has to do with anything. It says right here the police ruled it accidental after he lost control of his car."

"I figured you might say that." He places a second newspaper article in front of me, this one an obituary for Warren Clark.

As I read about his love for photography, I have to suppress the urge to roll my eyes or scoff, considering he eventually became one of the worst types of photographers in existence. During my time in the royal guard, I've had my fair share of encounters with the paparazzi. They're the worst of the worst, pushing all sorts of boundaries and barriers, putting lives at risk.

But as I reach information about his personal life and learn who his surviving family members were, I dart my eyes back toward Hayes.

"Callie and Jack Sloane were his kids?" I can't hide the disbelief in my voice.

Or the increasing suspicion.

"It seems an awful lot of tragedy for one family. Doesn't it? First, their father dies in a car wreck when he loses control of his vehicle. Then Jack also dies in a car wreck a few months before Callie disappears. Then, a few days after your brother said he'd look into this for me, he dies in a car fire that's nearly identical to the one that killed Callie's brother."

"Except for one thing."

"What's that?"

"The wreck that killed Adam wasn't ruled an accident. It was determined to be a planned, executed attack. By you." I pin him with a glare, studying his reaction.

But like all those weeks ago, there's no indication he's trying to cover up anything. He doesn't avert his gaze. Doesn't nervously fidget with his clothes. Doesn't repeatedly lick his lips or blink.

Instead, his stare is unwavering when he declares, "I had nothing to do with that."

I shouldn't believe him, but the more I learn about Callie, Jack, and their father, the more I can't ignore all the suspicious deaths.

"Regardless, there's no proof these car wrecks are related." I jab my finger at the newspaper. "Like I said, the wreck that resulted in Adam's death wasn't ruled an accident."

"Because there was a survivor," Hayes insists. "Did you ever stop to think what would have happened if there hadn't been anyone to make a statement about what she saw?"

Truthfully, I've never wanted to consider the possibility of Esme not surviving that horrible night. It's difficult enough knowing her life is constantly at risk by nature of who she is. I don't need to sit here and contemplate her death more than I already do.

"It still doesn't prove anything."

When Hayes parts his lips to argue once more, I hold up a hand, interrupting him.

"But I will admit it's suspicious. Especially if Adam was looking into this, as you claim."

"He was. And he knew I was onto something, that there was some connection between Callie's disappearance and her brother's death. Why else would he help me disappear when I told him about the man with a scar following me? There's something going on here. You know there is. Which is why I'm begging you to believe me." He pauses. "And help me."

I stare into the distance as I ruminate over everything he

shared with me. About both Callie and her brother observing a man with a scar following them before they died. How Hayes had seen that same man after publicly accusing Jameson Gates of murder. How not only Callie's brother died in a car wreck similar to the one Adam died in, but their father also did.

There's no smoking gun, so to speak, and each incident in isolation doesn't raise much doubt. But when you look at everything together, it's suspicious.

Like my brother often said. One time is a coincidence. Two times is a pattern. But three…

Well, three is reason for alarm.

And something in my gut tells me I have every reason to be alarmed right now.

Grabbing the glass off the table, I raise it to my lips and take a long sip, savoring the woodsy flavor as it travels down my throat and coats my stomach. Then I return the glass to the table and level my stare on Hayes.

"Okay," I say.

"Okay?" He arches a single brow.

"I'll look into this."

This is the last thing I should be doing right now, especially considering the risk if anyone finds out I'm not only aware that Hayes Barlow is alive, but that I'm helping him prove his innocence.

But my brother deserves justice.

I have a sneaking suspicion that justice hasn't been served.

"Thank you," he exhales, his expression awash with a combination of excitement and relief.

I hold my hand up. "That doesn't mean I believe your theory. Just that I agree something doesn't add up here. If I find you've lied to me or misled me in any way, I won't hesitate to turn you in. Or put a bullet in your head myself. Do you understand?"

With an unwavering gaze, he extends his hand across the table. "Agreed."

I stare at it for several long moments, at a crossroads. I just told him I'd help him, but this seems so much bigger than simply a handshake. Like the second I take his hand in mine, I'll embark down a path that there's no coming back from.

But Adam deserves the truth.

I deserve the truth.

Esme deserves the truth.

So, against my better judgment, I place my hand in his and give it a firm shake.

"Agreed."

PART II

Suspicion

CHAPTER FOURTEEN

Esme

I feverishly scrub my hands as I stare at my reflection in the bathroom mirror, my heart pounding a thunderous rhythm in my chest, my breath coming out in short gasps. But no matter how hard I scrub, I can't get what I just saw out of my mind.

Can't erase the blood covering my hands.

Most nights, I typically startle awake the second the man with the scar shoots Creed.

Not tonight.

Tonight, some outside force kept me under as blood sprayed everywhere.

No matter how hard I fought against the zip ties keeping me bound, I couldn't save Creed. All I could do was watch as his blood covered my face and hands, sobbing uncontrollably until my heart-wrenching cries woke me up.

I know it was only a dream. That it wasn't real.

But I still feel the spray of his blood as it splattered all over me. Still see the red staining my hands.

I fear I always will.

Scalding water stings my skin as I continue scrubbing my hands clean, searing pain intensifying with each stroke. But I keep going until I can't handle it anymore. With an anguished cry, I turn off the faucet and grab a towel. My hands tremble as I furiously wipe them. A part of me expects to see the white towel turn a crimson shade.

But it doesn't.

Further proof it wasn't real.

I pull my robe tighter around my body and make my way back to my bedroom, my eyes floating to the corner where Creed drew his final breath in my dream. I can't stay here. Can't get back in that bed. Not with the ghosts from my dream tormenting me.

Grabbing my cell off the nightstand, I send Creed a text asking if he'll meet me at the gym. I half expect for him to be asleep and not see my message, since it's only a little after four in the morning. Or for his message to go unread because my dream *was* real and he's dead.

Thankfully, his reply arrives almost immediately, telling me he'll be there, offering me a sliver of comfort.

When I arrive at the fitness center less than ten minutes later, he's already here, making me think he'd been at the palace when I texted him. It should have taken him close to a half-hour to get here from his house out in the suburbs.

Quietly dropping my bag on the floor, I'm careful not to immediately alert him to my presence. His body is tense and strong as he runs on the treadmill, sweat glistening on his toned arms and back that flexes as he increases his pace, eyes staring into the distance with an unbreakable focus and determination.

God, I miss seeing that same focus and determination in his expression as he makes love to me.

But we need to be smart.

Although, every night since the opera, I've hoped he'd sneak into my apartment.

He hasn't, though.

While I understand why, it doesn't make me miss falling asleep with his arms around me any less.

"Enjoying the show?"

The deep rumble of his voice snaps me back to the present, and I let my gaze drift up to meet his, a mischievous smirk curving his lips. In a heartbeat, all the unease I felt after waking from my dream vanishes. This is what I needed. A reminder of what's real.

A reminder that Creed's alive.

"Do you blame me?" I slowly saunter toward him as he hits the stop button on the machine, my body heating with every step. "It is quite…" I rake my eyes down his frame, my pulse kicking up, "tempting."

He groans, his muscles tensing as he grips the side rails of the treadmill. "You're making this bloody difficult, Esme." When he returns his eyes to mine, they're dark and dangerous, holding me captive.

"You're the one who insists we keep things platonic. If it were up to me, you'd be in my bed every night."

"If it were up to me, I'd be in your bed every night, too." He steps off the treadmill, his body so close I can feel the heat radiating off of him. He lifts a hand, gently grazing my hairline, smoothing back a wild strand and sending a wave of need crashing through me. "It's taken every ounce of resolve I possess to stay away. To refrain from sneaking into your bed. You have to know I'm always thinking about you." His lips hover tantalizingly close to mine. "Always craving you."

"Then have me, Creed," I beg breathlessly. "I'm yours."

"I plan on it." His mouth skims mine in a tease of a kiss before he pulls back. "But not yet."

I squeeze my eyes shut, pushing down the sexual frustration that's become worse every day.

"I'm going to need to stock up on batteries," I mutter under my breath.

"Batteries?" He scrunches his brows for a moment before his eyes widen in realization. Then his expression turns hungry as he leans toward me again. "Have you been getting yourself off without my permission, Esme?"

"Since when do I need your permission?" I spin from him, acting nonchalant as I make my way toward the scrimmage mats. But I can't ignore the thrill that rushes through me when I sense him stalking close behind.

"So you *have* been getting yourself off?"

"You can't expect me to go five months without an orgasm, can you?"

"No." He exhales a long sigh. "I just hate that I can't be the one to give them to you right now."

"If it makes you feel better, I think about you every time," I tease.

"I suppose I'll have to be happy with that consolation prize for now."

"I suppose you will."

"But you better be ready, Esme." He dips toward me, his voice dripping with sin. "The second I get those discharge papers, I'm coming for you. And I plan to make it so you can't walk for a bloody week."

A thrill rushes through me, my core clenching. I hoist myself onto my toes, my breath dancing on his lips. "I can't wait."

"Good." He winks and steps back, turning into the man

most people know him to be. Serious. Professional. Focused. "Should we review a few of the exercises we did last time?"

"Actually…" I clear my throat after taking a moment to compose myself. And tame my raging libido. "Can you show me how to escape zip ties?"

He doesn't immediately respond. Just stares, his analytical eyes sweeping over me.

"I'm constantly taught how to act in hostage situations to increase my likelihood of survival."

"And for good reason. What you do and say has a huge impact on that."

"But it's all premised on me waiting for help to arrive. Shouldn't I have the skills I need to help myself?"

"Escaping a situation where you're bound or restrained isn't always a golden ticket. Sometimes it can cause more harm in the long run. Like you've learned repeatedly, making your captor believe you won't cause any trouble can keep you alive long enough for you to be rescued."

"Please, Creed," I beg, my voice choked. "I don't want to depend on someone else coming to my rescue. What if that's not possible? Wouldn't you want me to know how to help myself? And I'm not asking the Creed Lawson who's a member of the royal guard." I approach him and lift my pleading eyes pleading to his. "I'm asking the Creed Lawson who I want to spend the rest of my life with."

He swallows hard. "You want to spend the rest of your life with me?"

"Of course I do." My expression brightens and I place a hand on my hip. "Do you think I'd resort to five months of only battery- and hand-powered orgasms for someone I didn't?"

He barks out a laugh, the sound echoing in the cavernous room.

God, I love that sound. What I wouldn't give to hear it all the time. I remind myself that in just a few months, I'll be able to.

"Okay…" he finally relents. "I'll show you how to escape zip ties."

"Thank you." I place my wrists together in front of me. "Tie me up."

He smirks, eyes darkening. "I like the sound of that."

CHAPTER FIFTEEN

Creed

"Let's practice one last time," I tell Esme an hour later, the mat below us littered with dozens of broken zip ties.

Her wrists are red and scratched from the pressure she's had to assert in order to break free. Regardless, she's refused any sort of tape to soften the blow, since she doubts her captors would be considerate enough to wrap her wrists before binding them.

I hate even hearing the mention of a captor when it pertains to her, but she has a point.

Which is why I agreed to this. I want her to have every tool available, should she find herself in a similar situation.

The more I learn about this man with a scar, the more I fear that could become a legitimate possibility.

"I'm not tired. I can keep going."

"You may not be tired, but your wrists need a break." I steal a glance at them, red and swollen with lines of chafed skin from being bound. "People are going to think you're into some kinky shit."

"Being tied up isn't that kinky."

"And what *do* you consider kinky?"

Truth be told, I'm not sure what her sexual tastes are these days. We've only spent two nights together in the past ten years. They were both bloody incredible, but I can only imagine she's matured from that summer when we were in our twenties. I hate thinking about her exploring her sexuality with anyone else, but I can't worry about that.

She's with me now.

That's all that matters.

"Play your cards right and maybe you'll find out this August." She winks, then spins around, moving her arms behind her, pinning her wrists together.

We've practiced all sorts of variations of this exercise. First with her wrists tied in front of her. Then with her in a chair, her wrists secured to the arms. But she insisted on this particular scenario — her wrists bound behind her as she lies on the floor. It makes me wonder if there's a reason behind it. I haven't pressed, though, focusing on teaching her the skills she needs for every situation.

I pull another set of zip ties out of my pocket and approach her. As I instructed, she's mindful not to fist her hands as I do so. Most criminals don't pay much attention to their hostages' hands, wanting to tie them up as quickly as possible. But with your hand flexed wide instead of scrunched into a fist, it makes your forearm wider.

The wider your forearm when being restrained, the more wiggle room you'll have when you eventually ball your hand.

I secure the ties and step back, giving Esme space to work.

She drops to the floor and finds a hard angle against the

wall, using the edge to weaken the zip tie enough to break free. After a few moments, she draws in a deep breath and closes her eyes.

Then, like I taught her, she makes a quick, decisive motion with both arms, causing the restraint to snap.

"Great job, Esme. You're becoming a real pro at this." I hold out my hand and help her to her feet.

"What can I say?" She gives me a brilliant smile. "I've got a great teacher."

"I'm glad you think so."

"Always." She tilts her head back, eyes locking with mine.

It's a simple word. One I've said countless times. But since the night we finally bore our souls to each other, it's taken on a different meaning. Now, even when we're in public, she finds a way to insert that word into her normal conversation. As if it's her secret way of telling me that she's still with me.

That she's still mine.

That she still loves me.

"Always," I repeat in a low murmur, resisting the urge to wrap my arm around her waist, pull her body to mine, and kiss her.

After several protracted moments, Esme clears her throat and steps back, putting space between us before I do something I'll regret. "I should get going. Let you get on with your day."

"Of course." Holding her gaze, I bow toward her. "Princess."

She bites on her lower lip, trying to reel in her smile. But the corners of her mouth betray her, lifting up despite her best efforts. She's always loved when I call her princess.

And I'm glad I'm the only one who can.

"Captain," she replies, eyes skating down my frame for a

beat. Then she slings her workout bag onto her shoulder and starts toward the door. She only makes it a few feet before stopping, whirling around to face me. Her lips part as if about to say something.

"What is it?" I move toward her.

She heaves a long sigh and reaches into the side pouch of her bag, retrieving her phone. After tapping at it for a few seconds, she offers it to me.

I take it from her, not immediately sure what I'm looking at. Until I notice the scar along the jawline of the man in the sketch.

"Is this who I think it is?" I arch a brow.

"It's not perfect, but I've determined it's all but impossible to draw sinister eyes or a malevolent sneer, regardless of how hard I've tried. But that's him. The man I've seen in my dreams. The same man I saw at the opera."

"You drew this?"

She nods, and I return my attention to the sketch, focusing on as many details as possible — the dimple in his chin, the angle of his almond-shaped eyes, the width of his prominent nose.

But the defining characteristic is that scar, long and jagged, running the entire length of his right jawline from his ear and curving up, stopping at his upper lip. I wonder what happened to cause such a prominent scar. Whatever it is, I bet he deserved it.

"Do you... Do you think you can find him for me?" she asks timidly.

"I've tried. I pulled information on everyone in attendance at the opera that night, performers and staff included. Broke protocol and sat through hours of security footage in the hopes of uncovering something." I lean toward her, lowering my voice. "No one had a scar."

"He was there, Creed. I saw him." She yanks her phone out of my hand, roughly shoving it back into her gym bag. "Callie did, too." She crosses her arms in front of her chest.

I blink, taken aback by her assertion. Hayes told me the same thing.

But how is Esme aware of this?

"How do you—"

"Jameson Gates."

I briefly close my eyes, unsure how I feel about her discussing this with Jameson Gates. And not because Hayes Barlow has accused him of being involved in the past, as absurd as the idea of someone as philanthropic as Jameson Gates being responsible for this is.

I don't like her talking to him because I can't do that. I can't stop by her apartment or her office and have a conversation without people starting to talk.

Without raising suspicion.

Hell, if someone learned about our early morning workout sessions, it would raise eyebrows, considering our history.

"What did he say?" I manage to ask through a clenched jaw.

"He just wanted to make sure I was okay. Then assured me I wasn't losing my mind. That Callie mentioned seeing a guy with a scar following her before she disappeared."

I nod, her statement similar to what Hayes told me.

"He thinks he may have some sort of connection to Silas Archer," she adds softly.

"Silas Archer?"

"You know Jameson and Callie had a thing, right?"

"I do."

In the months following his death, I repeatedly read my brother's report of the night Hayes Barlow accused Jameson

Gates of murder, if for no other reason than it was the last incident report he ever filed on the job and I wanted to read my brother's words. That included his notes about Jameson's secret relationship with Callie.

"Archer and his father wanted the two of us to be together—"

"And saw Callie as a threat to that," I say, filling in the blanks.

She shrugs. "It's just a theory, but considering Callie claimed to have seen a man with a scar before she disappeared, the same man who could very well be responsible for Adam's death, it's possible he's working for Archer. That he killed Callie. And is now going after anyone who could expose the truth."

I look into the distance, toiling over all of this in my mind.

Jameson's theory has some merit.

But how would he explain Callie's brother seeing the same man? And Hayes?

I can't bring that up with Esme, though. No one can know he's alive.

"That still won't make this guy suddenly appear on the security footage."

"I know. But maybe if you ran this sketch through a facial recognition program—"

"I'm not a forensics guy, Esme. I don't have access to that kind of stuff."

"Doesn't one of your old friends from special teams have a private security firm?"

"He does, but I haven't spoken to him in a while. And when I do call, it's with a favor that would require him to access government records outside the scope of his approved contracts?" I run a hand over my face. "I don't—"

"Please, Creed." She steps toward me, grabbing my hands in hers, eyes pleading with me. "I need to know who he is. Why he's haunting my dreams. And now my reality."

I pinch my lips together, not immediately responding. I want to shield her from whatever's going on. Keep her as far away from all of this as possible.

But isn't it too late for that? If her dreams are correct, this guy's already tried to kill her twice. I need answers before he tries for a third time and actually succeeds.

On a long exhale, I return my gaze to her. "I'll see what I can do."

CHAPTER SIXTEEN

Creed

I wipe the sweat from my brow, swallowing down a cough as dust kicks up in my face from yet another box stacked high in the garage that I haven't looked at in years. Since I moved in with Rory, I've avoided going through these. Today, it's a welcome distraction. Helps take my mind off this mysterious man with a scar. At this point, I could probably draw him from memory.

Unfortunately, Lucas, my friend from special teams, hasn't gotten back to me with any potential matches. I almost didn't reach out to him to begin with, not wanting to waste his time with something that might be nothing.

But when I paid Hayes Barlow a visit to show him the sketch, he confirmed it was an extremely close representation. After that, I had no choice but to ask Lucas for help, which he was happy to give me, despite the months that had passed since we've spoken.

I didn't expect he'd have an answer right away. But as the

days have stretched into weeks, I wonder if we'll ever find a name to go with the face.

In the meantime, I've also started to look into Silas Archer, see if there's anything in his background I find suspicious. As expected, that's also proved to be a dead end.

Everything's proved to be a dead end.

Which is why I came out to the garage. Thought by doing something completely unrelated, it would clear my mind.

Not to mention, this garage has needed a good cleaning for years. Since Rory already had a fully furnished house, I'd stored most of my things out here, thinking I'd need them once I moved out.

Little did I know it would be ten years before I'd finally do it.

Despite how overwhelming it all seems, going through these boxes has been therapeutic, like taking a trip down memory lane. I found some of my old military figurines from when I was a little boy. My graduation cap from secondary school. Even a framed photo of Anders, Esme, and me in the elephant boneyard, as we called the beach littered with driftwood near her family's villa on the coast. If I'd uncovered this years ago, it probably would have made my heart ache.

Now, it makes me even more excited about my future with her, regardless of the obstacles we'll need to overcome.

Dusting off another box, I set it on the workbench, the small space littered with bags of trash and donations. I lift the lid, expecting it to contain more mementos or paperwork I threw inside in the rush to pack up my old apartment.

Instead, it feels like all the air is sucked from my lungs when my eyes fall on my brother's belongings. A coffee mug with the royal guard insignia on one side, Captain Lawson on the other. A bag of his favorite chocolates he always kept hidden in the drawer of his desk at work. And a framed photo of him and Rory, an ultrasound image stuck in the corner. I pick it up, recalling this being displayed prominently in his office.

I'd forgotten Archie had given me all of Adam's things after he'd been promoted to Esme's CPO and took over my brother's old office. At the time, I was still numb. Still drowning in my grief. Still weighed down by the guilt of the way I'd treated Adam during our last conversation.

As much as seeing my brother's old things makes my heart ache, I find comfort in them, too. Instead of returning it to the shelves so another ten years can pass before I look at it again, I sit on the stool and sift through it, smiling at the memories that spring to the surface. Like the photo of us after I finished basic training. His old pocket knife with his initials inscribed on the handle. Even a bottle of his favorite scotch.

I stare at the label, remembering the two of us sharing a drink from this exact bottle when he told me Rory was pregnant.

When he begged me to look after her and their unborn child if anything ever happened to him. I tried to tell him he was being ridiculous, that he'd be around for a long time.

I wonder if he had a feeling in his gut he wouldn't and that's why he was so adamant I make him that promise.

Adam always had a sixth sense about this kind of thing.

What would his sixth sense say about this man with the scar and his connection to everything?

Pushing out a long sigh, I set the bottle on the work bench and continue sorting through the box. It's mostly filled with pens and other office supplies, which doesn't surprise me. Adam could never walk past a new notebook or set of pens without buying them.

I'm about to return everything to the box when something on the bottom catches my eye. It's just another notebook, but this one is dated just a week before he died.

I pull it out and run my fingers over my brother's familiar scrawl, remembering flipping through this notebook mere days after his death. Reading his notes about Jameson Gates' relationship with Callie Sloane was difficult back then, knowing they were some of the last notes my brother ever made. I couldn't even get through all of them.

But maybe revisiting them will help me get answers about this man with a scar.

Maybe he figured something out in his final days that could help.

Opening the notebook, I read through pages of notes Adam made about Jameson Gates' connection to Callie Sloane and why Hayes might think Jameson was involved in her disappearance. It's essentially the same information that was included in my brother's official incident report.

How Jameson claimed to have met Callie when he had a flat tire and she stopped to help him. How they dated in secret for months because of who he was. How after Jameson attended the King's Day gala and danced with Esme, the entire country salivated over the idea of them as a couple. How Silas Archer made a proposition for Jameson to marry Esme. How Jameson turned him down because he claimed to be in love with Callie.

Then how Callie broke things off a short time later. How that was the last time he spoke to her, even after repeatedly trying to call and text her. How he had no idea she'd gone missing until weeks later when Hayes Barlow, Callie's friend and boss, went to the police to report her missing.

How Hayes blamed Callie's disappearance on Jameson, despite there being no evidence to support it.

But that didn't seem to stop Adam from digging further.

As I flip through the pages, it's obvious he also spoke to Hayes, who essentially told him Callie wouldn't just disappear without saying goodbye. That he always thought Jameson had an ulterior motive in wanting to be with Callie.

I turn the page again, hoping to uncover more information.

All I find is a phone number. No name. Nothing.

It could be completely unrelated to this, but I know my brother. He was organized to a fault. He wouldn't jot down a number in this notebook unless it had something to do with what he'd been looking into.

Digging my phone out of my pocket, I punch in the numbers and bring it up to my ear, listening to it ring.

And ring.

And ring.

Just when it's about to go to voicemail, a woman answers. "Hello?"

"Hi. I, uh…" I clear my throat, taking a moment to get my thoughts in order. Truthfully, I hadn't expected anyone to answer. "I'm sorry for bothering you. My name's Creed Lawson. This may sound crazy, but I found my brother's old work notebook. He'd written down this number. I'm just trying to figure out why."

"Your brother was Adam Lawson, wasn't he?" the woman asks. She doesn't sound that old. Maybe in her thirties or forties.

"Yes. He unfortunately—"

"I know about your brother's death," she interjects, then adds, "I'm sorry for your loss."

"Thank you…," I trail off. "I'm sorry. What's your name?"

"Reagan. Reagan Fisher."

"Thank you, Ms. Fisher. How did you know my brother?"

"To be honest, I didn't really know him. We only spoke once."

"Can you tell me what about?"

"Jack Sloane."

The instant she says that name, my pulse kicks up, my mind racing with dozens of different scenarios. I quickly dig a pen out of the box and uncap it, scribbling down Reagan's name below her number in my brother's notebook before writing Jack's name.

"What about him?"

"Apparently, your brother had been going through Jack's phone records and saw a call to me a few days before he died. Jack, that is. Not your brother. Although, I guess your brother also called me a few days before his death, too. I…" She trails off, obviously unnerved by this revelation.

"What did you tell Adam about your phone call with Jack?" I press, pulling her attention back to me. "I understand it's been quite a few years, but any information you have could help."

I don't tell her *what* it could help with. Thankfully, she seems to know enough not to ask.

"I have a feeling I'll remember that phone call with Jack for the rest of my life. He didn't sound like the Jack I knew."

"What was your relationship to him?"

"We went to college together. Tried dating before we realized we were better as friends."

I continue making notes about practically everything Reagan says, not wanting to forget a single detail.

"And how did Jack sound when you spoke during that last conversation?"

"Uneasy. Crazed. Said he found something in his father's

things. A video he took the night he died. You know who his father was, correct?"

I nod. "I do. Did Jack tell you what was on the video?"

"He wouldn't say. Like I mentioned, Jack didn't sound like himself. Said he didn't know who he could trust. Who might have tapped his phone. He sounded like one of those conspiracy theorists, which was unusual for Jack. He was normally even headed. Kept going on and on about some huge coverup involving the royal family. Whatever he found certainly unsettled him, so I offered to reach out to my cousin, who worked at the palace. Thought if there was something that involved the royal family, maybe someone who worked for the royal household could help."

"What did he say to that?"

"He was grateful. Relieved, even."

"And who's your cousin?"

"Gianna Vale."

I stiffen, nearly choking on my own saliva. "Your cousin was Gianna Vale?"

"Yes."

I blink, my brain spinning with theories. Yes, this could simply be a coincidence.

But I'm starting to think there are just too many coincidences to write them off as nothing, especially since Gianna died just a few weeks after my brother.

"Did you ever learn what came of his conversation with Gianna?"

"She claimed he never showed up to the meeting I arranged, which wouldn't surprise me. Jack wasn't thinking clearly in the days before his death. It was almost like he was having some sort of psychotic break, which makes me wonder if there ever was a video or he'd just imagined it. And now with the latest news about his sister..." She exhales a shuttering breath. "That poor family has suffered tragedy after tragedy."

"They certainly have."

"I'm sorry I can't be more helpful. But that's all I spoke with Jack about during that phone call. All I told your brother, too."

"You've actually been extremely helpful," I assure her. "I appreciate you taking the time to talk to me. And for answering your phone in the first place. These days, most people don't."

"You've got that right," she laughs. "But I had a gut feeling it was important."

"That sounds like something my brother would say," I remark wistfully, staring into the distance for a beat before her voice pulls me back to the present.

"If I think of anything else, I'll be sure to call. And you're welcome to reach out if you have any more questions, as well."

"Thank you, Ms. Fisher."

We say our goodbyes, and I dash out of the garage and into the house, taking the steps two at a time as I dart up to my bedroom. I go to my desk and pull out the file containing all the research I'd amassed over the past few weeks, starting with Callie and Jack's father, Warren Clark.

He died in a car wreck a few hours before the avalanche that killed Esme's uncle, aunt, and cousins. After doing additional research into his "career", I learned he was credited with being the person to take the last photos of Prince Nicholas and his family alive. They weren't official photos, just candid shots of them leaving their ski villa the day before they perished. Based on all the photos he sold that week, it's obvious he'd been camped out in the area, hoping to snap as many shots as possible.

Couple that with the fact that Jack claimed to find a video from the night he died, it's probably safe to assume it was a video of Prince Nicholas and his family.

While I can understand why Reagan might think there may never have been a video, I'm not so quick to dismiss it. Not with everything else I know.

Especially considering she'd set up a meeting between Jack and Gianna Vale, who's also dead.

Is it possible Jack met with Gianna and gave her the video, which also made her a target?

And what could possibly be on that video that someone's willing to kill over?

CHAPTER SEVENTEEN

Creed

"Creed? Are you in here? Why's the garage door wide open?"

Rory's voice cuts through the comfortable silence, and I snap my eyes away from my laptop to see the sun has started to set.

I jump to my feet, cursing under my breath that I'd allowed myself to lose track of time. Last I checked, it wasn't yet two in the afternoon. Now, it's nearly six in the evening. I was so consumed with learning everything I could about Warren Clark that I hadn't given much thought to anything else — like the fact that Rory would be getting out of work and might question why I've been going through all the boxes in the garage.

I throw all the information I've amassed on Warren Clark back into a folder and shove it into my desk before slipping out of my room, closing the door behind me. I'm about to hurry down the stairs when Rory emerges onto the second floor landing, her suspicious eyes falling on my closed door.

I typically leave it open, since I generally don't have anything to hide.

These days, though, I tend to hide everything from her. Hell, I try to avoid her as much as I can.

"Have you been working in the garage?" Her question isn't accusatory. Just curious.

"Figured it was time to go through my old things. Get rid of stuff I don't need anymore."

"That's a good idea, considering most of that stuff's been collecting dust for years now. Just give me a few minutes and I'll come help you for a bit before I have to grab AJ from practice. I'd like to go through some of your old kitchen stuff before you get rid of it. See if there's anything we could use here, since a lot of our plates and glasses have seen better days." She starts to turn toward her bedroom.

"I'm not getting rid of my kitchen stuff," I tell her, the words leaving my mouth before I can stop them.

Maybe it's a good thing, though. It's already June. I've had plans to move out since the end of March. I've already signed a lease on a new place that starts a week or so after I return from this next trip to the States with Anderson. I can't keep putting this off. It will only make it more difficult. Hell, I've probably already made it more difficult than it has to be by waiting this long.

"I thought you said you were getting rid of things you don't need." She faces me, brows furrowed. "I figured that would be the first stuff to go—"

"I found a place in the city. I signed the lease earlier this week."

"You did what?" She steps toward me, her voice incredulous. "Why would you do that? And without consulting me? I get that the commute to the palace can be a bitch. I do it every day, too. But I chose this area because of the schools. You can't expect me to uproot our lives without being consulted. Expect me to be okay with putting AJ in a new school district that I've done absolutely no research on. AJ needs consistency in his life, and this—"

"I'm not planning on uprooting you or AJ."

"But you said—"

"I found a place. For me. Alone."

My words seem to echo around me as Rory gapes at me, face contorted in disbelief and surprise.

"You…" She swallows hard. "You're moving out?" Her voice rises in pitch at the end as she pulls her bottom lip between her teeth.

This is why I've avoided this conversation. I'm more than aware of Rory's abandonment issues. After growing up in the foster care system and essentially being moved from home to home, she never had much stability in her life. So when she finds security, she clings to it.

It's why she clung to me so hard after Adam's death. Unfortunately, I let her do it.

I can't keep letting her do it.

I need her to let go of me. For her own good.

And mine.

I draw in a deep breath, willing my voice to sound soothing. "It's time, Rory. It was time years ago. I just kept putting it off."

"But what about the promise you made your brother?" She throws her hands up in exasperation. "You swore you'd always be here for AJ. For me. You're just going to go back on your word?"

Truthfully, that promise has been one of the reasons I've avoided this for so long. Like my mum told me on Christmas,

Adam would have never asked me to make that promise if he knew I'd sacrifice my happiness in order to fulfill it. I doubt he anticipated I'd take my promise to the lengths I have. I allowed the remorse I felt after his death to cloud my rationale. To guilt me into making wrong decision after wrong decision.

No more.

"Adam wouldn't have wanted this life for me. Or for you and AJ. He would have wanted you to be happy. To live a full life. To finally move on."

"Move on?" she shrieks, her face reddening, the veins in her neck pulsing as she clenches her jaw.

"Yes, Rory," I reply, keeping my tone even despite the growing irritation and desperation in her own. "We all deserve to move on. It's been ten years. It's time."

"Maybe I don't want to move on, Creed. Did you ever stop to think about that? Maybe I'm not willing to just forget Adam."

"I'm not saying you need to forget him. But you can't stand there and claim this arrangement's actually been healthy. And I'm not just talking about us living together, but about everything else that's gone on, too. It's been so bloody toxic. You've got to see that. Hell, up until a few months ago, I let you crawl into bed with me and call me Adam while we fucked. Which we never should have done in the first place."

She purses her lips and crosses her arms over her chest, the fire in her gaze intensifying. "I never heard any complaints from you." She leans closer, her voice dropping to an icy whisper. "In fact, it seemed like you enjoyed it, Creed. Quite a bit."

I squeeze my eyes shut, refusing to play the blame game. It won't solve anything.

Nor will it change my mind.

Nothing will.

"It still doesn't make it right. It doesn't make *us* right." I gesture between our bodies. "After Adam died, I wanted to do right by him. Thought staying here with you was the only way to fulfill the promise I made. But by staying, I kept us trapped in the past. You deserve to have a future." I point to my chest. "I deserve to have a future." I gesture toward AJ's room. "*AJ* deserves to have a future. Don't you want that? For your son to be able to live without the ghost of his father constantly hovering over him? Over you? Don't you—"

Before I can finish my sentence, her hand connects with my cheek, the loud slap reverberating against the walls and ceiling.

I snap my mouth shut, blinking through the sting. But as much as my blood boils, I refuse to reciprocate.

"Fuck you, Creed."

"Rory…," I begin, unsure of what I can say to get through to her. *Is* there anything I can say to get through to her?

Should I have done more in those initial months following Adam's death to encourage her to get help? She did go to therapy and even joined a grief group at a local church, but after a while, she stopped going. She's started again here and there, but she never stuck with it. Maybe if I'd said something, pushed her harder to deal with her issues, she wouldn't be so dependent on me. On AJ.

And on Adam.

"You want to be rid of us so badly?" She holds her head high, the lines of her face radiating with anger. "Then sleep somewhere else from now on."

She spins on her heels and storms into her bedroom, slamming the door behind her, causing a photo of AJ and me to fall off the wall and crash onto the floor.

CHAPTER EIGHTEEN

Esme

"I apologize for the interruption, ma'am." My private secretary pokes his head into my office as I'm reviewing a speech I'll be giving this evening at a charity dinner benefiting cancer research initiatives that Jameson Gates asked me to attend.

I never thought I'd reach the point that I'd do Jameson Gates any favors.

But the more I've spoken to him over the past few weeks, the more worn out he seems with the weight of everything, the more I realize I'd allowed my imagination run away with me. Just like my father tried to tell me.

"I thought you'd already left for the day," I tell Lieutenant Hawkins.

"I just had a few things to finish up. I'm leaving now. I do have Captain Lawson on the line for you. You'd asked him to check in when he arrived in the States?"

"Of course." I smile, ignoring the fluttering in my stomach over the prospect of talking to Creed.

I hadn't asked Creed to check in, but if this is a way for us to talk while he's overseas with Anders, I'll happily lie.

"Thank you, Thomas. Enjoy your evening."

"You, too, ma'am."

I watch him retreat from my office. Once he closes the door behind him, I pick up the receiver.

"This is Esme," I say, keeping things professional in case I clicked on the wrong line.

"Your Highness," Creed responds with a seductive lilt.

"Captain." I lean further into my chair, kicking my feet up onto my desk. Hearing Creed's voice as I sit in this office brings back memories of our secret affair all those years ago. All the times he visited me under the pretense of planning a baby shower for Rory. All the ways he made my body come alive. All the things he made me feel.

They're still some of my fondest memories, despite how it ended.

And I can't wait to make even more memories with him soon.

"It's my understanding I asked you to check in with me once you arrived in America." My voice oozes with sarcasm. "I don't recall making that request. Are you sure you're not confusing me with some other girl?"

A raspy chuckle sounds on the line, making those flutters in my stomach increase even more. It's just a laugh, but the deep rumble does things to me.

Hits me in places I didn't think existed.

"Trust me, princess. I could never confuse you with someone else. You're one of a kind. At least in my eyes."

I sigh, basking in his words. It feels like it's been forever since we've been able to share a moment like this. I suppose that's the good thing about him being in the States. It's easier for him to reach out without raising suspicion.

"Okay then. Go ahead."

"Go ahead?" he asks.

"Yes. How were your travels?"

"Great."

"Pretty sure this conversation could have taken place over email."

"Then I wouldn't have been able to hear your voice. Or tell you to go check your gym bag."

"My gym bag?"

"I left you a present in it this morning."

I can hear the smile in his voice. Can picture the sensual smirk pulling on his lips. Can feel his eyes raking over my body as if he were in the room with me.

"So be a good girl and go to your private suite to find it. But don't open it until you FaceTime me back. I want to look at you when you do."

Excitement bubbles inside me. And not the kind of excitement a kid experiences on Christmas morning.

It's the kind of excitement that has my core clenching, my pulse quickening.

"Yes, sir," I say sweetly, then hang up the phone, jumping to my feet.

I fight the urge to sprint out of my office and toward my private quarters, remaining as calm as possible, especially when my butler greets me as I enter the living room, asking if I'd like any tea brought up to my suite.

I can't think about tea right now. Not until I know what Creed hid in my gym bag.

So instead, I tell him I need some time to myself and that

I'm not to be disturbed until Archie arrives to take me to tonight's event, which he reminds me is in less than an hour.

Hurrying into my bedroom, I close and lock the door behind me, doing a quick check of my reflection in the full-length mirror before finding my gym bag.

As promised, there's a medium-sized box wrapped in white paper with a red bow. I hadn't even noticed him sneak anything into it. Then again, I was too preoccupied with the intense workout he put me through before he had to get to the airfield.

Toeing off my shoes, I bring the box to my bed and hit Creed's contact in my phone to initiate a video chat with him.

He answers almost right away, his face filling my screen. His dark eyes are weary from traveling all day, a soft smile curling on his full lips. It's only been twelve hours since I last saw him, but the sight of him reminds me how much I've missed him in those twelve hours, especially when I thought I wouldn't see him for an entire month.

"Did you find it?" he asks without greeting.

I climb onto the bed, and use one of my pillows to prop up my phone, lifting the box so he can see.

"Good." He smirks, his pupils dilating briefly, making me think this box probably doesn't contain a bible. "Open it."

Biting my lower lip, I do as he asks, pulling the ribbon and lifting the top off the box. When I push back the tissue, my eyes bulge.

"Is that what I think it is?"

With a seductive gleam, he slowly nods. "I haven't been able to stop thinking about our conversation a few weeks ago. How you've resorted to hand- and battery-powered orgasms because of our…situation."

"And what does this have to do with that?"

I lift the curved vibrator out of the box. It's different from the one I typically use. Instead of being long, this one is U-shaped with one side thicker than the other, the thinnest part at the curve. It's almost as if it were designed this way to allow someone to wear it as they go about their day.

In fact, I think that's exactly why it was designed this way.

"Turn the power on, but don't use the remote control to start it."

My heart hammers in my chest as I follow his request, moisture pooling between my thighs. I show him the toy so he can see it's on, his gaze lingering on me.

"Good girl."

A shiver of awareness cascades through my body from those two words. I'll do whatever he asks if he keeps calling me his good girl in that raspy tone.

"Now what?" I ask, my mouth growing dry in antic-ipation.

"I want you to put it on."

Electricity heats my veins, desire pooling low in my belly. I steal a quick glance at the clock, noting that I have about forty-five minutes until Archie will be here. Normally, I'd already be working on my hair and makeup. That's what I *should* be doing. But looking presentable for this evening is the last thing on my mind right now.

Standing, I arrange my phone so Creed can see. With slow movements, I unzip my dress and leisurely slide the sleeves down my arms before pushing it past my hips, allowing it to pool in a pile on the floor. I unhook my bra, my panties joining the pile of clothes seconds later.

"God, I miss you," Creed groans, the intensity in his stare

scorching my skin. There's lust within, but also so much devotion.

"I miss you, too. Even when you're in the same country. I miss us."

"So do I. But until we can be us…" He playfully waggles his brow. "Give it a try."

I climb back onto the bed and spread my legs, not caring that Creed's currently getting a good show. It doesn't even faze me. I want him to see me like this. Want him to crave me more than his next breath.

Because that's how I feel about him.

Keeping my eyes glued on his, I ease the toy inside, biting back a moan at the sensation of fullness I've been desperate to feel for too long.

"Now what?" I pant.

His smirk becomes even more mischievous. Then I feel a low buzz, the surprise causing me to arch my back off the bed, gasping for air.

"I assume you felt that."

"Damn straight I did," I exhale, struggling to catch my breath.

"Good."

"Did you do that?"

"I have an app on my phone. So now I *can* give you an orgasm." He drops his tone to a sinful decibel. "I can give you *all* your orgasms."

"Then give me one now, Creed." I grab my phone as I lie against the pillows.

"Gladly." The word's barely left his mouth when the toy comes to life inside me again.

This isn't the first time I've used a vibrator. Hell, it's not even the first time Creed's used a vibrator on me, in so far as he's using it on me now. But every other time, I was able to anticipate the sensation and intensity.

Not today.

It's a vastly different experience to be at Creed's complete mercy. To have no control over what he does next. Sure, I could grab the remote and take control myself. But I love this more. Love how Creed knows just how far to push the intensity before dialing it back, leaving me desperate for more.

"God, I can't wait until I get to be inside you again, Esme," he grunts. "Do you have any idea how bloody difficult it's been?"

I moan as the vibrations increase, my breaths coming in heavy gasps. Every pulse of the toy sends shivers coursing through my body, driving me wild with need.

I've never been as desperate for release as I am right now.

But I don't want this to end. I want this to last. Want to lose myself in Creed's sensual voice and words.

"I need you, Creed," I moan, writhing against the bed as I chase that toe-curling sensation. "Need you inside me."

"I will be soon. But until then, imagine it's me driving into you." He increases the intensity, and I buck my hips, as if he were on top of me instead of thousands of miles away. "Imagine it's me licking your clit." He transfers the sensation to the outside of the toy, making me gasp, then moan.

I grip the sheets below me, circling my hips, squeezing my thighs together, desperate for release.

"Pretend it's me making you come, Esme." He increases the intensity yet again. This time is even more extreme. I try to fight it, wanting to savor in this for as long as possible. But it's a losing battle, especially when he rasps, "Come, Esme. Now."

His demand turns me into complete putty, my body

convulsing as I cry out, using a pillow to muffle my screams so my household staff doesn't come running.

"Fuck, yes. That's it," Creed groans, his expression tightening, jaw clenching. I'd been so lost in my own bliss that I hadn't even considered he'd be jerking himself off. "God, I love your face when you come."

"It's because you fuck me so good. I love when you drive into me. Love when you take me from behind. But you know what I love the most?"

"What's that, princess?" His breathing becomes even more labored, and I can hear the slick sound of his hand working his cock.

"When I'm on my knees before you. When you're fucking my mouth. When you're so deep I can barely breathe. And then when you come down my throat, forcing me to swallow every single drop. And I'll always swallow every drop for you."

"Fuck!" he roars, his breathing growing even more ragged in the seconds before he whimpers, his mouth opening as bliss covers his expression.

Neither one of us speaks for several moments, both of us struggling to catch our breath after such an intense orgasm. Sweat cools on my skin, my body still tingling from the aftershocks, even with the toy no longer vibrating.

A part of me wants to ask him why he seems to have had a change of heart, at least as it pertains to intimacy between us. From the beginning, he's kept the lines firmly drawn. While he technically hasn't touched me, this most certainly blurred any of those lines.

But I don't want to bring that up now. Don't want to do anything that could jeopardize having a repeat of today.

"That settles it, Captain Lawson," I finally manage to say through my labored breaths.

"What's that?"

I turn toward my phone, meeting Creed's gaze. "I'm going to need daily reports about how my brother's doing."

He doesn't say anything right away, simply stares at me. I half expect him to tell me we can't. That it's too risky.

Then a wicked smile lights up his expression. "For you, princess, that most certainly can be arranged."

CHAPTER NINETEEN

Creed

"What did you want to talk to me about?"

I take a refreshing pull from my beer, savoring in the cool liquid as I look around the relatively quiet West Village pub.

I've been in New York with Anderson for the past few weeks. While I typically enjoy the break that traveling with him affords me, I'm a bit on edge these days. Not just with the minor breakthrough I had regarding Warren Clark's death and the video he took, but also with how I left things with Rory.

The only good thing about being so far away from home has been the freedom that comes with being miles from prying eyes and eavesdropping ears, allowing me to talk to Esme every day.

Technically, it's allowed me to do *more* than talk to her every day.

Which has made me burn for her in ways I never thought possible.

Once I gave her that vibrator, I feared this would happen. But I hated the thought that she was sacrificing her needs for my peace of mind.

I can only hope this current arrangement will be enough to satisfy her over the next few months.

Can only hope that once I'm back in Belmont, I'll have the strength to resist the temptation to drive over to her apartment for a taste of what I'm so damn desperate for.

"Will you stop that?" Anderson barks out.

"Stop what?" I dart my gaze to him.

"I see what you're doing." He waves a hand around. "You're sweeping the room for potential threats. You don't need to. Kylian's in charge right now."

I glance toward where Lieutenant Kylian O'Kelly sits at the opposite end of the bar, a club soda in front of him. He scans the pub with his sharp eyes, looking for any suspicious activity, as he was trained to do.

"Occupational hazard." I return my gaze to Anderson, fighting my instinct to continue scanning my surroundings.

"I know." He brings his bottle up to his lips, taking a small sip from his beer.

While he's mindful of his doctor's recommendation to limit his alcohol intake, he'll sometimes sip on a beer or glass of wine at dinner. But he rarely drinks more than a quarter of a glass these days.

"So, what's up?" I ask again, doing my best to devote all my attention to Anderson. He specifically requested I have a beer with him. Begged me, even. Which leads me to believe this is important.

"I'm about to tell you something as my friend. I don't want you to go into work mode and think about what this means for me professionally. Not yet anyway. I just… I want to celebrate this moment with my friend."

"And what moment is that?"

He draws in a deep breath and runs his hands along his jeans, dropping his voice to a whisper. "I asked Nora to marry me."

I blink once. Twice. Allowing his statement to sink in.

Giving myself a chance to formulate my response and make sure it's done as a friend and not his chief protection officer.

As I've learned, the lines aren't always that clear.

Especially when something of a personal nature has such a huge bearing on his status as heir apparent, like who he's going to marry.

But he asked for a friend today. That's what I need to be.

"And she said yes?" I scoff.

Anderson playfully punches me. "Of course she did, you prick."

"I don't know." I shrug. "Thought maybe she'd like to explore her options for a little longer. See if there's someone better out there. Should I talk to her? Let her know how much of a pain in the arse you truly are?"

He laughs, a smile unlike any I've seen in a while lighting up his face. "Pretty sure she already knows."

I wrap an arm around him, giving him a quick bro hug. "Congrats, Anders."

He pats my back. "Thanks, mate."

"All joking aside, I'm happy for you." I pull back, keeping a hand on his shoulder. "Truly. Nora's a wonderful woman. She'd have to be to put up with all the shite that comes with dating you." My expression falters slightly as I drop my hold on him. "She *does* know what she'll have to put up with going forward, correct? Everything she'll have to give up? Her job? Her life here in New York? Her anonymity?"

"Of course she does," he reassures me. "I've been upfront and honest with her since the beginning. She understands as much as she can without experiencing it firsthand." He chuckles under his breath. "I often feel like a broken record with how many times I've warned her about what her future would look like if she chose this path. If she chose me. She even accused me of trying to scare her off with my incessant warnings."

"And yet she said yes." It's more of a statement than a question.

A wide grin lights up his face, eyes sparkling with barely contained joy. "She said yes," he repeats, almost as if in disbelief.

It's a far cry from the state he was in when he first met Nora.

And when he first lost Nora.

But sometimes we need to endure that soul-crushing loss to truly appreciate what we have. Kind of like I did with Esme.

"I'm happy for you," I say again, giving him another hug. Then I pull back, hesitating slightly as I ask, "And your family?"

"What about them?" He tilts his head.

"Do they know yet?"

He shakes his head. "I want to keep it quiet for now, at least until I have a chance to go through the normal channels."

I hate that Anderson and Esme can't just fall in love and decide to get married like the rest of the world. They're required to follow protocol and gain the king's approval to marry. I can only imagine how Anderson's grandmother will react to the news, especially with the referendum on the ballot this year. They've been saying a royal wedding could sway things. I doubt she anticipated the bride being an American commoner, though.

"I'll keep this to myself until you've spoken with him."

"That includes Esme." He gives me a knowing look.

"You have my word. Not a peep to anyone until you say it's okay."

Content in my reassurances, he tips his bottle toward me. "Thanks, mate."

I clink my beer with his, then take another long sip. I can't remember the last time I sat at a bar with Anderson and had a drink like this. It was probably the summer before I was sworn into the guard. After that, I did everything in my power to keep the lines firmly drawn.

Not anymore, though. I'm now counting the days until I can erase the lines altogether. And not just with Anderson, but also between Esme and me.

I *really* can't wait to erase those lines.

"Well, I should probably get back to my fiancée." Anderson sets his bottle on the bartop and pushes back to stand.

I drain the remainder of my beer and do the same, glancing toward Kylian and signaling we're ready.

"How does it feel?" I ask as we walk toward the door.

"What do you mean?"

"Calling her your fiancée."

He stops walking and squeezes my shoulder. "Bloody amazing." His expression lights up. "The only thing that will feel better is calling her my wife."

"Good for you, Anders. You deserve this." I give him one last hug, then step back, buttoning my jacket and transitioning into his chief protection officer.

"That reminds me…"

I whip my eyes toward his. "What's that?"

"Last weekend, Nora left a few things at the house in the Hamptons, including her passport. Do you mind taking a trip out there?"

"I can send one of the other guys so I can stay here with you."

"I'd feel better if you went," Anderson replies. "Plus, this would be good practice for Kylian, since it appears you've been prepping him to replace you?" He arches a single brow, and I nod slightly.

I haven't given my notice to retire yet. That would entail telling my father, and I know he won't be happy. But once I return home from this trip, I fully intend on breaking the news to him. Rip off the bandage, so to speak. While Rory's reaction to my moving out was less than optimal, I felt better once it was out there.

I'm sure I'll feel the same once I tell my father about my plan to retire.

Like Rory, he can scream and yell, but it won't change my mind.

Nothing will.

"Great. Kylian will stay with me and you can go to the villa to grab her passport."

"Right now?"

"I know it sucks, but Nora's stressed enough about every-thing as it is. I assured her I'd send my best man."

"Of course. I'll go grab it for her. Anything else you need while I'm out there?"

"If there is, I'll let you know," he replies with a smile.

I congratulate him once more, then talk to Kylian for a few minutes, making sure he has everything under control. Once I'm satisfied he'll be able to handle things, which I know he will, I hop into one of our SUVs and navigate away from the city.

As I expected, traffic is heavy, even though it's only two in the afternoon.

Another reason I could never live here.

After a three-hour drive that would make me want to gouge out my eyeballs if I had to suffer through it every day, I pull up to the gate of Anderson's beachfront villa. I punch in my code, and the gate opens, granting me access. I navigate the cobblestone path along perfectly manicured grounds, the pristine green grass the perfect complement to the bright oranges, yellows, and reds of the various flowers lining the path.

I put the car in park and climb out, stretching after the long drive. I tilt my head back, the sun warming my face as it moves toward the west.

But my moment of peace is cut short when my cell buzzes in my pocket. I pull it out, Anderson's name flashing on the screen.

"What's wrong?" I answer frantically. "Did something happen?"

"Calm down, Creed. Everything's fine. Except Nora found her passport. It was in her purse all along."

I sigh, pinching the bridge of my nose, hating that I made the trip all the way out here for nothing. And now I'll have to sit in that same traffic for another three hours. Probably longer.

"I'm on my way back then," I tell him, masking my aggravation.

"No need," he replies nonchalantly. "Why don't you take the weekend off? Stay at the villa."

"It's Wednesday," I remind him.

"Then take the rest of the week off."

"But I'm here to work."

"Kylian has things under control. And before you say you can't because you don't have any clothes or toiletries, I've got you covered. Your suitcase is in the back of the SUV. Although, I did have to get my personal shopper to pick up some shorts and swim trunks for you, because you had absolutely nothing for a stay at the beach."

"Anders..." I begin, a sneaking suspicion settling in my stomach. "What's going on?"

"Consider this a retirement gift. Don't worry. I wouldn't be so cheeky as to just give you a few days off and call it a gift. Your real present is waiting inside. Have fun, mate. And I don't want to see your ugly mug back in the city until Sunday."

"But I don't—"

"Bye, Creed." He ends the call, leaving me bewildered.

And curious.

I scoot around to the boot of the SUV, clicking the button on my key fob for it to open. Like Anderson claimed, my suitcase is sitting there, packed and waiting for me.

I grab it, then click the rear door closed before climbing up the elaborate stairs, punching my code into the keypad. When I step inside the grand foyer, dropping my suitcase by the door, I'm surprised at how quiet it is. Normally, this place is buzzing with staff, especially in the summer.

Not today, though.

I wonder if Anderson gave them the rest of the week off, too.

When I hear footsteps, I dart my eyes toward the great room just as a body comes into view, wearing a bikini and a sheer coverup, legs seeming to go on for miles.

I blink repeatedly to make sure I'm not seeing things. Make sure this isn't a figment of my imagination. A manifestation of my deepest desires. But when Esme saunters up to me, surrounding me with her addictive scent, I know it's not. Know she's real.

"You're here."

She slowly nods, but doesn't make a move to touch me. "I'm here." Her lips curve into a smile. "Anderson wanted to do something nice for you as a retirement present. So did Archie."

"Archie?" I lift a brow.

She shrugs. "He knows how we feel about each other and was happy to help Anderson. He's staying at a hotel down the street and will leave us alone as long as you check in with him once a day, since he'd rather not lose his job over this. But don't worry," she adds quickly. "He knows you haven't officially given your notice yet. You can trust him to stay quiet about your retirement… And me."

I shake my head, overwhelmed by the lengths both Anderson and Archie have gone in order to make this happen. To give me the best gift I've ever received.

Slowly moving toward her, I rake my gaze down her body, moistening my lips as desire blooms inside me. "*You're* my retirement present?"

"I hope you're not disappointed that you didn't get some expensive watch or monogrammed cufflinks."

I grip her hip, yanking her body against mine. She gasps, my touch taking her by surprise. I understand why, considering I've resisted any sort of intimate touching between us.

But right now, in this place, I can do whatever I want without fear of someone learning the truth.

For the next five days, it's just us.

"This is the best present ever."

Then I slam my lips against hers.

CHAPTER TWENTY

Esme

I've forgotten how much I love this man's kisses. Forgotten how amazing his mouth feels as it moves against mine. Forgotten how much a single swipe of his tongue against mine ignites me on fire.

I wasn't sure how Creed would react to Anderson's plan. We may have spent every night since he left for New York getting each other off during phone sex, but we haven't been physically intimate since our one night together.

Three months ago.

He seemed so steadfast in his resolve against any physical intimacy.

Not anymore. Not here. Not in this place where it's just us.

We're back in our bubble where we can be free to love each other without anyone using our love against us.

Creed tears away from our kiss, his heavy pants filling the space. "Bedroom. Now."

A shiver trickles down my spine from the dominance in his voice. But if Creed wants to go to the bedroom, I'm only too happy to oblige. Even with all the fun we've been having these past few weeks, I'm desperate for the real thing.

I grab his hand, and pull him from the foyer, our steps quick as we head up the winding staircase and onto the second floor landing. I continue down the corridor, passing several guest rooms before finally reaching the room at the end.

The second the door closes behind us, I'm in his arms again, his mouth claiming mine in a kiss I feel in the depths of my soul. Invigorating. Enthralling. Consuming.

His desperate hands roam my body, pushing my sheer coverup down my arms. Then he finds the string securing my bikini top and yanks, the material loosening before it falls to the floor. He steers me across the room, his lips not breaking away from mine even when the back of my legs hit the mattress. His tongue continues tangling with mine, fingers caressing the contours of my frame, smoothing along my hipbone before dipping into my bikini bottom.

"Creed," I whimper into his mouth, the promise of his touch driving me wild.

Then he moves his hand between my legs, spreading my moisture around.

"Always so wet for me, aren't you?"

I gasp when he thrusts a finger inside of me, the sensation of fullness almost too much, especially when he presses his thumb against my clit and pinches.

"Always so greedy for me."

"Please," I beg, every stroke and pinch making me desperate for more. I need him everywhere. Need him inside of me. His mouth on me. His love surrounding me.

"Please what?" He moves to my neck, tongue tracing a delicious circle just below my earlobe. "Tell me what you want, Esme." His voice becomes less demanding. More sensual. But it still turns me on. "Tell me what I can do for you."

"Make me come, Creed. God, I need to come so bad."

"Gladly." He abruptly steps back, leaving me a panting bundle of need, every inch of me screaming for release.

"Creed, wha—"

Before I can utter another word, he hooks his fingers into my bikini bottoms and drags them down my legs. With an arm wrapped around my waist, he lowers me onto the bed, his body covering me as his lips find mine.

But unlike our previous kisses, this one is slow, sensual, affectionate, his tongue sweeping mine so gently I nearly cry.

I wrap an arm around his shoulders, savoring in every swipe, every nip, every caress. It still seems surreal that I'm here. That we're together.

When Anderson called last week and asked if I'd fly out here as part of Creed's retirement gift, I jumped at the opportunity to have five days alone with him. Even if he insisted on following the rules and not being intimate, I would have been happy just to spend time with him.

But god, am I glad he's thrown away the rules for now.

Like all those years ago, the rules don't matter in our bubble.

My skin lights on fire as he moves from my mouth and down my body, the roughness of his unshaven jawline a stark contrast to the tenderness as he circles my nipple with his tongue. I rake my fingers through his hair, nails digging into his scalp, every swirl of his tongue and nibble of his teeth propelling me higher.

"Please, Creed," I beg again. "I need you."

He glances up, eyes meeting mine. "And I'll always give you everything you need… Princess." Smirking, he snakes down the rest of my body, pushing my thighs wider.

My chest heaves as I stare down at him, time seeming to stand still as I wait to feel his mouth on me. I'm about to lose my bloody mind, hunger and raw need rioting inside me.

Finally, he drags his tongue down my slit, and I release a moan, my body momentarily going slack against the mattress.

"You taste so fucking good," he groans. "So needy. So desperate for me. Aren't you?"

"Yes, Creed. Yes…" I exhale, moving with the rhythm he sets. It won't take long for me to detonate, the past few months nothing more than intense foreplay, all leading up to this moment.

"God, I've missed the taste of your cunt. Missed fucking you with my tongue and fingers." He slips two fingers inside me, stretching and massaging as he presses his free hand against my stomach, limiting my movement.

Allowing him to be in complete control of my body and orgasm.

"Missed having you come all over my face." He twists his fingers, hitting that spot he knows sets me off.

And that's exactly what happens.

I try to arch my back as my orgasm races through me, blinding me to everything, but Creed keeps me pinned to the mattress. His tongue laps at me, his fingers continuing to torture and tease, drawing out my bliss in an orgasm unlike any I've ever had.

My body's still quivering when he finally pulls back and stands, practically ripping his clothes off before crawling back onto the bed, bringing his erection up to me.

His eyes lock on mine as he eases inside, both of us moaning in unison at the sensation we've been craving for too long now. At the connection we've missed these past few months.

He covers my body, resting his forehead on mine as he remains fully seated for several seconds, allowing me to get acclimated to his size after so long without him.

"I've missed this," he whispers tenderly.

I run my hand up and down his back, relishing in the feeling of his muscles. "I've missed this, too."

He cups my cheek. "I love you, Esme."

My heart swells in my chest at the sincerity and affection in his declaration. I never thought I'd find something like this. Never thought I'd experience the kind of love they write about in books or show in movies. I didn't think it existed.

Creed proved me wrong.

"I love you, too." I curve toward him, our lips touching in a soft kiss.

When I wrap my legs around his waist and circle my hips, he deepens our exchange, slowly retreating then thrusting back inside me, each drive more exhilarating than the last.

"So fucking good," he grunts, burying his head in the crook of my neck, his breathing ragged. "You always feel so fucking good. I just..." He pulls back, eyes locking with mine. "I can't get enough of you, Esme." He lowers his mouth to mine. "I'll never get enough of you."

I lose myself in his kiss once more, each swipe of his tongue and rock of his hips pushing me higher, my body a complete slave to him. It doesn't matter how much I try to fight it. How long I want this to last. I'm completely powerless when it comes to how easily Creed makes my body sing. I cry out, wave after wave of euphoria crashing through me.

"That's my girl." He straightens to kneel, increasing his motions. "Think I can get one more out of you?"

"I don't…" I shake my head, my mind a blank slate from the bliss still consuming me. I doubt I could put together a coherent thought right now if my life depended on it.

A mischievous grin teasing his lips, he hooks one of my legs over his shoulder as he curves toward me, the shift in position making him feel even bigger and deeper.

"I've always liked a challenge. And you're my favorite challenge to date." He presses his lips back to mine before straightening once more. Then he brings his thumb up to my mouth. "Suck."

A rush of desire shoots through me, turning me on even more, something I didn't think possible with the aftershocks of my orgasm still ravaging me.

But I do as Creed asks, parting my lips and allowing him to slip his thumb inside. I wrap my mouth around it, tongue swirling, tasting me and him in one intoxicating combination.

"Enough!" he growls, his chest heaving through his labored breaths.

I open my mouth, and he lowers his thumb to my clit, increasing his rhythm again.

I whimper at the sensation of him moving inside me and rubbing my clit.

"Is this what it feels like, Esme?" he grunts. "When I tell you to wear your toy and make you come, is this how it feels?"

I moan, my pulse racing, core clenching with impending release.

"Tell me," he demands when I don't immediately answer. "Tell me if this is what it feels like."

I swallow hard, shaking my head. "It's not." I train my gaze on him. "This is better."

"Good girl." He drives into me with even more ferocity, leaning down and taking my nipple between his teeth. But that's not what sets me off one last time. It's when he pinches my clit between his thumb and forefinger, the combination of pleasure and pain too much for me.

"Creed!" I cry out, my screams echoing around us.

And for the first time, I don't have to muffle them. Don't have to hold them in. I'm free to be as loud as I need. And soon, Creed joins me, his own grunts mingling with mine as he succumbs to his release, collapsing on top of me when he has nothing left to give.

Our heavy pants fill the room as I run my fingers up and down his spine, relishing in the feel of his body against mine. What I wouldn't give to stay here forever. To never be apart from this man.

"So I take it this retirement present doesn't suck," I remark as we continue to hold each other, neither one of us in any rush to pull away. To have even a breath between us.

Creed rolls onto his side, but brings me with him, caressing the contours of my frame. "I wouldn't say that."

"Hey! I flew all the way out here for you."

"And I appreciate that." His eyes darken once more. "But I'd quite like it if my retirement present sucked. At least certain parts of my body." He waggles his brows.

"Is that right?" I hook my leg over his waist.

"Absolutely."

"Well, then… What kind of retirement gift would I be if I didn't fulfill all your wishes over these next few days? So consider me to be at your complete and total disposal." My lips skim his. "Your deepest desires, your darkest fantasies… I'll make them all come true."

I push him onto his back and crawl on top of him, snaking down his body, not surprised to see he's already getting hard again. He digs his fingers into my hair as I swirl my tongue around his tip.

"This may just be the best gift ever," he says as he guides himself into my mouth.

CHAPTER TWENTY-ONE

Esme

"I don't think I've ever worked so hard for my food in my entire life," Creed grunts as he brings his oyster knife back up to the shell, looking for that sweet spot in the hinge where he can get some leverage, just like I showed him. After a few wiggles, he's able to slide the knife in, twist it, and pry open the oyster. Then he hands it to me so I can sever the muscle from the shell before adding it to the rest of the oysters.

We'd have a lot more if we didn't keep eating them as we shucked.

But that's all part of the fun about having oysters.

"You can't expect me to come to Long Island and not get oysters. Blue Points are found here. They're some of the best oysters around."

He pries open yet another oyster, then hands it to me. "And the biggest."

After severing the muscle, I add some of the shallot

mignonette I made, then bring it up to Creed's mouth. "But so delicious."

He parts his lips and I tip it back into his mouth, watching as he swallows.

"I can't disagree with you there. Although there's something in this kitchen I find much more…satisfying." He loops an arm around my waist and pulls me against him.

"And what's that?" I ask breathlessly.

"You don't know?"

I chew on my bottom lip, playing coy.

He curves toward me, his mouth skimming mine. "You, Esme." He moves a hand to my face. "You satisfy me in ways I didn't think possible."

I moan, surrendering to his kiss.

This entire scenario is a double-edged sword. While it allows us to finally be together and not worry about getting caught, it will make returning to the real world all that more difficult. Especially now that I've been able to enjoy Creed's kisses whenever I want. It'll make me want to steal more kisses.

I remind myself that's the precise reason things have to be this way. So that one day, I *can* steal all the kisses I want.

Creed slowly curves back. "Come on. These oysters won't shuck themselves." He releases me and picks up his oyster knife, getting to work on prying open another one.

"True, but I think the oysters wouldn't mind waiting so we can go for round three. Or is it four?" I waggle my brows.

His eyes darken as he leans toward me, taking my bottom lip between his teeth. "You're insatiable, Esme."

"I *have* been eating oysters. They have amino acids thought to increase sex drive."

"All the more reason for me to keep shucking."

He leaves a kiss on my lips before devoting his attention

to opening the oyster, a silence settling over us as we get back to work.

"I don't want you to think I'm only interested in sex with you," he says after a beat.

"I know you're not. You tell me practically every day how much you love me."

He sets the knife on the counter and wipes his hands on a kitchen towel. It's so normal. So domesticated. And I love everything about it. Love the possibility of being able to do more of this in the future.

It brings into focus just how much things have changed between us.

The last time we cooked dinner together, I refused to think about the possibility of having more nights like that with him in the future. Back then, I didn't think there *was* a future with us. Didn't think I'd ever find the strength to go against centuries of tradition and fight to be with someone I loved.

Hell, I didn't think I'd actually ever love anyone.

Now, I can't stop thinking about my future... A future with Creed.

A smile tugs on my lips when I picture what that future might look like. About cooking dinner together every night. No more waitstaff. No more cooks preparing every meal.

Just me, Creed, and this love we've found.

And maybe, at some point, a few little ones running between our legs, something I never truly wanted until now.

With Creed, I want it all.

"That may be true," he continues. "But I want to show you how much I love you. Don't get me wrong. I like the sex. Hell, I bloody love the sex." His pupils dilate, lust flaming within. "The things you do to me, Esme... The things you make me feel." He licks his lips, taking a minute to compose himself. "I didn't think these feelings were possible."

"Me, either."

He inches toward me, mouth skimming mine. "I didn't think this kind of love was possible."

"Me, either," I say again, melting into his kiss before he retreats.

"Which is what I want to show you this week. I want to show you how much I love you." A boyish smile teases his lips. "Want to cook dinner with you. Want to bring you coffee in the morning. Want to lounge on the couch as we watch a movie and I rub your feet."

"It all seems so…normal."

"But that's what I want with you. What I want to give to you. A taste of normal in a life that's been anything but normal for you."

"That sounds…" I trail off, searching for the right word.

"Boring?" He laughs nervously.

I hoist myself onto my toes and touch my lips to his. "It sounds absolutely incredible."

With a smile, he kisses me, briefly swiping his tongue against mine before pulling back, returning his attention to the oysters.

Over the course of the evening, Creed keeps his word. He gives me a taste of something normal. We shuck oysters together. We get our hands dirty as we devour a pot of peel-and-eat shrimp I've always wanted to try. And we enjoy a bottle of wine as we share our hopes and dreams for our future.

A future we're now happy to talk about.

"Have you given any more thought to starting a community restaurant?" Creed asks as he sips on his wine after we've finished off the Chilean sea bass I prepared for our main course.

It was a veritable seafood feast, but considering where we are, I needed to take advantage of all the fresh seafood available. It would have been a shame not to.

"Community restaurant?" I dab at my mouth with my napkin.

"You'd mentioned something about that at the soup kitchen."

"Oh." I blink repeatedly. "Right."

I'd completely forgotten about our discussion that day. Considering I'd nearly been killed minutes later, a conversation I had with my temporary chief protection officer seemed rather inconsequential.

But Creed hasn't forgotten about it, despite everything that transpired.

"You remember that?"

The corners of his mouth lift up, peace washing over his expression. I don't think I've ever seen Creed look like this. Like he's not carrying the world on his shoulders. Like he's finally free to be happy.

"I remember everything you've ever said to me, Esme." He holds my gaze, allowing his statement to sink in. "Have you thought about actually opening something like that? You seemed quite passionate about it when you told me."

"I guess with everything going on with Anderson and the referendum, I haven't really thought about it again. Truthfully, even when I did tell you about it, it wasn't because I had plans to do something about it."

"Why not?"

I give him a knowing look. "I don't get to make decisions like this. Everything I do has to be carefully examined for potential consequences to the monarchy." I avert my gaze. "I learned a long time ago that sometimes it's better not to hope or dream when someone will always stand in the way of those dreams."

He grabs my hand in his. "But you didn't give up hope on me. On us."

"I almost did," I admit with a slight laugh, the tension lightening. "If you didn't barge into my apartment that night—"

"Then I'm bloody glad I did."

I lean toward him, touching my lips to his. "So am I."

"But still…" He brushes his thumb across my knuckles. "I want you to have it all, Esme. Believe me. I know how difficult this world can be. I'm still struggling with it myself. I've been putting off telling my father I'm retiring because I know it won't go over well, especially since my retirement will mean that, for the first time in centuries, there won't be a Lawson in the royal guard, not with him having to retire next year when he turns sixty-five. But I want you to have everything. I hate seeing your talents go to waste because of who you are. Plus, just because they turned you down years ago doesn't mean they'll turn you down now. Your father's not the same man."

"I know." I pull my lips between my teeth.

The truth is, I have no doubt that my father would support this venture if I brought it up to him again.

"Then why haven't you—"

"What if it fails? What if I put all this time and effort into it and it completely flops? I'm not sure I'm ready to deal with the smug look on my grandmother's face when that happens."

"*If* that happens," Creed corrects. "There's no guarantee it'll flop."

"But there's also no guarantee it'll be successful."

"Listen, Esme. I know what it's like growing up with huge expectations placed on your shoulders. Maybe not to the same extent as you and Anders, but for as long as I can remember, my path in life has been dictated for me. Straying from that path was not an option so I never dared to dream of anything different. Hell, I never dared to dream at all. Until now. It's terrifying, yet freeing at the same time. The best dreams often are, I suppose."

I can't help but smile as I listen to Creed's words. "So what's your new dream?"

"You mean other than you?" He winks.

"Yes. Other than me."

He pushes out a long sigh. "Right now, I'm just focused on getting through these next few weeks with as little difficulty as possible. After that, I'm not quite sure, apart from keeping my girlfriend satisfied." He flashes a mischievous smile as he curves toward me. "I'm not quite sure if you heard, but she's a complete minx in the bedroom."

"Say that again," I exhale.

"You're a minx in the bedroom."

I shake my head, pulling back to meet his gaze. "Not that."

"Then what—"

"You called me your girlfriend."

He straightens, blinking repeatedly. "I guess I did."

"Is that what I am? Your girlfriend?" I tease.

He cups my cheek. "You're so much more than that. But for now, I guess that's the best title for you."

I lean into him. "I like the idea of being your girlfriend. Of you being my boyfriend."

He groans, his grip on me tightening. "Say it again."

"You're my boyfriend."

In one swift motion, he yanks me off my chair, forcing me onto his lap, my legs straddling him. "Again."

I drag my tongue along his jawline. "Boyfriend."

"I didn't think anything would turn me on more than the sound you make when you come, but hearing you call me your boyfriend is a damn close second."

He covers my mouth, his tongue swiping against mine as he stands, easily lifting me with him. I wrap my legs around his waist, both of us kissing and laughing as he carries me to the couch.

As he makes love to me, I can't help but be filled with hope for my future with Creed. It's something I never dreamed of, but it's now somehow within reach.

Maybe some of my other dreams are within reach, too.

CHAPTER TWENTY-TWO

Creed

The moonlight shines through the windows of the opulent bedroom, casting shadows along Esme's face as I watch her sleep. I should get some rest myself, considering in a few hours I need to say goodbye to her.

As much as I've enjoyed our time together, I fear it's only going to make the next few weeks all that more difficult, especially now that I've had a taste of what our future will be like.

Regardless, I wouldn't trade these past few days for anything. Even if it all implodes tomorrow, I'll carry the memories we made for the rest of my life. From waking up with her in my arms. To spending our afternoons by the pool. To strolling along the beach and collecting seashells. It's been nothing short of perfect.

Which is why I don't want to fall asleep. Don't want to waste a second of what little time I have left with her before we have to go back to the way things were. I remind myself it's not forever. That in a few weeks, it will all be over.

That we'll finally be able to be together.

It doesn't make this any less difficult, though.

As I admire how peaceful Esme looks, especially since her nightmares haven't plagued her this week, my phone buzzes on the nightstand. I'm about to silence it, figuring whatever it is can wait until the morning.

But when Lucas' name flashes on the screen, I bolt upright, hope filling me that he's found something about the man with a scar. Doing my best to remain as quiet as possible, I slide out of bed, padding on light feet across the bedroom and into the hallway.

"Hey, Lucas," I whisper, making my way down the stairs, through the foyer, and into the kitchen, sitting at the table in the breakfast nook.

"Is this a bad time?"

"No. I'm in the States, so it's the middle of the night."

"Shite. I'm sorry. We can talk later."

"It's okay. I was awake anyway. Did you find something?"

By the way he pauses before answering, I sense he did.

"I'm sorry it took so long. I had a few of my computer gurus work on enhancing the sketch to turn it into a three-dimensional rendering of what he'd look like. Unfortunately, that didn't return anything. I thought for sure we'd get something based on that scar. It's a pretty distinguishing characteristic."

"Yes, it is."

"Unless it's recent. Or at least recent enough that any photos on file wouldn't have it."

"So you took the scar away?"

"We did. And also aged him down a bit. Once we did that, we got a hit."

I swallow hard, an uneasy feeling settling in my stomach. This is what I wanted. What I'd hoped for, especially after Hayes confirmed that Esme's sketch bore a strong resemblance to the man he saw. But I can't shake the feeling that whatever Lucas is about to tell me is going to make things worse.

"Who is it?"

"I'm so sorry, mate."

"Who is it?" I ask again, this time much more forcefully.

"Kane Kingsley."

"Kane Kingsley?" I repeat, scrunching my brows.

By Lucas' demeanor, I'd have thought it would be someone I knew. Or at least a name I recognized. But I've never heard of him.

"And he is?"

"You don't know?" He sounds genuinely surprised.

"If I did, I wouldn't be asking."

"I guess I've been in the private security business so long, I assumed everyone's heard of him. I don't know if I'd consider him a legend. More like a ghost story you tell new recruits. Someone I didn't think was real. He's nicknamed the *Angel of Death*."

"*Angel of Death*?"

"He's an assassin, Creed. At least that's how the story goes. And not just your run-of-the-mill hitman."

"I didn't realize there is such a thing," I joke, trying to cut through the turmoil filling me at the idea that the person Esme's been seeing in her dreams, who she saw at the opera, is a notorious assassin.

I worried it would be something like this. After all, a handful of people who claimed to have seen him ended up dead. That still doesn't make the confirmation of my fear any easier to swallow, though.

"This fucker doesn't have a conscience. Doesn't care who he gets in bed with as long as the money's good."

"I doubt anyone who kills people for a living could be considered to have a conscience."

"But this guy really doesn't. He's the guy you call when no one else will take the job. Nothing's off-limits. Including children. I'm not saying anyone who works as a hitman is honorable, but most of them draw the line there. Not this guy."

"Jesus," I exhale, pinching the bridge of my nose. "What can you tell me about him? What's his background?"

"I'll send you his information in an encrypted file, but long story short, he was discharged from the military after two years of service. According to his records, he was an incredible sniper, but a little too…excitable. And off balance."

"Off balance?"

"They tried to work with him. Get him counseling, since he was such a great shot and the powers that be hated losing someone like that. But in the end, he became too much of a liability, especially when he decided to do target practice on a small village. Killed dozens of men, women, and children."

"Fuck."

"It was covered up, blamed on a local extremist group. But officials knew they couldn't risk a repeat, so he was discharged. The last known record of him is his discharge papers. After that, he essentially disappeared. Became a ghost. Someone who only remained alive in legends… Until you gave me this damn sketch. Where did you get it?"

I chew on my bottom lip, unsure what to tell him. It's not that I don't trust him. Lucas was on special teams with me. He was essentially my mentor. We faced death together.

Saved each other's lives more times than I can count. If there's anyone in the world I *can* trust, it's Lucas.

"It was a friend," I tell him finally. "She asked if I knew someone who might be able to figure out who it is."

I hope that's enough to satisfy him. He's not the type of person to pry. He knows me well enough to realize if that's all I tell him, that's all I will. I have no desire to go into the details about how the Princess Royal has been having night terrors where she sees this man try to kill her. How at least two people claimed to have seen him in the days leading up to their deaths.

How I'm bloody petrified it's only a matter of time until Esme joins them.

"A word of advice, if I might…" Lucas breaks through the silence.

"Yes?"

"Keep an eye on this…friend. If she's gotten close enough to be able to sketch his likeness, you can guarantee she won't live to talk about it. Not for much longer, anyway. He's not referred to as the *Angel of Death* for fun. It's because once you see him, you can safely assume that your number's up."

I push down my mounting anxiety, telling myself he's probably exaggerating. He said himself that the stories about this man are just that — stories.

But I also know Lucas. He's not one to get worked up about much. He's even headed. Practical. Methodical. For him to warn me like this, he must know there's something to these stories and rumors.

There must be some basis in fact.

Based on what little I've learned from Hayes and Esme, I fear these ghost stories are more real than any of us want to believe.

A motion out of the corner of my eye pulls me out of my thoughts, and I snap my gaze up as Esme moves toward me, concern etched in the lines of her face. No doubt she noticed the worry covering my expression.

I quickly straighten and clear my throat. "I have to go. Thanks for the update."

"You bet. We'll talk soon."

"Thanks, mate." I end the call and set my phone onto the surface, my mind reeling with dozens of thoughts about what could be going on, each scenario worse than the one before.

"Is everything all right?" Esme saunters toward me and sits on the table in front of me.

"Everything's fine," I assure her, smoothing my hands up her bare legs, pushing the silky material of her robe to the side.

"Your face a few seconds ago said otherwise. Was that your private security friend? Did he get a hit on the sketch?"

"Not yet," I tell her with a straight face, praying she can't see through the lies.

I hate keeping the truth from her, but I know Esme. If I share what I know, she'll look into him, which could put her life in danger.

When I joined the guard, I swore an oath I'd do whatever was necessary to protect the royal family above all else.

I can't knowingly put her in harm's way without breaking that oath.

And telling her about this notorious assassin who appears to be after her would do just that. For now, I need to put my oath above any promise I made her.

"He just wanted to let me know they're still working on it. But these things can take time, especially since they need to turn your sketch into a three-dimensional rendering in order to run it through facial recognition. Just be patient." I squeeze her thighs. "If anyone can get answers, it's Lucas."

"Then why did you look so…upset when I first walked in?"

I force her legs apart, settling between them. "I'm just not looking forward to leaving you later today."

She studies me for several long moments, and I fear she's about to call me out on my lies. Instead, she reaches for the sash on her robe and tugs, allowing the material to fall off her body.

"It's not later yet."

CHAPTER TWENTY-THREE

Creed

I stare at the ceiling, my mind consumed with all things Kane Kingsley. Not even the feel of Esme's finger tracing a circle against my chest can ease my worry.

Can make me stop going through every scenario possible, wondering about his connection to everything I've learned over the past several weeks.

As much as I'd love to stay here with Esme, I'm now desperate to get back to Belmont. Go through my brother's things again to see if anything stands out.

All I do know is Jack Sloane found one of his father's tapes, the content of which somehow involved Prince Nicholas and his family, and people started turning up dead. What could be so inflammatory that people would need to lose their lives?

I refuse to entertain the notion of Esme losing her life over whatever it is, too.

Which is why I need to keep her in the dark, despite any promises I made.

"I can hear you thinking," she murmurs in a lazy voice, pulling me back to the present.

"You can hear me thinking?"

She tilts her head, eyes meeting mine. "I can." She smiles sadly. "Are you sure—"

I silence her question with a kiss, not wanting her to press the issue of my conversation with Lucas again.

Not wanting to lie to her again.

"I'm sure," I tell her, rolling onto my side to face her. "I just hate having to leave you." I feather my mouth against hers. "I don't want to lose you."

My confession falls from my lips before I can stop it. I didn't mean to say that. Didn't mean to give voice to the fear that increases with every passing moment, especially since she's about to get on a plane to go back to Belmont, and I'll be in the States another week. Thousands of miles away. Unable to get to her if anything goes wrong.

"You won't," she whispers against my lips, dragging her fingers up and down my spine. I arch into her, wanting to savor every touch. Every caress. Every brush of her mouth. "Like we swore all those weeks ago. And every day since. Today." She presses a kiss to the side of my mouth. "Tomorrow." She leaves a kiss on the other side. "Always."

"Always," I murmur, coaxing her lips to part, finding some solace in her promise as she breathes into me, her kiss and touch giving me life. Giving me hope. Giving me faith that no matter what happens over the next few weeks, we'll get through it.

We didn't come this far to lose everything we fought for in the last quarter.

And I'll be damned if I lose Esme.

She swipes her tongue against mine, her little whimpers driving me wild. Just like they did all those years ago.

I slide my hand down her side, her body trembling in response. Digging my fingers into her hip, I force her onto her back and settle between her legs.

"One last time, Esme," I growl, rocking my hips against her, feeling how wet she already is. How desperate she is for me.

I bury my head in the crook of her neck, relishing in the salty-sweet taste of her skin. She moans as she circles her legs around my waist, nails digging into my scalp, igniting a hunger only this woman can satisfy.

"Take me, Creed," she begs, rubbing her slickness against my erection. Her restrained need is palpable as she grinds harder and faster. "I'm yours."

"Mine." I trail kisses across her jawline, snaking down her body to take a nipple in my mouth, tongue licking, teeth biting. I skim my hand along her curves, her breath hitching as I slip my fingers between her thighs and spread her wetness around.

"Yours," she says again, as if she can sense I need yet another reminder.

"Mine," I repeat one last time as I line myself up at her entrance.

My body quivers with anticipation when I press my hips forward, inch by incredible inch. She parts her lips, a noiseless gasp falling from her throat as I fill her. Once I'm fully seated, I lean forward, my fingers linking with hers. Our eyes locking, I slowly move against her, each rhythmic tilt of my hips showing her much I crave her. How much I need her.

How much I love her.

How big the depth of my love for her truly is.

And as I peer into her eyes, I see how big the depth of her love for me is, her lip quivering, eyes welling with tears.

"I know, baby," I croon, kissing away her tears as I continue moving inside her, each thrust making me love her a little more.

Making me hate the idea of leaving her a little more.

"God, do I know."

I tighten my hold on her hands, her body tensing around me, signaling she's close. She whimpers, closing her eyes, but I need them open. Need to peer into them.

Need the reminder that she's still here.

"Look at me, Esme."

My voice isn't demanding like it usually is when I utter those words. Instead, it's needy. Desperate.

She returns her gaze to mine, so much love swirling in her green orbs.

"Stay with me."

"I'm with you," she manages to choke out.

"And I'm with you." A small smile curves on my lips as I swallow through the emotion building in my throat. "Today." I kiss away another tear sliding down her cheek. "Tomorrow." I touch my lips to her other cheek, like we always do whenever we make this pledge to each other. "Always."

"Always," she repeats.

I move my mouth against hers, our tongues tangling as we succumb to the sensations coursing through our joined bodies.

This isn't the first time we've had sex.

Hell, it's not even the first time we've made love.

But it's the first time it's felt like this.

Like this truly could be forever.

But as we come down from our state of hyper-arousal

and I hold her in my arms, that unsettled feeling returns, reminding me that everything's about to change.

And not because we'll have to go back to pretending we're nothing more than mere acquaintances the second we walk out of this house.

This is something much bigger.

Something much more devastating.

All I can do is pray I'm wrong.

CHAPTER TWENTY-FOUR

Creed

I stare out the window of the plane, counting down the minutes until we finally touch down in Belmont. I've never been so anxious to get home as I am right now. Normally, the flight from the States goes by quickly, since I usually sleep the entire time.

But I haven't been able to sleep a single wink.

Hell, I haven't been able to sleep much since Esme left. I know she's in good hands. Archie's one of the best protection officers we have. He'll do everything in his power to keep his safe.

But with all the uncertainty about Kane Kingsley, I hate not being near her.

I usually pride myself on being able to perform my duties with as few distractions as possible.

This week, I've been more distracted than ever.

Partly because of what I know about Kane Kingsley.

Partly because of what I *don't* know about Kane Kingsley.

I have a feeling what I don't know is even worse than what I do, something I didn't think possible mere days ago.

I lean my head against the window and close my eyes, hoping the drone of the jet engine and gentle rocking of the plane can lull me into a quiet moment of rest. But it's short-lived, the shrill sound of my phone forcing my eyes open yet again.

Pulling my mobile out of the inner pocket of my suit jacket, I glance at the screen to see a text from Anderson's private secretary. I assume it's to review the same things we discussed yesterday regarding our plan for arrival. In accordance with Anderson's request, I told him to keep Nora's presence in the country quiet for now so they're not swarmed with reporters and photographers when we land. This entire way of life is going to be a big change for her. He wants to make the adjustment as easy as possible.

But when I open the text and see screenshots from dozens of different news websites, some reputable, some not, I fear that will no longer be possible. Not with the headlines announcing Anderson's engagement to an American commoner, along with a picture of them kissing, a very large diamond on an important finger.

"Fuck," I curse under my breath, jumping to my feet.

"What is it?" Kylian asks, quickly standing and approaching.

"Look." I hold out my phone for him to see one of the many screenshots Anderson's private secretary shared with me.

His eyes scan the screen for a few seconds before widening, darting to meet mine once more. Then he leans toward me, glancing around the cabin at the rest of my men. "They're engaged?"

I give a small nod.

"Did you know?" he asks softly.

My lack of response is the only answer he needs.

"That's what he wanted to talk to you about at the pub. Isn't it?"

"He told me as a friend. Not his chief protection officer," I attempt to argue in my defense.

"You know damn well the two aren't always mutually exclusive. That sometimes you have put your oath to the crown above any friendship."

"He wanted to keep it quiet until he could go through the proper channels." I pinch the bridge of my nose, a stress headache forming behind my eyes. "Said she was only going to wear the ring in private."

"That doesn't look private to me." He gestures toward my cell.

"I know." I run a hand over my face, silently berating myself for not being more observant. For not realizing that Nora was wearing her ring in public.

For not seeing those bloody photographers in the first place.

Instead, I was distracted by Kane Kingsley. By why he'd been paid to kill Jack and Callie Sloane. And most likely my brother and Esme, too.

"Well, get your game face on," I tell Kylian. "Because we're about to land in a bloody three-ring circus. Hope you're ready for it."

"Is anyone ever ready for something like this?"

I blow out a long breath. "Doubtful."

As I walk through the administrative corridors of the palace several hours later, I can't help but feel like a condemned prisoner. Several members of the king's staff whisper amongst themselves, no doubt about the events of the day and the role I played in this giant mess.

Much like I predicted, the second the plane touched down earlier this morning, we were greeted by a massive amount of reporters and photographers. Anderson didn't seem all that bothered by it. Either did Nora. Instead, she held her head high and ignored all the rude questions and comments flung her way.

It helped that Anderson didn't let go of her hand from the second they stepped off the plane until the instant I dropped them off at his estate. And when I saw the affection in his gaze as he looked at her, I considered that maybe I worried for nothing.

Maybe it won't be so bad.

Maybe it's not as big of a deal as I feared it would be.

At least that's what I thought before my father summoned me to the palace.

It's the last thing I want to do after being gone for the past several weeks. I just want to go home, even if I'm not quite sure I have a home to go home to.

But I know how these things work.

They need someone to blame for what happened today, and I have a feeling that's going to be me.

When I reach my father's office, I pause, mentally preparing myself to get reamed out.

I know I fucked up. Know I should have been more observant and seen the photographer snapping Anderson's photo. Berating me won't change things now.

My father doesn't care, though. He's never been one to miss an opportunity to remind me just how much I fail to live up to his standards.

There was once a time I might have cared.

While I still take my duty to the crown — to Anderson, in particular — quite seriously, I'm no longer desperate for my father's approval.

Not when I doubt he'll ever give it. Too bad it took me thirty-six years to finally realize this.

Drawing in a deep breath, I bring my hand up to the door and knock.

"Come in," he orders, and I turn the knob, slipping inside. The door's barely closed behind me when he asks, "Did you know?"

I part my lips, his question taking me by surprise. I'd expected him to scold me for being careless and not seeing the photographers watching Anderson. Keeping the paparazzi far away from the royal family is a huge part of what we do. I hadn't expected him to ask if I knew about the engagement, though.

"Answer me," he demands when I don't immediately respond, his voice a deep rumble. He crosses his arms in front of his broad chest. I can feel the weight of his disappointment pressing down on me like a heavy burden. "This engagement. Did. You. Know?"

I glare at him for several long moments, unflinching and filled with contempt. Then I give a subtle nod.

"For fuck's sake, Creed." His chest heaves, face reddening with rage, the vein in his neck throbbing. He clenches his jaw, mouth drawn into a tight line as his nostrils flare. "And you didn't think to inform anyone? Are you really so dense that you didn't think his engagement would have far-reaching implications?"

"Anderson—"

"*Prince Gabriel*," my father corrects me.

"Prince Gabriel," I repeat.

But for the first time, referring to him as his regnal title feels strange, especially when these days he truly does feel like my friend again.

"He asked me to keep it to myself for the time being."

"Did you forget the oath you took? It's your duty to put the safety of the royal family above all else, regardless of any request Prince Gabriel may have made. You should have foreseen that keeping this to yourself would put his life in danger, particularly if word got out. Which is exactly what happened."

"He didn't share it with me in my professional capacity, but as a friend."

"*You are not his friend!*" he roars, his voice bellowing against the stark walls of his office, spittle forming in the corners of his mouth. "You never have been. You never will be. You're his protection officer. His *chief* protection officer. And if you expect to continue performing these duties that you swore under oath you would, you need to remember what's important. And that's the oath you took, Creed. Nothing else. Do you understand?"

"What if I don't want to perform these duties anymore?"

The words leave my mouth before I can stop them. But this is as good of a time as any to finally tell him. My anniversary date will be here in just six more weeks. It's time to put the wheels in motion so I can officially start training Kylian to take over.

"What are you talking about? That's preposterous. You're a Lawson. You—"

"I'm retiring."

He stares at me, not immediately responding, his face frozen in shock.

"In August, I'll have eighteen years of military service under my belt," I continue. "With my consideration for special teams, I can retire with full benefits and honors.

That he always put his duty to the crown above his own family.

I refuse to do that to *my* family.

To Esme.

"I'll fight for her," I insist through gritted teeth, every muscle in my body wound tight with conviction. "Even if it's the last thing I do. I don't care if a bunch of old blowhards don't want us to be together. Don't care if *you* don't want us to be together. You can't stop us from loving each other."

"What about everyone else in your life?" he asks, his face less than an inch from mine. "Have you stopped to think about how this might affect us?"

"I don't—"

"You had a front-row seat to the circus that erupted the second the world learned Prince Gabriel was engaged." He points out the window, photographers and reporters still lining the perimeter of the palace, waiting to catch a photo of anything that could help them make headlines.

"How those bloody pappos will stop at nothing to learn everything they can about Nora. Reporters are camped out at her friends' homes in the States. Their work. Her family's, too. Do you think I'd still be allowed to fulfill my duties to the crown if my only remaining son dated the Princess Royal?"

"I didn't—"

"Didn't think about that?" he snips out. "That's pretty damn clear, Creed. I bet you didn't consider your mum wouldn't be able to leave the house without being hounded. And what about Rory and AJ? Your nephew wouldn't be able to go to school without reporters following him. Forget about being able to play footfall or have a normal childhood. He can kiss that goodbye. And Rory most likely wouldn't be allowed to keep her job in His Majesty's private secretary's office, not with all the extra attention she'd receive."

I swallow hard, my expression blanching. I knew it wouldn't be a walk in the park. That I'd have to give up my anonymity to be with Esme.

I didn't consider that the people close to me would have to make that sacrifice, as well.

"How will she provide for AJ? You're already abandoning them."

"I'm not—"

"And now you're going to do something that may very well cause her to lose her job? To put AJ's life in danger?" He sneers. "All because you want to get laid?"

My body trembles in anger, my chest rising and falling in short, rapid breaths. I try to rein it in, but it's already taken control, pummeling through me like molten lava. My vision tunnels until all I see is the man standing before me, reminding me how inferior I am.

Before I can consider the consequences, I reel back, my fist connecting with his jaw with an audible crack, his face snapping to the side.

He doesn't immediately move, head turned away from me as several painfully long seconds tick by.

Finally, he straightens and wipes away a few drops of blood from his lip. I fully expect him to give me a dose of my own medicine. To deliver a harsh blow to my jaw. After all, that was his form of punishment when we were growing up. If Adam hit me, I was allowed to hit him in return, and vice versa.

He doesn't, though.

Instead, he peers at me with icy eyes that radiate contempt.

"Just remember the guilt you carried after Adam died. If you choose this path and anything happens to AJ or Rory because of this, their blood will be on your hands." He points a finger in my face. "And I'll do everything I can to remind you of that until I draw my last breath." He pushes past me, jostling me roughly as he strides to the door.

Just before he steps into the hallway, he meets my gaze one last time. "You've always been such a bloody disappointment."

Then he slams the door closed behind him.

CHAPTER TWENTY-FIVE

Esme

I toss my cell beside me as I collapse onto the bed, pushing out a long sigh. I didn't expect my brother to answer my call, not with all the crap he's been dealing with since the bloody pappos posted those photos and the entire country lost its goddamn mind.

He's doing the right thing by focusing on Nora and making sure she adjusts to all of this, despite some of the horrible things being said about her. And I get the feeling those negative sentiments aren't just from the small yet vocal minority of our citizens who hate the idea of the future king marrying a foreigner. An American, no less.

I sense some of them are also coming from within the royal household itself.

I just hope Nora doesn't let them get to her. That she realizes what she has with Anderson is worth it.

I *need* her to realize Anderson's worth it, if for no other reason than because I need Creed to realize it when we face this same thing in the coming months.

The sound of a door opening cuts through my thoughts, and I sit up in bed, darting my eyes toward the hallway. It's after ten, so my staff has left for the evening. There are only a few people who have the code to get in, narrowing down who it could be.

My bare feet barely make a sound as I glide down the carpeted hallway, tightening the sash on my silk robe. Did Anderson sneak out of his apartment once Nora was asleep to come talk to me about everything? That's the only explanation I can think of.

But as I step into the living room, I come to an abrupt stop, realizing there's another explanation for who might sneak into my apartment without knocking.

A man who's done it several times before.

But a man who I didn't think would risk it now.

Creed's gaze burns into me, the turmoil and distress within stealing my breath as he stalks across the room, mouth set in a determined line. My pulse skyrockets, heart thrashing in my chest with every step he takes until he reaches me. When he does, I don't have a chance to ask what he's doing here before he clutches my cheeks and crashes his lips to mine with an intensity that shakes me to my core, sending shockwaves through my body.

His kiss is powerful. Consuming. Anguished. As if my mouth on his is the only thing able to quiet the storm raging inside of him.

He moves a hand to my back, yanking me against him. His possessive grip holds me captive as he deepens the connection we share.

When I'm not sure how much longer I can go without

taking a breath, he breaks our kiss, our heavy pants filling the room.

"Is everything—"

"Tell me you love me." His voice is choked, strained...pained.

"Is this because the royal household isn't happy with the idea of Anderson marrying someone normal? I promise that won't be us. They tried to dictate who I could be with before and it blew up in their face. They won't dare try it again."

He vehemently shakes his head, screwing his eyes shut. "That's not it." Leaning his forehead on mine, he draws in a shuttering breath, bringing his hands back to my face. "Please, Esme. I need to know you love me." His gaze locks on mine. "Please."

I part my lips, searching his expression for a clue as to what brought this on, if not the royal household. But if Creed needs my reassurance, I'm more than happy to give it to him.

"I love you, Creed Lawson."

He expels a long breath, tension rolling off him.

"Today," I continue, hoisting myself onto my toes and kissing the corner of his mouth. "Tomorrow." I brush my lips to the other side before placing my hand over his heart. "Always."

"Always," he repeats, closing his eyes as he wraps himself in my promise.

"Always," I say once more, mouth skimming his in a ghost of a kiss.

But it doesn't stay that way.

He clutches my hip and yanks me against him, his free hand going to my hair. His lips are consuming, demanding attention as they move hungrily over mine. I whimper into his mouth, the roughness and desperation in his kiss lighting me on fire, making me burn for him.

Making me want to spend all night showing him just how much he means to me.

How much I can't live without him.

How much I love him.

He steers me out of the living room and down the hall toward my private suite, navigating the path with ease, his lips never breaking from mine until we reach the bedroom.

When we do, he brings our kiss to an end and peers at me, indecision swirling in his eyes.

This isn't the first time he's snuck into my apartment. And it's not the first time we've been intimate here.

But when we started down this path back in March, Creed was adamant we draw firm lines. That we refrain from any sort of behavior that could put his career at risk, at least while we're in Belmont.

I need to respect those boundaries. Need to respect his need to retire from the military with honor. If nothing else, Creed Lawson has always been a man of honor.

But when he reaches for the tie on my robe and tugs, it's obvious that doesn't matter. Not right now, anyway.

Neither one of us says a single word as he strips me of my clothes. As I rid him of his. As he lays me on my bed and crawls between my legs.

Creed and I have had sex more times than I can count, especially during our brief escape in the Hamptons. But as he slides into me tonight, it feels…different. So much more intense. More poignant. More meaningful.

I've always felt Creed's love whenever we've been intimate. Even during those wanton, carnal moments when he's demanding I take his cock like a good girl or when he's yanking on my hair as he pounds into me from behind.

Regardless of whether he's rough or sweet, I always feel nothing but pure adoration radiating from every touch. Every kiss. Every whisper.

But tonight, it's…more.

More of everything I've come to crave from him.

Our fingers intertwined, his hips rock in perfect harmony with mine, his eyes glued to mine. I can't look away even if I want to. But I don't. I want to stay in this moment with Creed. A moment that's both heartbreaking and fulfilling at the same time.

There are no harsh grunts. No lust-filled declarations of how amazing he feels inside me. Because there are no words in existence to properly convey the depths of what we feel for each other.

Instead, we share our feelings with our bodies. With our souls.

With our hearts.

Once we've come down from our orgasms, Creed collapses on top of me, the only sound in the room that of our heavy breathing. He doesn't say anything. Doesn't explain the desperation that seems to drip from every inch of him. Doesn't share why he holds me in a way that makes me fear it's the last time he ever will.

And I don't ask.

I just bask in his love, unable to shake the uneasiness inside me that everything's about to change.

And not for the better.

CHAPTER TWENTY-SIX

Creed

The world is quiet as I drive away from Esme's apartment the following morning. The first hints of light are beginning to illuminate the horizon in shades of pink and gold, announcing the arrival of a new day.

I don't know what came over me last night. Why I snuck into Esme's apartment, knowing full well what could happen if I was caught.

After everything my father said to me, the way his disappointment stung, I needed to see her. Needed to lose myself in her. Needed to feel something other than the crushing weight of despair I was left with after my father stormed off.

And for a while, feeling Esme wrapped in my arms helped ease my mind.

But in the quiet of the night as I listened to her gentle breaths beside me, my father's words found their way back to my subconscious, repeating like a broken record player, torturing me with the truth I'd been content to ignore for too long.

I can't ignore it any longer.

As much as I hate to admit it, his concerns *are* legitimate.

If I were to openly date Esme, it would make headlines. Reporters would hound my parents, Rory, and AJ. My father would most likely be forced out of the guard early. I wouldn't want someone on my team who could be a liability. And that's precisely what my father would become. A liability. A target himself.

Worse, it would destroy any chance AJ might have at a normal childhood. He's already been through enough. Can I really put him through even more trauma?

I'm not sure I can.

But I'm not sure I'm ready to give up on Esme yet, either. On *us*.

No matter what choice I make, I stand to lose something. It's just a question of what's more important.

What I can stomach living without.

The streetlights cast a yellow-orange glow over the trees and hedges that line the peaceful streets of the subdivision where I've lived for the past decade. Slowing my speed, I turn my car into the driveway and kill the ignition, peering through the windshield at the Queen Anne-style dwelling. I should feel a hint of sadness over the idea that I'll soon no longer call this place home.

I don't think it ever *was* a home, though. I don't regret being here for Rory and AJ. But I never felt like I belonged here. Instead, it felt like a waypoint. Like I've been waiting for a connecting flight that's been permanently delayed.

I step onto the driveway and make my way up the path toward the front door. If Rory hadn't texted and asked me to stop by before work, I doubt I would have come here. I probably would have gone straight to Anderson's estate, showered in the staff quarters, then tried to get a little sleep in my office there.

Considering Rory's been cold at best over the past few weeks, I was a bit surprised to get her text. I'm hopeful she's finally realized this needs to happen. That I can't stay here anymore.

That I don't think she and AJ should stay here anymore, either.

I try to be as quiet as possible as I input my code into the keypad. Thankfully, she hasn't changed it since kicking me out, and the door beeps, granting me entry. I slip inside, careful to keep my steps light so as not to wake up AJ.

But when I tiptoe into the kitchen, expecting to see Rory sitting at the table, she's not there. Someone else is.

"AJ…" I move toward him. "What are you—"

"Is it true?"

I stop in my tracks, raking my gaze over him.

I've only been gone a few weeks, but he looks even older than he did the last time I saw him. The boyish cheeks he once had are more angular, his nose becoming more defined. If he had facial hair and laugh lines around his eyes, he'd be a mirror image of my brother, right down to the hardened stare and how he crosses his arms in front of his chest, as Adam so often did whenever he was berating me for something I'd done.

"Is what true?" I ask hesitantly, unsure what he's referring to. It could be any number of things. That I'm retiring from the guard. That I punched his grandfather. That I failed to consider the potential ramifications to his life and safety when making promises to Esme.

"That you're moving out."

I expel a breath, somewhat relieved this is all he wants to talk about.

While I'd hoped to tell him my reasons before his mother made me out to be an inconsiderate bastard, I can't rewind the clock now. That ship has sailed. Instead, all I can do is give him the one thing he deserves... The truth.

Or as much of the truth as is appropriate to share with an almost ten-year-old boy.

"Not right away. I still have a lot of packing to do."

"But you *are* moving?"

With a slow nod, I pull out a chair and sit beside him. "I'm sorry, buddy. I hate to disappoint you, but—"

"I think it's a good thing."

I straighten. "You do?"

A smile teases his mouth. Even his smile reminds me of Adam, the sheepish grin he'd try to hide.

"Yeah. And I'm not just saying that because Mum said I could turn your old room into a video game room. You're not married to Mum or anything. You should have your own place."

"So you're not upset? I wanted to talk to you about it myself, but...well, things don't always work out as planned."

"Nah. I get it, Uncle Creed. I'll miss having you around, but you deserve to be happy. Live your own life."

I stare at him, blown away by his level of maturity. I don't know many boys his age who would initiate this kind of conversation. Then again, AJ had no choice but to grow up quickly.

"Thanks, buddy." I open my arms and he slides off his chair, walking into my embrace. I close my eyes as I squeeze him tightly.

These days, the hugs are few and far between, especially

now that he's almost ten. But today, he doesn't try to shorten it or push away because he's worried about who might see.

"This means you'll be the man of the house now." I pull back, keeping my hands on his biceps. "You'll need to look after your mum. Help her out around here. Are you ready for that responsibility?"

"You know I am. I've been mowing the lawn for her this summer. And taking out the trash. And helping her put away the groceries."

"Good." I squeeze his arms, heart swelling with pride.

Being a parent is a strange thing, even if I'm not technically his dad. I still spent the past decade helping to raise him. There are countless times I wondered if I was screwing everything up. If I was doing enough. If I was causing him more harm than good.

But when I see how well-adjusted he is, despite the obstacles he's overcome, I'm reassured I did a pretty good job. We all did.

"Just promise you won't forget me," he says after a beat. "That you'll still come to as many of my football matches as you can." He pulls his lips between his teeth to hide the subtle quiver in his chin. "You're the closest thing I have to a dad."

I pull him back into my chest and kiss the top of his head, reminded of all the times I got up in the middle of the night with him when he was a baby so Rory could sleep. How I'd lay him on my chest as I lounged on the couch, watching some action movie with huge explosions. Over time, it seemed AJ preferred to fall asleep to those movies.

"No matter where I live, you'll always be a huge part of me, AJ." I tousle his dark hair. "You'll always be my family. Nothing will ever change that."

A floorboard creaks nearby, and I look up to see Rory

watching us. I part my lips to explain why I'm here, considering it's more than apparent AJ stole Rory's phone to text me. But instead of the fury and disappointment I saw in her expression during our last conversation, there's understanding. Acceptance.

She gives me a small smile, then mouths, *I'm sorry*.

I nod slightly. *Me, too*, I mouth back.

I should feel a sense of relief over the fact that Rory has accepted my leaving and moving on. If this happened yesterday, I would have.

But that was before my conversation with my father.

Before he reminded me of all the consequences of my actions.

Before I realized everything Rory and AJ would have to sacrifice for me to be happy.

They've already sacrificed so much.

Can I really ask them to sacrifice even more?

CHAPTER TWENTY-SEVEN

Esme

"They just pulled up, ma'am," Lieutenant Hawkins announces, peeking his head into a sitting room at the palace where I've been waiting for Anderson and Nora to arrive.

I can only imagine the nerves plaguing her today. Yesterday was such a whirlwind that I didn't have a chance to talk to either of them. Which is why I made sure I got here early so I could see how Nora's handling all of this before she's sucked into the three-ring circus.

It doesn't matter how much Anderson may have warned her about what to expect once she was part of this world. Nothing can adequately prepare someone to be thrust into the spotlight overnight.

It's what happened to us when our uncle and cousins died. At least we had each other to lean on.

I need to make sure Nora has someone she can lean on, too.

That she still has a sliver of normalcy in a world that will eventually become anything but.

"Thank you, Thomas," I tell my private secretary as I stand, following him down the corridor, the palace buzzing with more activity than normal.

That's to be expected on the day the king formally announces the Crown Prince's engagement.

I make my way down the grand staircase and step into the elaborate foyer as a dark SUV pulls in front of the entrance. When I spy Creed jump out of the driver's seat, I can't hide the smile the tugs on my lips, my body tingling with electricity, especially as I think of all the things I experienced mere hours ago when Creed snuck into my apartment.

"Your Highness."

I snap out of my growing inappropriate thoughts, darting my eyes to my right. Creed's father approaches and bows toward me, his tall frame imposing. He wears his dress uniform, medals lined across his chest. It's not his normal attire, but today's not a normal day.

"Major-General Lawson." I force a smile, pushing down any unease from being in his presence, considering I was just fantasizing about his son.

If anything, though, my nerves only increase around him, especially when his analytical gaze rakes over me, a combination of disappointment and ambivalence in his stare.

Or maybe it's merely my guilty conscience rearing its head, making me question if I'm doing the right thing by coming between Creed and his legacy.

Between Creed and his father.

"I trust you enjoyed your time away last week?"

I keep my expression relatively disinterested, not wanting

to give away the fact that I spent my break with his son buried between my legs.

"I did. It was precisely what I needed."

"Is that right?" He arches a single brow.

"The ocean always refreshes me."

Thankfully, Anderson and Nora enter the foyer before he can ask any more prying questions.

"Excuse me, Major-General," I say politely, putting as much space between us as possible, unable to shake the feeling that he knows about Creed and me.

Is that why Creed came to my apartment last night, desperate for me to tell him I love him?

"Of course, ma'am."

I glance his way, my nerves unraveling under his calm expression. But I can't worry about that right now. Not when I see how anxious Nora appears, a faint sheen of sweat dotting her porcelain skin. She may look every part the American princess the palace PR team wants her to be, a near mirror image of Grace Kelly, but I can tell how uneasy she is, her blue eyes skittering around the foyer as she nervously fiddles with her strawberry-blonde waves.

"Nora…" I don't even wait for her to greet me, as I'm supposed to. Instead, I wrap her in a tight hug. "Breathe," I whisper into her ear. "It'll all be over soon." I pull back, not looking away until I see her shoulders rise and fall.

"Thank you," she says softly with a slight tremble in her voice.

I give her one more reassuring smile, then drop my hold on her, facing Anderson. "And fuck you very much, big brother. I have to find out you're engaged from the bloody pappos?"

"Sorry, Ezzy." He kisses my cheek. "I'd planned on telling you in person." He gives me a knowing look. I don't have to ask to know he hoped to tell me when we were supposed to meet for brunch before I left New York. Instead, I opted to spend those few hours with Creed. "Things didn't exactly go as planned."

"I'd say." I wink, returning my attention to Nora to ask how she's been coping, when my eyes fall on Creed.

"Your Highness." He bows in my direction, his posture stiff, demeanor aloof.

"Captain Lawson," I reply cautiously.

He seems…different. I can't quite explain it. Granted, I didn't expect him to pull me into his arms and kiss me like he was able to when we were in the Hamptons. Like he did last night. Still, there's something off. A war being waged within his dark eyes.

"Excuse me," Creed's father interrupts, stepping between us, creating a barrier.

Creed averts his gaze, looking anywhere but at me, as if he were a teenager who was just caught with his first *Playboy*.

"His and Her Majesty are ready for you in the private drawing room," Major General Lawson tells my brother. "We shouldn't keep them waiting."

"Of course," Anderson replies with an air of authority.

"I'll see you out there anyway." I tell him before turning toward Nora, wrapping her in another hug. "Congratulations, sweetie. And I promise, it'll be worth it." I give her one last squeeze and step back.

They follow Major-General Lawson toward the grand staircase, Anderson's hand firmly placed on Nora's lower back, a reminder he's with her. As they're about to disappear down the hallway toward my dad's office, I notice Creed's father glance back at him, something unspoken passing between them.

"Excuse me, ma'am," Creed says, bowing slightly toward me.

But before he can retreat, I grab his forearm. "Are you okay?"

He darts his eyes to my hand before meeting my gaze. "I'm fine," he says softly, stepping away from me. Smoothing a hand down his dark suit jacket, he glances over his shoulder to make sure no one witnessed me touching him.

It's not like I kissed him. Or even hugged him. Yet based on his reaction, you'd think that's precisely what I did.

"No you're not." I drop my voice to a barely audible level. "Why did you really sneak into my apartment last night?"

"Esme." My name is a warning, but I'm not backing down. Not from this conversation. He may not have wanted to talk about it last night, but there's something bothering him.

"Creed," I reply, mimicking his tone.

He stares at me for several long moments, constantly scanning the area for anyone who might see us together.

But there's nothing wrong with us talking.

At least I didn't think there was.

Now, I'm not sure.

By the look on his face, either is he.

"I had a bad day yesterday," he finally admits with a sigh. "That's all. They're blaming me for the leak."

"But you had nothing to do with that."

"No, but I could have prevented it."

"How?"

"Because it's my job to protect your brother. I should have seen the photographers snapping their photo. Should have realized Nora was wearing the ring. Should have at least let his private secretary know he proposed."

"You knew?"

"I… Uh… Yes." He widens his stance, holding his head high. "He told me. As a friend," he adds. "Not as his chief protection officer."

"And I'm assuming a certain member of the royal guard told you in no uncertain terms that you can't be both," I say, putting the pieces together.

No wonder he was so distraught last night, so desperate for my reassurances that I love him. I can only imagine the lashing out his father gave him for putting his friendship with Anderson over his job as a royal guard.

"He did. Which is when I told him I was retiring."

"I assume that didn't go over well."

"If by not going over well you mean it ended with me punching him, then yes."

My gaze widens, jaw dropping. "You punched him?"

I sensed Creed's father wouldn't be all that supportive of his plans to retire. I never expected for it to end in a physical altercation.

"He, well…it doesn't matter." He leans toward me. "But right now, I'm under a lot of scrutiny. More so than usual."

"So you need to be extra careful not to step even a toe out of line."

"It may not make any sense because I gave my notice but…"

"You need to retire with honor. On good terms."

He nods subtly. "Last night can't happen again. *Won't* happen again. And I think it best if we put some space between us, including our morning workouts. I don't want to give anyone more fuel for the fire, so to speak."

"Okay then." I force a smile, hating the idea of keeping my distance from him yet again.

I knew it would be difficult to come back to our regular

lives after we spent all that time together in the Hamptons. After we had a taste of what it would be like to be a real couple.

The only thing that makes this remotely easy to handle is that it's only for a few weeks. That soon, Creed will no longer be in the royal guard.

But as he bows toward me and addresses me as he's been trained, I can't shake the feeling that there's something more to his changed demeanor.

CHAPTER TWENTY-EIGHT

Esme

"Earth to Ezzy. Are you even paying attention to what you're doing?"

I blink, snapping my eyes up. Harriet and Marius sit on the other side of her kitchen island, where I'm currently making a sauce to accompany the duck I'd prepared for our monthly dinner party.

Although, it appears I'm actually *burning* the sauce instead.

To say I've been distracted lately is putting it mildly. I thought I'd be happy now that Creed's retirement is less than two weeks away. But lately, he's been…aloof. Distant.

I know he's had bigger issues to concern himself with, like the added publicity of my brother's engagement, which has required Creed to not only provide Nora with her own protection team but to amp up Anderson's detail.

Regardless, I can't help but feel like something's different. That he's purposefully avoiding me.

"Shite," I curse under my breath, taking the nearly scorched saucepan off the burner and dumping out the contents, hurriedly collecting the ingredients to make a new sauce.

"Someone's distracted today," Marius remarks.

"There's just a lot going on," I lie, taking a large sip from my glass, the red wine warming me as it travels to my stomach. "Between all the craziness with Anderson and the referendum, I have a lot on my mind."

"And you're sure that's the only thing on your mind?" Harriet waggles her brows, pinching her lips into a knowing smirk.

"I… Well, of course. What else would I be thinking about?"

"I don't know…" Marius leans back in his barstool, crossing a leg over his thigh. "Maybe a certain member of the royal guard's upcoming retirement."

"I guess." I shrug.

Earlier in the summer, I would have been thrilled that Creed would be retiring in just a few more weeks. Now I'm no longer certain about him.

I'm no longer certain about *us*.

Marius straightens. "You *are* still planning to be together, right?"

I feverishly whisk the bubbling red wine in the saucepan, not wanting to burn it yet again. Once it's reduced, I add in the broth and seasonings, then turn the heat down to a simmer.

"Ezzy?" Harriet presses when I don't respond.

Placing the whisk on the resting spoon, I wipe my hands on a nearby dishtowel. "I think we are."

"But you don't know?"

"It's just… He's been distant lately." I hold up a hand to

cut them off, already sensing their argument. "I know he's been busy. That he's had double or triple the work to do with the announcement of Anderson's engagement." I take a long sip of my wine. "But it's almost like he's been avoiding me ever since…"

"Since what?"

I part my lips, unsure where to even begin. There's so much I haven't told them. Not because I don't trust them. We just haven't had time to catch up like we once did.

"Since we spent a week together in the Hamptons."

Their eyes widen. "The Hamptons?"

"Anderson wanted to give Creed a retirement gift."

"And that gift was you?" Marius remarks.

"It was. Although, I definitely benefited from it, too." My cheeks heat from the memories of that week. Waking up in Creed's arms. Making love first thing in the morning.

Being able to kiss him anytime I want.

"Then what happened?"

I shake my head, staring into the distance as I attempt to formulate my thoughts. Pinpoint one thing that happened to make me question everything.

But there hasn't been. Just a feeling in my gut.

"I don't know. I came back home. Creed went back to Manhattan to be with Anders before they flew back here. Then there was the leak about Anderson's engagement. But he came over to my apartment that night."

"Who?" Harriet furrows her brow. "Anders?"

"Creed. He snuck in. And he was… I don't even know how to explain it. He begged me to tell him I loved him. Like he physically needed my assurances to breathe."

"And did you?" Marius asks softly.

"Of course. Because I do love him. Since then, things

have been…different. Before that week in the Hamptons, we'd get together in the morning to work out."

"Is that what kids are calling it these days?" Marius smirks.

"That's not what I'm talking about, Mari. We really did meet in the palace fitness center and he gave me self-defense lessons. They've helped me feel less anxious. More in control."

Marius' playful expression sobers, and he gives me an understanding smile. "I get it."

"But you can't fault him for not showing up," Harriet states. "He's got a lot on his plate right now."

"I get that he's busy. I get things are complicated. And I'm trying not to be the clingy girlfriend, or whatever I'm supposed to be. But even on the rare occasion we do see each other, he sticks to protocol."

"Do you blame him?" Harriet remarks. "You agreed to keep your distance, not cross those lines like you did all those years ago."

"I understand that. And I completely support him wanting to make as few waves as possible, especially considering he got his ass handed to him after Anderson's engagement was leaked."

"Your brother blamed Creed for that?" Marius asks, aghast.

"No," I interject quickly. "Not Anders."

Realization washes over both their faces.

"His father," Harriet breathes.

I give a small smile, neither confirming nor denying. I don't have to. They know how his father can be.

"And I don't blame him for keeping the lines between us firmly drawn until he retires. I just…" I expel a long breath, trying to find the words I need. "He's not the same as he was in the Hamptons. Or before."

"It's natural for things to feel different, especially after you had a glimpse of what it's like to be together," Marius assures me. "You were free to be yourselves without a single care about who might learn the truth because there was no one around *to* learn the truth. You had to know things couldn't stay that way once you left. Not while Creed's still in the guard."

"It's more than just that, though. I can't explain it, but I can't shake this strange premonition that something's wrong. That it's more than just redrawing the battle lines, so to speak." I pull my lips between my teeth. "Maybe after seeing all the shite Nora's had to put up with, he changed his mind. Because if he were to be with me long term, that's exactly what he'll have to put up with." I swallow hard through the lump building in my throat, a few tears escaping at the thought of Creed walking away. "Maybe he's finally realized I'm not worth it."

"Oh, Ezzy…" Harriet slides off her stool and steps around the island, wrapping me in her arms. "You know how much Creed loves you. He's wanted you since you were teenagers." She pulls back, but keeps her hands on my biceps. "Plus, you can't compare Creed to Nora. Creed grew up in this life. Hell, he's been your brother's chief protection officer for the past six years now. He knows what the two of you have to deal with better than anyone. And yet, he's willing to turn his back on the only career he's ever known to be with you. Willing to turn his back on his legacy. That's got to count for something. Don't you think?"

"I know." With a long sigh, I push out of her hold, wiping my cheeks with my arm as I return my attention to the sauce. "Which is why I'm so confused. One second, I feel like I'm losing him. The next, I remind myself of all the hoops he's willing to jump through for me. Everything he's giving up."

"Listen, Ezzy," Marius begins, sliding off his barstool and approaching me, clutching my biceps. "You can talk to us about this until you're blue in the face. But we can't give you the answer you need. Only one person can. If you're uncertain about your future, bring up your concerns with Creed. In the highly unlikely event he *is* having second thoughts after witnessing the circus around Nora, you deserve to hear it from him. I may not be the best person to give relationship advice, considering I've avoided all serious relationships as much as possible, but you need to talk to each other. Not let your mind wonder with what he could be feeling or thinking. Go straight to the source. Okay?"

I push out a long breath and nod. "Okay."

"And like Mari said," Harriet adds, playfully nudging me. "It's highly unlikely he's having second thoughts. He'd be a complete fool if he was."

"But if he is, he'll have me to deal with." Marius puffs out his chest. "He may be able to snap my neck with his bare hands, but I got your back." He winks. "We both do."

"Damn straight we do." Harriet lifts her glass, and I grab mine off the counter, all of us clinking them together.

My friends are right.

I deserve an answer.

Even if it's not the answer I want to hear.

CHAPTER TWENTY-NINE

Creed

I sit in the security office of Anderson's estate, surrounded by a dozen glowing monitors, the room illuminated only by the faint blue light of the screens. I scan each one for any sign of unusual activity as Anderson plays host to a variety of diplomats, aristocrats, and business moguls in the grand ballroom. Considering he'll be king in a few years, he needs to get used to this kind of thing.

As does Nora.

Despite the early hiccups, she's adjusted easily to her new role as the Crown Prince's fiancée. She's actually been a breath of fresh air from all the stuffy tradition that's plagued the royal family for years. Instead, she follows her heart.

She reminds me of Esme in that way.

But I'm trying not to think about Esme.

Not because I don't love her with every beat of my heart.

But because I still don't know what to do about our future.

I'd hoped by keeping my distance over the past few weeks, I'd have a bit more clarity.

Instead, I'm more confused than ever.

One minute, I convince myself it'll all work out. That Rory and AJ will be okay with whatever attention they may receive if I were to publicly date Esme.

Then I remember how much the media hounded Rory after Adam's death.

For weeks, she couldn't leave her house to grab a gallon of milk without a reporter shoving a microphone into her face, asking how she was coping with the prospect of giving birth and raising a child without his father in the picture.

Can I force her to endure that again? Can I force *AJ* to endure that, too?

A sharp rap on the door pulls me back to the present, and I quickly scan the various monitors, making sure I didn't miss anything while I was lost in thought.

But I haven't. Everything is exactly as it was mere seconds ago. All the guests still mingle in the ballroom, a few members of my team interspersed among them to keep a closer eye on things. The perimeter of the property is still secured, no cars having approached the gate in over an hour now. And each entry point is protected, no one able to gain access without being on the approved list, everyone having passed a full background check.

It may be overkill, but without being able to uncover any more information about Kane Kingsley and his possible connection to the attempt on Esme's life, I can't take any chances. Instead, I've been cross-referencing a file I put together containing all the information I could get on Kane Kingsley in case anyone bearing even a slight resemblance to him appears.

"Come in," I call out, returning my eyes to the cameras

covering the ballroom, a moment of panic seizing me when I can't find Esme among the guests. "Did you finish the last perimeter walk?" I ask, assuming it's Kylian here to report back after doing a foot patrol, something I insist on since my cameras can't cover every square inch of this property.

"In these heels?"

I snap my head up, eyes falling on Esme wearing a stunning emerald green silk dress, the deep V bringing attention to her ample cleavage. I should be relieved she's here, that she's safe.

But at the same time, the last thing I need is to be alone in a small space with her.

And during a function with hundreds of people in attendance, including various members of the royal household who could walk in on us at any moment.

"Esme, I—"

"I shouldn't be here." She squeezes her eyes shut, pinching her lips into a tight line. "I know, Creed." When she looks to the ceiling, I notice unease and apprehension flash on her expression.

It's obvious the past several weeks have been just as trying for her as they've been for me. I haven't helped matters at all. If anything, I'm the reason she appears weary and exhausted.

"I just…" Her tongue darts out to moisten her lips, and she meets my gaze again. "I needed to talk to you. I…" She trails off, her attention fixated on something on my desk.

I follow her line of sight, my heart falling to the pit of my stomach when I see what she's looking at.

Kane Kingsley's military photo, as well as the three-dimensional rendering of her sketch, the similarities unmistakable, despite the lack of scar in Kingsley's file photo.

But that's not what causes the hurt and disappointment

to cover her expression. It's all the background information I've amassed, too.

Information I purposefully kept from her.

With slow steps, she walks toward me and picks up the file. I don't even bother hiding it.

"What is this, Creed?" Her voice is strained. Choked.

I swallow hard. "His name is Kane Kingsley."

"I see that." She sets her jaw, but still can't hide her quivering chin, tears welling in her eyes. "How long have you known about him?"

My chest tightens as I rub the back of my neck, an emptiness settling in my stomach. I could lie and say I just found out about him. That I was planning on telling her but was trying to get more information first.

But I can't disrespect her by adding more lies on top of the ones I've already told her. It'll only make matters worse.

"A while."

She levels her fiery stare on me, green orbs flaming with anger. "You found out in The Hamptons, didn't you? That's what that phone call was about. Why you've been distant since then. Because you've been keeping this from me. Because you've been lying to me, even when I asked if you'd found anything. Isn't that right?"

I shake my head, wanting to tell her this isn't why I've been distant. Then again, it would probably hurt her infinitely less than the truth. Still, I can't bring myself to lie to her.

I also can't bring myself to tell her the real reason.

"I did it to protect you, Esme," I finally say. "This guy…" I grab the file back from her. "He's not a good person. He's a bloody assassin!" I lean into her. "He's known as the *Angel of Death*, for crying out loud. Do you want to know why?"

She blinks repeatedly.

"Because if you're unlucky enough to see him, you can all but guarantee to die soon. I'm sorry I didn't tell you about him, but I made an oath to protect you. Not put you in the line of fire."

"That wasn't your decision to make, Creed! All my life, every decision has been made for me. You of all people should know how that's affected me. How it *still* affects me. I didn't ask you to find out who he was as a member of the royal guard. I asked you as the man I love. Who I thought loved me."

I step toward her. "And I do, Esme."

"Obviously not enough to tell me the bloody truth."

"I didn't have a choice. While I'm still in the royal guard, I have to put my oath first."

She barks out a laugh. "You didn't seem to have a problem forgetting that oath any of the countless times you fucked me in the Hamptons. Or when I was on my knees for you. You seem to be more than happy to forget that oath when it benefits you. Don't you?"

"That's—"

"Different?" she shoots back, her voice echoing around us.

I cringe, worrying someone might overhear. But I don't bother trying to hush her. I doubt it would work right now, anyway.

"No, it's not, Creed. You always have a choice. And this time, you chose wrong." She spins around, stomping toward the door.

"Esme, please." I move toward her, grabbing her forearm to prevent her from leaving. "You need to understand."

"Oh, I do understand." She smiles sadly. "I just can't

believe it took me this long to realize that when it really matters, you'll never choose me." Her voice catches on her last words.

Then she rips her arm from my grasp and storms out of the office, slamming the door behind her.

CHAPTER THIRTY

Esme

I hurriedly swipe at my cheeks as I study my reflection in the bathroom mirror, drawing in several deep breaths in the hopes of regaining my composure.

If I were anyone else, I'd be able to leave and put the pieces of my broken heart back together in private, preferably with a bottle of wine and a tub of ice cream. But since I learned the truth at a diplomatic event, I have no choice but to stay, pretend everything's fine when it feels like my life's falling apart more and more every day.

I don't know why I hoped Creed would run after me. Swear his love for me. Realize he fucked up and vow never to choose the crown over me again.

But he didn't.

Solidifying my belief that he'll never choose me. Not when it matters. Maybe that's why he's been distant. Not because of the truth he's been keeping from me. But because as his retirement drew near, he's been questioning whether he can actually go through with it.

If he can walk away from his legacy for me.

I thought this was finally our chance to be together.

Apparently, I'm not enough for him.

I'll never *be* enough.

I push down more tears threatening to fall, rebuilding the wall around my heart, brick by painful brick. Then I fix my mouth into the practiced smile I've perfected over the years.

The one that manages to hide everything under its false veneer.

After one last check of my appearance to make sure I've successfully hidden all evidence of a broken heart, I open the door, heading toward the formal ballroom. But before I can rejoin the party, a motion out of the corner of my eye catches my attention. I snap my head to my right, inhaling a sharp breath when I see Creed rushing toward me. His long strides are swift and determined, his piercing gaze radiating an intensity that makes my heart both soar and break at the same time.

He grabs my hand, pulling me away from the open doors of the ballroom and into a darkened corridor. Laughter and jovial conversation from the party still find its way to us, the happy atmosphere at complete odds with the heartache plaguing me.

And, by the look of things, plaguing Creed, too.

"Please, Esme," he whispers, his dark eyes reflecting an emotion that matches my own. "You have to believe me when I tell you that taking away your decision-making ability never entered into the equation. I just want to keep you safe. That's all. I love you. Today. Tomorrow. Always."

This is what I wanted — for Creed to run after me and tell me he loves me.

But they're just words. Now more than ever, I need action.

Placing my hands on my hips, I hold my head high. "Prove it."

"Prove it?" He furrows his brow. "I've told you time and again how I feel about you. You know how much I care about you. How much—"

"Right here. Right now." I turn from him and march into the foyer, positioning myself in front of the open doorway of the ballroom, where I'm in full view of all the guests.

Where Creed would be in full view, too.

"Kiss me," I beg softly, eyes glossing over.

He stares at me for several long moments. "Esme…"

"Please, Creed," I choke out, swallowing down a new wave of tears.

I know I'm asking the impossible of him. Know he's still a member of the royal guard and if he does this, it won't end well for him. Even if he only has a few weeks left until he's set to retire, he'll no longer be able to retire with honor.

But I need to know he wants me. Need to know he'll put me first. Need to know the crown won't always come between us.

To my surprise, he steps slowly toward me, stopping several inches away. His eyes dart toward the ballroom, scanning the hundred or so guests mingling around the large space, including several important members of the royal household. When he looks back at me, he traces his gaze over my lips, making me think he's about to kiss me.

Then his shoulders fall and he shakes his head. "I… I can't."

My knees buckle, a vice squeezing my heart as I suck in a shuttering breath. But I force myself to stand tall, show no emotion. I can't. Not when I'm on full display like this.

Instead, I spin from him and re-secure the mask I've worn most of my life, plastering a fake smile on my face and pretending Creed didn't just rip my heart out of my chest.

As I re-enter the ballroom, I'm immediately stopped by some ambassador and his wife to discuss one of my charity initiatives. I barely hear a word they say, though. How can I when the sound of my heart breaking is more deafening than anything else in the room?

I worried something like this might happen when he grew distant.

I thought we were stronger than this.

I guess I was wrong.

"My apologies," I say when a silence falls over the conversation, the expectant expressions surrounding me indicating they're probably waiting for a response. "I'm needed somewhere else right now."

The ambassador and his wife bow their heads slightly, and I make my way through the ballroom, my heels clicking against the marble floor. I slip through one of the open sets of double doors and onto the verandah, a summer breeze caressing my skin.

A few people mill about, smoking and laughing, but I ignore them, heading toward the ledge and placing my hands on it for support.

I scan my surroundings, about to do my counting exercises to help reduce my anxiety, but all that does is bring up more memories of Creed.

I have a feeling *everything* will bring up memories of Creed.

"Want to talk about it?"

Startled, I whirl around, pushing down my surprise and fixing my expression. A tall figure looms a few feet away, a smile tugging on his lips. But it doesn't reach his eyes like it once did.

"Talk about what exactly, Mr. Gates?"

"For starters, what has you all worked up." He narrows his gaze. "Or perhaps, I should say *who* has you all worked up."

"I…" I shake my head, squaring my shoulders. "I'm fine. Thank you for your concern." I turn back around, soaking in the stunning gardens on my brother's property.

"Well, it's good to know some things never change," Jameson remarks as he moves to stand beside me.

"And what's that?"

"That you're still a damn good liar."

"I'm not lying. I—"

"You're not?" He arches a disbelieving brow. "Don't forget. We once spent an entire summer trying to fool the country. Hell, the world." He playfully nudges me. "I'd like to think I've picked up on a few things. Learned when you're pretending to be okay even though you're not." His smile falls. "Like right now."

I push out a long sigh, on the verge of insisting yet again that I'm fine. But over the past few months, Jameson has proved to be trustworthy. He didn't keep me in the dark about anything. In fact, he took the initiative to visit me the day after I saw the man with the scar to tell me he believed me. He's one of the few people who *has* been honest with me. Who hasn't purposefully kept the truth from me.

It's only right I return the favor and not keep the truth from him, either.

"Kane Kingsley," I announce in a determined voice.

He blinks, confusion furrowing his brow. "I'm sorry. I don't—"

"The man with the scar. That's his name."

He doesn't immediately respond. Just stares, eyes wide, lips slightly parted. Then he nods. "I see." Placing his hands on the ledge, he peers into the distance, a contemplative expression creasing his brow. "How did you find out his name?" He glances my way.

"I sketched his face and gave it to Cr—" I stop short. The mere mention of his name leaves a sour taste in my mouth. "A friend."

"And he helped track him down?"

"More or less."

"What do you know about him?"

"Not much, I'm afraid." I roll my eyes. "Apparently, he's too dangerous for me to know about." I can't subdue my biting tone, making it more than obvious I'm upset over this. "All I do know is he's some sort of trained assassin who's known as the *Angel of Death* because once you see him, you're as good as dead."

He nods slowly, seeming to process this information. I can only imagine how he must feel to finally know the name of the man who killed Callie after all these years.

"I'm sorry for ruining your night with this information," I say after several moments of silence. "I just thought you should know. If this is the guy who killed Callie, someone obviously hired him for a reason. Someone who wanted to make sure she disappeared without a trace. I just…" I grab his hands in mine. They're cold, despite it being a warm summer evening. "Be careful."

"You, too, Esme." He shifts our hands, running his thumbs over my knuckles like he once did whenever I needed reassurance during a public event. "And thanks for telling me. You did the right thing."

I hold his gaze for a beat, my eyes scanning his frame.

The last time I saw him, I thought he looked worn out. I figured it was due to the news of Callie's death.

But he looks even more tired tonight. His once broad shoulders seem small and hunched over. Shadows loom beneath his eyes, and there's a gauntness to his cheeks.

As if he's withering away in front of me.

I part my lips to ask if he's okay, but before I can, he releases me and bows. "Enjoy the rest of your evening, ma'am." Then he spins from me, hurrying inside.

I blink, momentarily taken aback by his abrupt departure. But when I look around the verandah and notice Silas Archer watching us with interest, I understand why he left so quickly.

I consider approaching him, see what he knows about Kane Kingsley.

But something prevents me from being so bold. It was one thing to share what I know with Jameson.

It's another to confront Silas.

As much as I hate that Creed kept the truth from me, he wouldn't have risked our relationship if he didn't think there was a real threat to my safety.

And I have a feeling Kane Kingsley is one of the biggest threats to my safety there's ever been.

PART III

Truth

CHAPTER THIRTY-ONE

Esme

"**P**ardon the interruption, ma'am," my butler says, poking his head into my office as I stare at my laptop screen, my eyes glazed over from having spent the better part of the morning trying to find out everything I can about Kane Kingsley.

Hell, I've spent the better part of the past week trying to find out everything I can about Kane Kingsley.

But like Creed warned me, the man's a ghost. That didn't stop me from trying, though. And I've tried everything. Yet I still came up empty.

"Mr. Gates is here to see you. He mentioned it's regarding what you discussed last week?" He arches a questioning brow.

I perk up, trying not to get my hopes up. But Jameson's father founded a private military company. Maybe he used some of the resources available to him to get more information than I have access to. I probably should have given him the sketch I'd done instead of Creed. I foolishly thought I could trust him.

"You may show him in."

"Certainly."

With a subtle nod, my butler retreats. Seconds later, Jameson steps into my office, looking more unkempt than he did last week, his complexion pale, eyes lifeless.

"Your Highness." He bows in my direction.

"Mr. Gates." I jump to my feet. "Are you okay?"

"I apologize for the surprise visit. I just…" He rubs the back of his neck. "Would you like to go for a walk in the garden? I always enjoyed spending time with you out there." He meets my gaze, almost pleading with me to agree. If getting some fresh air makes him more comfortable, I'm happy to grant his request.

"I'd like that."

His body relaxes as he expels a long breath. "Thank you."

I nod, skirting around my desk toward the double doors that lead to the gardens. Jameson jumps in front of me and opens them. I give him a polite smile and step out into the sunlight, basking in the warmth on my face. But any sense of relaxation is short-lived when I glance over at Jameson, who appears on edge once more.

"Is everything okay?" I ask again.

"That's a loaded question."

"You don't seem like yourself lately," I remark, unsure how to politely tell him he looks like crap. Then I lower my voice. "Did you discover something about Kingsley?"

"You could say that."

"What is it? I've searched everywhere, even used my clearance to look into intelligence databases—"

"I know."

"You do?" I stop walking, furrowing my brow. "How?"

He glances up at the sky, pinching his lips together. Then he looks my way. "Would you like to sit?"

I have a feeling whatever he's about to tell me won't be good news. But if it has to do with the man who killed Adam and who tried to kill me, I need to know.

My heels crunch on the gravel as I walk toward a bench. A gentle breeze carries the sweet aroma of various types of flowers, a few bees drifting from bloom to bloom, gathering nectar. As we sit, a small bird on the edge of the white marble birdbath assesses us curiously before preening its glossy feathers.

"The truth is, I've known about Kingsley for a while now," Jameson says after a few moments.

"Because of Callie, right?"

"No." He shakes his head gravely. "I knew about him even before Callie. I knew he killed her brother, Jack."

I blink repeatedly, confusion knitting my brow. "I don't—"

"Listen to me, Esme." He grabs my hands, clutching them. But his grip is weak. "I plan to disclose everything I'm about to tell you to the privy council tomorrow. I'm not trying to avoid responsibility. In fact, I'm done avoiding responsibility. Done being a pawn in this game for fear of what could happen. I've stayed silent for years now. Allowed the threat of prison, or worse, to control me. I'm done with that."

"Okay…" I draw out, still unsure what's going on.

"Kingsley killed Jack and Callie Sloane because of a video recording their father made nearly thirty years ago."

"Who was their father?" I ask, feeling somewhat naïve that I hadn't taken the time to learn that myself. I was so focused on the man with the scar that I didn't consider learning more about Callie's family.

"A man named Warren Clark. He was a paparazzo."

"And what was on this recording?"

He pulls his hands away, running them along his pants, the seconds stretching as I await his response. Then his eyes lock on mine.

"The murder of your uncle, aunt, and cousins."

His statement forces all the air to whoosh from my lungs. It's a good thing I'm sitting. Otherwise, my knees probably would have buckled under the weight of his admission.

"But they weren't murdered. They died in—"

"An avalanche?" he interjects, his voice heavy with skepticism. "That's what they made the world think to cover up the truth. And the truth is that Kane Kingsley was paid to dispose of your family and make it look like an accident."

"By who?"

"Silas Archer." He pauses, then adds, "Who did so under the direct orders of your grandfather, King Theodore."

My mouth falls open, my heart dropping to the pit of my stomach. I can feel my face drain of color, a thousand questions racing through my mind.

But one in particular is at the forefront.

"Why?"

"I don't know. Archer's always remained tight-lipped about that. All I know is, for the past ten years, he's made it his mission to eliminate anyone who could expose the truth." He swallows hard. "As has my father."

"And what's your father's role in all of this?" I tilt my head, still reeling from the bombshell Jameson just dropped.

"You know he was once in the royal guard. Correct?"

I nod.

"He was on Prince Nicholas' team."

"Let me guess. He was supposed to be on watch that night."

"Archer gave him a huge payout to turn a blind eye, more or less. But he did more than that. He helped. And after the dust settled, he left the guard and started his own security company with the money Archer paid. You don't think it's a coincidence we're routinely awarded all the big government contracts, do you? My father essentially blackmailed Archer into making sure he gets them every year in exchange for his silence. And loyalty."

"And Warren Clark?" I press, needing answers. Needing all of this to make sense.

Needing someone to pay.

"Clark observed Kingsley and my father dragging six unconscious bodies from their house and up the mountain. He made sure to document it."

"Instead of calling the police. Typical paparazzo," I mutter under my breath.

"I agree." He meets my gaze, sympathy and compassion filling his orbs. "At some point, they were alerted to his presence. He tried to get away, but they pursued and forced him off the road. He died on impact. Kingsley and my father confiscated the camera they found in the passenger compartment. Thought he was only shooting stills."

"But he had a video camera," I say, filling in the blanks.

"He must have hidden it somewhere else in his car. And for nearly twenty years, that video was stored away in a box of his belongings. Until Jack Sloane found it."

"How did you learn he had it?"

"He reached out to a friend whose cousin worked for the royal household. Thought he was doing the right thing by exposing this huge coverup. Unfortunately for him, that person was Gianna Vale."

I close my eyes as another puzzle piece snaps into place.

"Even worse, he told her the copy he'd given her was just that. A copy. That he was hanging onto the original for security purposes and would be going to the media if nothing was done to right this wrong. She told Archer about it and he had Kingsley do what he does best."

"Kill him, but make it look like an accident."

Jameson nods.

"And Callie?"

He runs a hand over his face, his shoulders falling. "Until that point, I had no idea about any of this. After they killed Jack and couldn't find the recording, they targeted his sister. Thought she was the most logical person who might have it. But they couldn't keep killing people. That wouldn't make the recording appear if it was hidden. So my father recommended they change tactics. Suggested getting someone close to Callie. And since I had a way with the ladies once upon a time…" He laughs under his breath, which soon turns into a coughing fit.

"They asked you to get close to her to find the recording."

"I thought I was protecting my legacy," he says in a strained voice once he gets his coughing under control. "I knew what they'd done was wrong. But I'd also grown accustomed to a certain…lifestyle. I didn't want to lose that."

"So you helped cover up the murder of six people just so you could continue buying expensive cars and jetting around the world?" I shoot back, my voice full of venom.

"I didn't say what I've done is right. I know it's not. At the time, I didn't care. I was egotistical. Narcissistic, even. So I agreed to help my father. Then something happened I didn't anticipate." He smiles sadly. "I fell in love with Callie. I wasn't lying when I told you I loved her. I did. But I knew there was a ticking clock hanging over her. Knew the second I found the recording, they'd kill her, even if she was clueless as to the contents."

"Which is what happened."

"Yes… And no."

"No?"

"After dating her for months, my father was tired of waiting. Thought I'd gotten too distracted. So they made her… disappear. Unfortunately, they underestimated her relationship with Hayes. They knew she worked for him, but didn't think he'd go to the lengths he did to bring attention to her disappearance. The last thing they wanted was for anyone to look into it. So Gianna suggested manufacturing a news story that would bury any mention of a missing woman." He gives me a knowing look.

"That's why we dated."

"And why we were nearly engaged after Hayes accused me of killing Callie. It was just a ploy to manipulate the headlines. Make sure no one looked hard enough to uncover the truth."

"But Adam did. Isn't that right?" I press, my blood boiling at all the lives lost because of this.

Because of my grandfather and Silas Archer.

"They killed him, and planted enough evidence to pin it on Hayes. Two birds. One stone, more or less."

"And you were still okay with all of this? Still didn't think it was getting out of hand and to just come clean?" I lean toward him, throat tight. "Adam trusted you."

"Which is why I'm going to come clean tomorrow morning at the privy council meeting. Tell them everything, starting with the murder of Prince Nicholas and his family, all the way to the attempt on your life last year and how they framed Charles Thacker for that, too."

"Are you only telling me all of this in the hopes of cutting a deal?" I seethe. "Because I'll do everything I can to make sure you serve every minute of the maximum sentence. I—"

"I'm tired of people getting hurt, Esme. That's all. When this began, I thought once Callie died, it would be over and we could go back to our lives." He licks his lips. "Now I realize it won't ever end. Not when there are people out there who might expose the truth. Or who are smart enough to look beyond what you're told and question everything. People like you and Creed. I'm just…" He hangs his head and stares at his feet. "I'm tired of all the blood on my hands. So if I can prevent even more blood from spilling, I'm willing to do that, to hell with the consequences."

I scrutinize him for several long moments, searching for any sign of deception. He seems repentant. But one thing is gnawing at me.

"Why me?"

He shakes his head. "What do you mean?"

"If you're planning on coming clean at the privy council meeting tomorrow, why tell me all of this now?"

"I guess for insurance purposes."

"Insurance?" I furrow my brow.

"Let's just say I've been on borrowed time for a while now. After our conversation last week, I needed to do something. Needed someone to know the truth. All of it." He reaches into his suit jacket and retrieves a flash drive, extending it toward me.

"Is this what I think it is?" I ask in a shaky voice as I take it from him.

"It is."

"How did you—"

"Callie," he answers with a nostalgic gleam in his eyes. "I actually found it fairly early on in our relationship."

"But you kept it to yourself because you knew what would happen once they had it."

He nods.

"And after they killed Callie?"

"I don't know…" He pushes out a long sigh. "I guess I didn't want them to have it. Wanted them to believe they ruined their one shot at finding the recording. Liked watching them squirm trying to find it. So I carried on as if it was still out there."

My fingers close around the small, cold metal stick. It almost seems to throb in my hand with the weight of its secrets. I can only imagine how much it's burdened Jameson over the years.

"Yet you kept this to yourself, even after Adam was killed. After I was nearly killed, too. Twice."

"Like I said. My actions have been anything but conscionable. I can sit here and apologize for them, but it won't make them right. Won't erase what I've done. Won't bring back anyone who lost their life because of me. Hopefully, this will make sure nobody else dies in order to protect this secret."

I lift my eyes to his, a part of me wondering if this is just another manipulative game. But what could he potentially have to gain by admitting his involvement? Sure, Silas Archer and his father are much more involved, but Jameson is just as responsible. Just as culpable.

Maybe he really is doing this to make amends.

This may be the first honorable thing he's ever done in his life. It makes the sting of learning I was right about him all along a little easier to swallow.

"Well…" I pull myself to my feet, keeping the flash drive clutched tightly in my grip. "Thank you for coming clean."

"You'll keep that safe?" He stands, glancing toward my hand.

"Of course."

"And your apartment will be secure?"

"This entire complex is secure."

"I understand that." He hesitates, licking his lips. "But can you put in a request for additional protection? At least for the next few days? What I'm planning to do tomorrow is going to piss off a lot of people. I'll be on the official visitor log here, which means they may turn their ire on you. I hate to have put you in this position in the first place. Unfortunately, you're the only person in my life I trust. Who I know will do the right thing with this information."

Jameson's not even a friend. He's more of an acquaintance than anything. Someone forced into my life ages ago by someone trying to manipulate me. The fact I'm the only person who he can trust is incredibly sad.

"I'd just feel better knowing someone was here with you. Someone on your protection team."

"I'll have Archie arrange full-time security for the next few days."

He seems to find relief in this, his shoulders falling. Then he bows toward me. "Your Highness." He lifts his eyes to mine, his voice quivering as he says, "It's been an honor."

"Mr. Gates."

As he retreats from me, I can't shake the premonition forming in my stomach that this may be the last time I ever see him.

CHAPTER THIRTY-TWO

Jameson

I step into the foyer of my house, feeling infinitely lighter than I did when I left for Esme's apartment. If you'd told me years ago that I'd admit to the role I played in all of this, I wouldn't have believed it.

I would have argued I'd never betray my father like that. That I'd never do anything that could put the lifestyle I've grown accustomed to at risk.

A terminal diagnosis puts things into perspective, though.

I should have been content to go to my grave without a single person knowing the truth. But the sicker I got, the less I was able to stomach that idea, especially with the knowledge that Esme's been looking into Kane.

It's only a matter of time before Archer and my father succeed in silencing her, for once and for all.

I can't have her blood on my hands, too.

Not anymore.

I toe off my shoes as I shrug out of my jacket, draping it

over the polished mahogany banister before tugging off my navy blue tie, the sound of rustling fabric filling the cavernous space. Gripping the railing, I pad up the winding staircase, the carpet soft on my feet, and slip into the owner's suite, heading straight for the bathroom.

The counter is cluttered with dozens of pill bottles, each filled with drugs that promise to give me a little more time. Most people would be devastated upon learning they only had months to live.

Not me.

There's no doubt in my mind I'm finally getting what I deserve after all the horrible things I've done. Confessing my sins won't bring back those I've hurt.

Won't bring back Callie.

But at least I can leave this life with a clear conscience.

Or as clear of a conscience as a man who's done horrible things can have.

If I can leave this world with even a shred of dignity, maybe I can find the peace I never did before.

I bypass most of the bottles, going straight for the painkillers. I don't bother counting them out, just dump several into my hand. Returning to the bedroom, I grab my favorite bottle of scotch off the wet bar and toss back the pills, washing them down with a few large swallows. Mixing opioids and alcohol is frowned upon. But I have stage four pancreatic cancer. I'm already dying. May as well enjoy the ride on the way out.

Facing your own mortality is a strange thing. Eye-opening, humbling, but strange all the same. You have no choice but to reflect on your life. Ask yourself if you've lived a good life. If you have any regrets.

At least, that's what I did when I received my diagnosis and my doctor said I had six months at most, the cancer having already spread to other parts of my body, making it incurable.

I was angry at first. Told the doctor I had more money than many small nations put together and can afford whatever treatment was available.

That's when I learned money isn't everything.

Because no amount of wealth can save my life.

But I can do everything in my power to save other people's lives. To make peace with my regrets.

To save my soul.

Which is why I knew I had to tell Esme the truth.

Now that I've told her everything and gave her the recording to back it all up, the weight that had been crushing me for too long has evaporated, my conscience finally at peace.

I'm still not a good person. I've never purported to be.

But I can die knowing I've done at least one good thing. That after years of hurting people, I've done something to help instead.

I take another long sip from the scotch, savoring the smokey flavor on my tongue, relishing every drop as if it's my last. If there's a heaven and the powers that be decide I've been repentant enough to deserve a spot, I pray they offer a decent selection of single malts.

Just as I'm about to take one last swallow, a clicking echoes behind me, cutting through my moment of peace. But I don't need to turn around in order to know there's a gun currently aimed at me. I should have anticipated this. After all, I've noticed Kane following me these past few days.

But I never could have anticipated the voice that booms moments later, demanding, "Why did you do it?"

I'd expected Kingsley to be the one to end my life. To stop me from doing what I've already done.

I never expected for it to be my father.

I slowly turn around, barely even registering the gun pointed directly at me. It doesn't scare me. Nothing does anymore.

"It was time for the truth to come out." My voice is even. Calm. Serene.

Which angers my father even more, his grip on the gun tightening, knuckles becoming white.

"*Bullshite!*" he roars, spittle forming on the corner of his mouth, the vein in his neck standing out like an exposed root. "The truth was never supposed to come out. We all agreed to protect the truth by whatever means necessary. And now…" He shakes his head, lip curling in a sneer. "I never thought my own son would betray us."

"Just trying to make peace with the part I played." I hold up my hands, gazing into his eyes with unwavering determination. But he can barely look at me. I'm not sure if it's my betrayal that has him unable to meet my gaze.

Or because he doesn't want to look into my eyes as he kills his only son.

I doubt that matters to him, though.

He was never much of a father. Which is probably why I went along with all of this for so long. I thought if I did everything asked of me, he'd finally be proud of me. I'd finally have his approval.

It took learning I was dying to realize I no longer cared about any of that. That the only person I need to be proud of is myself.

And I'm definitely proud of my actions today.

"Go ahead," I goad him. "Just do it. I'm ready. But it won't change anything. The truth is protected. Along with that recording you've been after all these years."

He blinks repeatedly, jaw dropping open in surprise. "You… You found it?"

"I've had it all this time. After what you did to Callie, I decided to hold on to it as insurance. And that's exactly what it is. Insurance that even after I'm gone, the truth will come out. The truth should have come out a long time ago. It should have come out after you killed Callie, but I was too naïve, allowed you to convince me that I'd be the one blamed for it. I was so desperate for your love and respect that I did whatever you asked. But I'm done with that. I—"

A deafening bang reverberates through the room, my chest burning with a searing pain. I look down at my shirt, the crimson stain stark against the crisp white. My back collides hard with the wall as I stumble backward, my failing vision focused on the man before me.

Crazed laughter erupts in my throat as I think of the irony of it all.

This man brought me into this world.

And now he's the reason I'm leaving it, too.

I clutch my chest, the world growing fuzzier with every passing second. With my last ounce of strength, I say, "You lose."

Then the darkness takes over.

CHAPTER THIRTY-THREE

Esme

I stare at my laptop screen, reading yet another article written about the avalanche that killed my aunt, uncle, and cousins. I've spent the past several hours learning everything I possibly could about it, especially after watching the recording contained on the flash drive Jameson entrusted to my safekeeping.

A part of me expected it to be some wild prank. For it to contain anything other than the story he shared with me.

But it didn't.

The video was dark and grainy, but there was no mistaking a much younger Henry Gates helping a man with a bloody gash along his right jawline dress six limp bodies in ski attire, then drag them up the ski run. At least now I know how Kane Kingsley got that scar. It gives me a sense of vindication to know he got it when he tried to hurt my family, that someone fought back enough to permanently scar him.

Regardless of the fact that they were murdered, not a

single report mentioned the possibility their deaths were anything but accidental. Or that a charge had been set off causing the avalanche in the first place. Why would anyone question it? They all died as a result of blunt force trauma, a logical death after falling victim to an avalanche.

Never in a million years would I have thought they were murdered.

And the worst part is they were killed at my grandfather's direction.

Why? Why would he want not only his first-born son and wife killed, but also their four children? His grandchildren?

These questions have plagued me for hours, making it impossible for me to think about anything else.

The only possible answer I've been able to come up with is that perhaps they could have exposed something that would have destroyed him.

And, in turn, the monarchy.

But what could that have been?

And what did my cousins have to do with it?

They were all older than me, but still only teens at the time, ranging in age from thirteen to sixteen. Why the need to silence them, too?

My body sags in the chair, and I close my eyes, fingers massaging my temples in the hopes of warding off the headache I feel forming. All I can hope is that Silas Archer answers all these questions once Jameson shares this information with the council.

Which begs the question of whether my grandmother knows any of this. I may not have the best relationship with her. She's never been warm or nurturing. But I struggle to believe she'd condone the murder of her son and four of her grandchildren. She may be set in her ways and stubborn, but she's not vicious.

Not capable of something like this.

I drag myself from my chair and roll my neck, trying to relieve some of the tension. Then I slip out of my office, padding on light feet through the administrative wing and toward my living quarters.

My apartment is relatively quiet now that my staff has left. Normally, I'd be the only one here at this hour, since I don't feel the need to keep my staff around twenty-four / seven.

But as I promised Jameson, I asked Archie to set up a security presence in my apartment for the next few days. If he thought it an unusual request, he didn't question it.

"Everything okay, ma'am?" Archie asks when he passes me in the hallway, probably on his way to do yet another exterior patrol.

I don't know how these guys spend hours patrolling and watching their surroundings on the off chance there's a threat. I'd be bored out of my mind. But as I've learned, being selected for the elite protection squad is an honor for most military men. One they take extremely seriously.

Which is why it was unfair of me to ask Creed to do something that could jeopardize his position and put a mark on his otherwise exemplary military record. But between the secret he kept and his growing distance, I needed to know he still wanted me. That he hadn't changed his mind. That he still chose me.

I *needed* him to choose me.

"Everything's fine." I flash Archie a small smile. "I'm just going to make some tea. Would you like a cup?"

"I can do it," he offers, but I wave him off.

"I'm perfectly capable of boiling water for tea. English Breakfast okay?"

He nods. "I could use some caffeine."

"I figured."

"I need to do another perimeter check. I won't be more than a few minutes."

"I'll have a cup of caffeine ready for when you get back," I say, then continue past him toward the kitchen.

I set the kettle on the stovetop and ignite the gas, the blue flame hissing to life. Finding a couple of infusers in one of the drawers, I scoop some leaves into them before placing them in a pair of tea cups.

As I wait for the water to boil, my thoughts go back and forth between my grandfather, Jameson Gates, and Creed.

Especially Creed.

Did I throw away the best thing to ever happen to me because of my stubbornness? Creed was just trying to protect me. As for the distance I've felt, can I really blame him for putting space between us? I couldn't have expected things to be like they were in the Hamptons when we were free to do whatever we wanted without fear of anyone seeing us.

We don't have that same luxury here.

Not yet, anyway.

I grab my mobile from my pocket and navigate to my text conversation with Creed, fingers poised over the screen as I debate what to say. If I should even say anything.

But I need to.

So I start typing out a message apologizing for my behavior. Tell him I was wrong to put him in a position where he could potentially risk losing everything he's worked toward since enlisting in the military. That I was selfish to ask that of him, considering all the sacrifices he's repeatedly made, not just for me but also his country.

Before I have a chance to hit send, the kettle whistles, pulling me away from my thoughts. I place my phone on the island and turn off the burner, then pour steaming water into each cup just as I hear the front door open.

"Tea's ready, Archie," I call out.

I work on steeping the tea, expecting Archie to appear in the kitchen at any second.

But he doesn't.

Figuring he may not have heard me, I walk into the living room. "Archie, your tea's…"

"Sorry, princess." Silas Archer curls his lips into that same sinister smile he always wears. His eyes are menacing in the low light, his voice unnerving. "Captain Walsh won't be able to join you for tea. He's…indisposed at the moment."

A subtle ping sounds from somewhere in the distance, and all I can do is pray that sound isn't what I think it is. But when I hear a thud behind me and whirl around as Kane Kingsley emerges from elsewhere in my apartment, hands covered with dark leather gloves, holding a gun with a silencer attached, I know I won't get my wish.

Not when he drags Archie's lifeless body behind him and tosses him into the corner.

I should be more frightened at seeing the man who's haunted my dreams for months standing in my house, especially with everything I know about him.

But all I can think about is that my chief protection officer just lost his life for me.

Again.

Thanks to Kane Kingsley.

Again.

"Now princess…"

I snap my eyes back to Silas as he advances toward me. But with each step, I take one in retreat, looking around my living room for something, *anything* I can use to protect myself.

As I back against a bookshelf, my eyes settle on the lamp placed on a nearby side table. Out of options, I lunge for it, figuring it's better than the weapon I don't have.

Before I can attempt to hit Silas over the head with it, Kane reaches out, stopping my arm in mid motion, his strength easily overpowering my own. When he squeezes, his grip so tight I'm positive he's on the brink of snapping my bone in half, I drop the lamp. It crashes to the floor, glass shattering around us.

"I believe you have something that doesn't belong to you," Silas finishes, malevolent eyes searing into me, sending a chill down my spine.

But I refuse to show fear, even though I'm bloody petrified right now. I need to keep my head on straight. It's the only way I stand a chance of making it out of this.

Lifting my chin in defiance, I yank my arm from Kingsley's grasp, placing my hands on my hips. "Technically, nothing in my apartment belongs to me. It all belongs to the monarchy. *I* don't even belong to myself."

Silas narrows his gaze on me. "Don't play games. You know what I'm talking about, princess. Now hand it over."

"Hand what over?"

"Jameson Gates paid you a visit earlier today and gave you something. I'm going to need it back. So you can either be a good little girl and give it to me now, or you can do things the hard way. Either way, it won't end well for you. It just depends on how much you want to suffer. How much you want your friends and family to suffer, too."

I look between Silas and Kane, knowing full well what they're capable of. At least Kane.

But I also know what's on that flash drive. Know these two bastards have killed countless people to keep the truth hidden. I refuse to do anything that will help them continue to escape responsibility.

"Over my dead body."

Silas smirks. "That can be arranged."

His words barely register before the cold metal of a gun connects with my temple in a sickening thud that sends me spiraling into darkness.

CHAPTER THIRTY-FOUR

Creed

I take a long pull from my bottle of beer, the icy liquid refreshing. Wiping my sweat-stained brow, I glance around my new townhouse, the box-filled rooms slowly taking shape into furniture-adorned spaces.

But even after spending all day unpacking dozens of boxes and putting furniture together, it hasn't quite distracted me from what's weighing heavy on my mind.

What's *been* weighing on my mind for over a week now… Esme.

The way she begged me to kiss her. Love her.

Choose her.

It should have been so easy for me to give her what she needed and kissed her. Years ago, I would have.

Hell, just a few weeks ago, I probably would have, too.

But after my father opened my eyes to the reality that my decision didn't only affect me, but also all the people close to me, I'm no longer sure about my path.

If I ever was to begin with.

I glance at the clock on the stove, debating stopping here and watching the football match while I wait for my food delivery to arrive.

But I'm so close to having my kitchen unpacked. While I may not be the best cook in the world, I'm looking forward to not ordering take out for every meal.

I take another drink of my beer, savoring in the cold liquid, then use my knife to cut through the tape on yet another box, this one containing more pots and pans I'd forgotten about. I consider rearranging the cupboards to make room for them when a knock reverberates through the quiet space.

"You can just leave it," I call out, assuming it's my food delivery.

"Open up, Creed. Right now."

The hairs on the back of my neck bristle, my body freezing at the sound of my father's urgent tone.

I leave my beer on the counter and go to the front door, drawing in a deep breath to calm my nerves over the prospect of dealing with my father. No doubt he's here to talk to me about what happened at Anderson's party last weekend. Truthfully, I'm surprised it took this long for the rumors to reach him. I may not have kissed Esme, but plenty of people saw us talking. In his mind, that's probably just as bad as if I had kissed her.

I pull back the door, but barely have it cracked more than a few inches before my father pushes his way inside, throwing a paranoid glance up and down the street before locking us inside.

"Get your shoes on. We need to go."

My brows knit together. "And where are we going?"

"We don't have time for this, Creed. Put your goddamn shoes on. We'll leave through the back. My car's in the alley."

An unsettled feeling settles in my gut that something's wrong. And that feeling increases when sirens wail in the distance, my father's eyes widening in panic.

"*Now, Creed!*"

I don't question him. Instead, I do as he asked, hurriedly grabbing a pair of shoes I'd left in the foyer. Heart hammering, I rush through the house and down into the basement, throwing the back door open to see my father's SUV idling in the alley, as promised. Just before I step outside, I double back toward my tool cabinet and open the bottom drawer, retrieving the gun and holster I stashed there. Then I slip into the alley behind my father.

"Probably a good idea," he says as I attach the holster to my belt, confirming my suspicion that something is drastically wrong.

I start toward the front passenger seat, but he stops me with a hand on my forearm, shaking his head.

"In the back. And stay low. There's a blanket on the floorboard. Use that to cover yourself."

I hesitate, about to press for information yet again.

But as the sirens get louder, I sense whatever's going on isn't good. And those sirens are coming for me.

Not wasting a second, I duck into the back seat. I barely have the blanket on me before my father pulls down the alley, maintaining a moderate speed so as not to draw attention to himself.

Neither one of us says a single thing for several long minutes as I attempt to get my breathing and heart rate under control, my mind spinning. When I'm confident we're several kilometers away from my townhouse, the sirens no longer audible, I lift back the blanket slightly.

"Now do you want to tell me what's going on?"

"Fuck if I know."

"Okay…" I draw out, more confused and uneasy by the second.

"All I know is those sirens you heard are members of the royal police heading to your townhouse to execute an arrest warrant."

"Arrest warrant?" I shoot up, meeting his eyes through the rearview mirror. The warning within has me lying back on the floor, covering myself with the blanket once more. "For what?"

"Murder."

"Murder? Who's dead?" I swallow hard, unsure I want to hear the answer, panic squeezing my heart.

"Jameson Gates was found dead from a gunshot wound to his chest earlier this evening."

I push out a long breath, momentarily relieved. For a second, I feared he'd tell me it was Esme. That Kane Kingsley got to her despite all the steps I took to keep the truth from her.

But that relief is short-lived, considering someone still lost his life.

And I'm being blamed for it.

"You don't seriously think I'm responsible, do you?"

"If I did, do you think I'd be risking arrest myself by hiding you?" he retorts.

"Probably not."

"*Definitely* not." He pushes out a breath. I can picture the frustration in the lines of his face. "But someone on Gates' household staff claims a man matching your description forced his way into the house. Stated she heard shouting, that you two got into a heated argument about Esme. That you threatened him to stay away from her. That Jameson told you he and Esme were in love and would be getting married, at which point you shot him."

"That's a bunch of bull!"

"I know that, son. Unfortunately, this witness statement was enough for a judge to sign off on an arrest warrant. Especially when other witnesses claimed to see you and Esme involved in a pretty heated conversation last weekend at the Crown Prince's estate."

"But it wasn't about Jameson Gates. She barely even speaks to him! It was about…" I trail off, mind racing. Then I sit up, not giving a fuck who might see me. "Has anyone checked on her?"

"She requested additional security over the next few days, which also led many to believe she considered you a threat to her and Jameson Gates' safety. The last check-in was thirty minutes ago and was all clear."

"But has anyone actually spoken to her?" I demand.

"Why do you ask? What do you know?"

"Maybe nothing." I run a hand over my face. "The heated discussion people saw between Esme and me was about a man named Kane Kingsley." I pause. "The man with the scar."

"Creed," my father warns.

"He's real. I know you told me to drop it, but Esme sketched his face. I asked Lucas to help see if he could put a name to the face and he did. Kane Kingsley. He's—"

"I know who Kane Kingsley is," he interrupts, his voice grave. "He's bad news."

"Which is why I kept his identity a secret from Esme. But she found out. That's what we fought about." I swallow hard. "Because I kept the truth from her to keep her safe. Because I chose my job over her."

Something resembling sympathy flashes in his eyes before he returns his gaze to mine.

"What happened next?"

"She went back to the party, but I observed her talking to Jameson Gates for quite a while. What if…" I silently curse under my breath. "She told him. I know she did."

"How do you know?"

"She told me Jameson paid her a visit the day after she saw the man with a scar at the opera. He told her he believed her. That he knew the man was real. That Callie mentioned seeing him a few days before she died, which they framed on someone else. And now Jameson's dead and someone's trying to frame *me* for it, to the extent of bribing a witness to lie."

"You don't know that for sure," my father attempts to argue.

"You're right. I don't. But I don't think it's a coincidence that Gates is now dead. And if he's dead, there's a damn good chance Esme's…"

My father slams on his brakes before I can finish my thought. I brace myself against the front seat, holding on tightly as he yanks the SUV in the opposite direction, returning to the city.

"Thanks for believing me."

"I may not always agree with your actions," he begins, his eyes finding mine in the mirror once more. "But you're not a killer. And I'll be damned if I'm going to let anyone think you are."

"Even though by helping me you could be considered an accomplice?"

"Some things are more important. I should have realized that when we lost Adam." His voice wavers with emotion, regret filling the lines of his face. "I've been a shite father.

I'm sorry it took my son being accused of a crime he didn't commit to open my eyes. I promise to do better. Be less of a stubborn are."

I give his bicep a final squeeze. "Me, too."

CHAPTER THIRTY-FIVE

Esme

Pain rips through my skull like a raging river, each pulse sending me crashing against the rocks. I try to move my arms, only to be met with resistance.

With a gasp, I open my eyes to see the familiar surroundings of my bedroom as I lie on the floor. I wrack my brain, trying to put together the pieces of how I got here.

Maybe I'm asleep. Maybe this is yet another iteration of the same dream that's been plaguing me for months now.

"It's okay," I assure myself, like Creed told me to do whenever having a night terror. "It's just a dream, Esme. You'll wake up soon, and it will all be over. You're fine. You're safe. You're—"

A cackling laugh cuts through, startling me. A chill races up my spine as a voice taunts, "Don't you realize? You're already awake?"

I push myself to my knees, the position awkward, but it allows me to see a figure moving in the shadows. The ball of dread in my stomach grows heavier with each thundering footstep until he emerges into the light.

Silas Archer.

His dark eyes narrow on me with a predatory gaze, his lips curling into a menacing smile. In a heartbeat, the events of the past twenty-four hours come rushing back, starting with Jameson Gates paying me a visit and ending with Silas and Kane breaking into my apartment.

"My father trusted you," I sneer, my voice filled with rage. "And this is how you repay him?"

"My loyalties have always been to your grandfather, first and foremost. Regardless that he's been dead for nearly thirty years." He slowly makes his way across the room, remaining the picture of precision, his suit perfectly tailored to his long and lean frame. Grabbing the chair beside my desk, he pulls it toward me and sits down.

"So much so that you did his dirty work for him? Had his son and grandchildren killed?" My throat tightens, nausea swirling in my stomach. I swallow down the bile rising up. "Do you have no compassion? It was bad enough you had my aunt and uncle murdered. But their children, too?" My voice trembles as tears threaten to fall. "How could you?"

"I swore to protect the monarchy at all costs. And that's what I've spent my life doing. Protecting the monarchy. No matter the cost," he spits out with venom, his eyes burning with determination.

"How can you claim to protect the monarchy when, had you not killed him, my uncle would have *been* the monarch? How can you—"

"Because he was about to destroy everything!" His face contorts with exasperation as he jumps to his feet, a wildness about him. "She got into his head, made him forget his duty. His obligation. Where his loyalty should be."

"Who did?"

"Who do you think? Evelyn."

I furrow my brow, confusion deepening with every second. "My…aunt?"

"She convinced him to walk away from his duty. His birthright."

"She did?" I'd never heard about any of this.

Then again, I have a pretty good feeling *why* I'd never heard about any of this. Silas made sure of it. Or, more appropriately, my grandfather did.

"Do you know how bad that would have looked for the monarchy? King Theodore couldn't have that. But he couldn't risk the truth getting out, either. That's precisely what that little bitch convinced Nicholas to do. Tell the world the truth."

"And what truth is that?"

Silas hesitates, obviously unsure how much to disclose. I shouldn't want him to tell me. If he does, that most likely means he's planning to kill me. But I need to know I'm risking my life for a reason.

"Your grandfather did what he had to do," Silas finally says, which only increases my confusion.

"Forgive me if I don't agree with that statement, not when he had you kill his son and grandchildren."

"He didn't ask me to kill his grandchildren."

"So that's supposed to make it better?" I shoot him a derisive look. "Because they were simply unintended casualties?"

"They weren't his grandchildren."

"I don't see…" I trail off, his statement not immediately sinking in. When it does, my mouth falls open, my eyes widening. "They weren't?"

Did my aunt have an affair that resulted in my cousins?

Could this be the secret my grandfather didn't want to get out? But if that's the case, why would my uncle walk away from the royal family after learning his wife had an affair? It doesn't make sense.

"They were his children," Silas states.

"His…children?" I squeak out, a heaviness settling over me.

"Nicholas and Evelyn were married for quite a few years without conceiving a child. People were starting to talk. Wondered if they were able to have children and what that might mean for the monarchy. We knew Evelyn was fertile. She'd been examined before King Theodore approved of their marriage."

I push down the bitter taste in my mouth at the reminder of how fucked up this world is. Most parents want to make sure their children marry someone they love. Someone they hope to grow old with. Not us. The only requirement is that our chosen spouse can provide an heir.

"But Uncle Nicholas wasn't fertile," I say, filling in the blanks.

"This was before IVF, so that wasn't an option. Because of that, King Theodore needed to take matters into his own hands. He needed to ensure the bloodline continued."

"And Aunt Evelyn was okay with this?" I ask incredulously.

"She was reminded of her duty to the crown." Silas lifts his chin.

"So he raped her," I snip out.

"No. She had a choice."

"I highly doubt she thought she did." I bark out a disbelieving laugh. "Did Uncle Nicholas know what his father did?"

It's one thing to learn this about my grandfather. He was

never a warm person. But Uncle Nicholas was always kind. Always smiling. Always loving. I don't want to think he was a willing participant in this.

"Not until Evelyn went back on her word and told him the truth."

"I imagine that didn't go over very well."

"Of course not! And because she couldn't keep her mouth shut, Nicholas threatened to go public unless King Theodore agreed to remove him and his children from the line of succession. But Theodore knew something like that would raise eyebrows as to why the heir apparent was so eager to relinquish not only his birthright but also that of his children. Or who everyone *believed* to be his children."

"Maybe he should have thought of that before he raped my aunt just to produce a few heirs."

"He did what was necessary to—"

"I don't want to hear you say it was necessary to kill six people in order to protect the monarchy. He was so worried about the truth of his actions getting out? Did he not think what would happen when people found out they were murdered?"

"I assured him that would never happen. And it's a promise I plan to keep."

"How? By silencing everyone who could potentially expose the truth?"

"This would have ended years ago if Jameson had just handed over the recording when he found it. If you're so worried about more people losing their lives, I suggest telling me where it is."

I hold my head high. "I don't know what you're talking about."

Without hesitation, he lifts his hand, delivering a harsh

slap to my face. I somehow manage not to lose my balance, remaining sunken on my knees as I blink through my tears.

"I warned you. We can do this the easy way or the hard way. I'm happy to trade places with Kingsley. His methods are somewhat…unusual. By the end, you'll be begging him to put an end to your suffering. So if I were you, I'd give me what I want. Save yourself the hassle…" His mouth twists into an evil smirk. "And the torture, really."

"You want to know where it is? Well, I'll give you a little clue." I glower at him, my expression a mask of steel, my heart pounding. "You can tear apart this entire place, and you'll never find it. You're going to kill me anyway? Go ahead and do it. But believe me when I say you won't get away with it. Not this time. If a princess ends up dead, someone is bound to ask questions."

"Do you honestly think I haven't already thought of that?"

He returns to the chair, his face mere inches from mine, but I refuse to flinch. Refuse to show any fear.

"It's all quite perfect, really. Several guests mentioned seeing you and Captain Lawson get into a somewhat… heated argument last weekend. Couple that with the fact that Jameson Gates was just found murdered and an eyewitness observed a man matching Lawson's description breaking into the house, and overheard a loud altercation inside, it was enough to convince a judge to sign an arrest warrant."

"No." My breathing comes in shallow gasps, the room spinning around me. Not just because he's trying to frame Creed. But because Jameson's dead.

"Oh, yes." He flashes a smile, then frowns. "And when they find your body, it won't be too much of a stretch to tie him to your murder, as well. After all, he does have a history of sneaking into your apartment undetected. Does he not?"

"You…" My voice catches. "You won't get away with this," I say once more, but this time my words lack any sort of conviction.

"Oh, but I already have." He smirks, then leans toward me, barely a whisper separating us. "Now tell me where it is. And maybe I'll put in a good word for Captain Lawson. Provide an alibi for him, since he doesn't exactly have one."

I blink, a part of me considering his offer, if for no other reason than to protect Creed. Save him from all of this.

But I know Creed. He'd be pissed if I traded his freedom for the truth.

So instead, I glower at Silas. "Go ahead and kill me, because I'm never telling."

With a deep sigh, he pulls himself to his full height once more and retreats from me. My palms sweat as I watch his every move, unsure what he's going to do next.

Truthfully, I don't really want to know.

"I was afraid you'd be difficult."

He pulls a knife from the inside pocket of his suit jacket. Lifting it in front of his face, he inspects it with a smile that causes my muscles to tighten. Then he closes the distance between us, my resolve withering away to nothing when he presses it against my throat.

"Trust me, princess."

I tense, doing everything to prevent my body from trembling, not wanting to show him even an ounce of fear.

"We have ways of getting the information we need." He drags the knife from my throat and toward my blouse, slicing off each button. "Do I need to have Kane come in here? Give you a bit of…" He licks his lips, eyes skating down my body, focusing on my chest. "Encouragement?"

"Why? Can't get it up yourself so you need him to do

your dirty work for you? Is that the only way you can get your kicks now? By watching someone else get off?"

I'm breaking every rule I've ever learned about what to do when held hostage. I was trained to be agreeable. Not do anything to make them angry.

But all my training has involved being abducted by someone for ransom, usually by a terrorist group wanting to make a name for themselves.

We never covered being abducted by a high-power player in our own government hoping to cover up criminal acts by a former monarch. I could be wrong, but I'm pretty sure the rules are vastly different.

"You think you're so smart? I guess I'll just have to prove that I have absolutely no problem getting it up."

Panic races through me as he steps directly in front of my face and starts to unbuckle his pants.

Then a gunshot pierces through the rustling of his zipper, his hand frozen mid-way down as my heart skyrockets into my throat.

Silas' eyes fly to the closed door, holding his breath as he listens intently for further movement. But there's nothing for several long moments. That doesn't put him at ease, though. Especially since this gunshot wasn't from a silencer.

Quickly zipping his pants back up, he tightly wraps his fingers around my bicep and yanks me to my feet.

"Let's go." He brings the knife to my throat with one hand and roughly forces me to walk.

I have no idea what's going on, if that gunshot was from someone here to help or Kane killing yet another innocent person.

All I can do is pray it's not Creed. That he was smart enough to stay away once he learned he was being framed for murder. He wouldn't come here, would he? Not after our argument.

But I know better than that.

After all, he kept me in the dark about Kane Kingsley because of the oath he made to protect the royal family above all else.

No doubt, that oath is exactly what will bring him here, despite the risk.

When another shot thunders through the air followed by an ear-piercing wail, I stiffen, my heart pounding in my chest. Silas is momentarily caught off-guard, too, his grip on my arm loosening. But he recovers before I can attempt to free myself.

"Move," he hisses into my ear, pushing me along the corridor, not allowing me to stop even when another shot rings out.

And another.

And another.

Reaching my office, Silas kicks the door open, using me as a human shield. A familiar figure whirls around at the sound, gun raised, ready to fire.

Until his gaze lands on me.

And the knife held to my throat.

"If I were you, I'd drop your weapon," Silas sneers, digging the blade even harder into my flesh. "Unless you want the princess' next breath to be her last."

CHAPTER THIRTY-SIX

Creed

"Stay down," my father orders softly as he slows the car to a stop, the sounds of the city filtering into the SUV when he lowers the window.

I hear a subtle beep, indicating he's most likely at the staff entrance to the Gladwell Palace complex. After a few seconds, he urges the car forward at a slow speed before putting it in park a minute later.

"Anything look out of place?" I ask, desperate to see something, *anything* that tells me Esme's okay.

"Not…really." My father's voice certainly doesn't instill any confidence in me, and I try to sit up, but he pushes me back down to the floorboard.

"But—"

"You need to stay hidden," he says, his words clipped and urgent.

"What do you see?"

"Nothing. I just… It could be nothing, but I have a feeling in my gut that something's off. I'll go check it out."

"I'm coming with you." I start to rip the blanket off me again.

And yet again, he pushes me back to the floor.

"There are cameras everywhere. You'd better believe they're watching every single one of them for any trace of you."

"I know how to avoid them. How do you think I've snuck into her apartment all the times I have?"

"Of course." I can hear the exasperation in his tone. But there's also a hint of humor. "All the same, it's too big of a risk right now. You need to stay hidden until we can figure out why someone's trying to frame you. Understood?"

I want to protest. Tell him Kane Kingsley is most likely trying to frame me because I found out he killed Adam. Which is why my father shouldn't go into Esme's apartment without backup.

"If I don't make contact in three minutes, you can come in," he offers after a few moments, sensing my hesitation.

I part my lips once more, on the verge of insisting I go with him. But my father's just as stubborn as me. Probably more so. I'm wasting time by arguing with him.

"Fine," I agree reluctantly, still not liking anything about this.

"Good." He opens the door, his feet crunching on the gravel as he steps out. The last thing I hear are his retreating footfalls before silence surrounds me.

I strain to listen for any indication that everything inside is okay and I was worried unnecessarily. I'd feel better if I could at least see something. But I promised I wouldn't take any unnecessary risks. Removing this blanket while sitting in a compound swarming with security would most certainly do just that. So I stay hidden.

Until the unmistakable sound of a gunshot reverberates in the night air.

Panic races through me, urging me into action. I rip off the blanket and leap out of the car in less than a second, my gun drawn. I barge inside Esme's apartment, quickly scanning the room for any threats. When my eyes land on Archie's body in the corner, the life long gone from his eyes, my heart drops to the pit of my stomach, throat tightening.

I look up at the ceiling and say a silent prayer that he didn't suffer, then continue on light feet, stopping in my tracks when I hear a low groan from a few feet away. I tighten my grip on my gun, gaze constantly sweeping through the dimly lit room as I cautiously move closer, unsure if it's friend or foe.

As a low light reveals a pair of shoes peeking out from behind the couch, I struggle to push down the knot of emotion that bubbles up inside of me. I know those shoes. They're the same ones my father likes to wear when on duty.

I hurry toward him, bile rising in my throat at all the blood drenching his shirt. For a split second, guilt freezes me in place, a voice in my head telling me I caused my brother's death. And now, I could very well be responsible for my father's, too.

But I refuse to think about that. Instead, my training kicks in, and I focus on what's most important.

And right now, that's helping my dad.

"Was it Kingsley?" I ask as I kneel beside him, careful to avoid the blood staining the carpet. When I rip his shirt open to see what I'm dealing with, I try to find some solace in the fact that he was hit closer to his shoulder.

But that still doesn't mean he'll survive. He needs help, and fast.

"Yes, but don't worry about me." He swats me away, stubborn as always. "Find her. I'll call this in. Let them know we have a potential hostage situation." He manages to prop himself up against the back of the couch, wincing from the pain. When I don't immediately move, he pins me with a glare, pulling his phone from his pocket. "Go," he orders. "I'm not your priority. She is."

I hate leaving him when it's obvious he's in bad shape. But he's right. From the beginning of my career in the royal guard, I was trained that when it's between saving a team member or guaranteeing a royal's safety, we have no choice but to choose the latter.

Even if that means choosing the royal family over your own father.

Which is exactly what I have to do.

Swallowing down the ache in my chest, I pull myself to my full height and move toward the corridor, remaining alert for any sound.

"Creed?" my father whispers just before I disappear.

I glance back at him.

"You were never a disappointment." A peaceful smile crosses his expression. "I'm sorry I made you think you were."

"I'm sorry, too." I hold his gaze for a protracted beat, then force myself to look away, tiptoeing down the corridor toward the sound of drawers opening and papers rustling.

As I grow closer to Esme's office, the double doors cracked open a few inches, I'm mindful of my surroundings, remaining as silent as possible. When I reach the end of the hallway, I flatten myself against the wall and peek through the crack, relieved when I don't find any sign of Esme.

Especially since Kane Kingsley is inside.

But if she's not here, where is she? Did she escape?

I should leave, continue my search. But I struggle to walk away when I have a clear shot of the man who killed my brother.

And countless other people.

If I don't take this shot now, I risk him getting away, evading capture for another ten years.

Killing more people.

Eventually killing Esme.

That's all it takes for me to justify my decision.

Slowly lifting my weapon, I carefully push the door open a little more to get a better view of him as he ransacks Esme's bookshelf, flipping through each book before tossing it, as if searching for something.

But as I do so, the hinges on the door creak.

He whirls around, grabbing his weapon off the shelf and pointing it in my direction in one swift move.

I don't hesitate to fire, my shot hitting him in the hand. The gun clatters to the floor, along with chunks of flesh and bone. Groaning, he clutches the remains of his hand, squeezing it in an effort to staunch the bleeding.

"It'll be kind of hard to be a hired gun when you no longer have a hand," I muse, a sense of vindication filling me as I watch him scrunch his face up in pain.

"I can still fight," Kane roars, charging toward me. But he only manages a few steps before I pull the trigger again. This time, I hit him in the knee, sending him tumbling to the floor, blood soaking the area rug.

I cluck my tongue mockingly. "For someone who's supposed to be a good shot and have all this incredible talent, you're not very good," I remark sarcastically.

Part of me feels guilty for taking pleasure in his suffering.

The other part knows how much he deserves it.

Hell, he deserves worse than I could ever do to him in good conscience.

"I was good enough to kill your brother," he strains to say. "I didn't even have to shoot him. Just had to run him off the road." He flicks out his tongue, his dark eyes shining with a crazed glint. "I hear he was burned to a crisp when they put out the flames. I would have loved to see that. But I get queasy from the smell of burning flesh."

Blood boils in my veins, and it takes everything I have not to end him for once and for all. But I want this man to suffer a little longer for everything he did to my brother. To Esme. To all the people he's harmed during his pathetic life.

So instead of aiming at his chest, I point my gun at his groin, finding delight in the terror flashing across his features. He attempts to roll away from me, but I press my foot against his shattered knee, preventing him from escaping his fate.

An agonizing howl echoes in the room, jarring the crystal chandelier above.

But that's nothing compared to the scream that rips from him when I shoot him in the crotch.

"Whoops. Sorry. I was aiming for your hip."

With a sadistic grin, I shift my gun a little to the left, shooting him in the hip, as well.

"Please...," he begs, face contorted. "Please stop."

"Now you want compassion when you've never offered anyone else the same luxury?"

"I'm not the one to blame here. I was just following orders." His Adam's apple bobs up and down. "I didn't have a choice."

"That's where you're wrong. There's always a choice. Like right now, I choose to show you compassion."

His expression lights up with hope. "You do?"

"This is me showing you compassion." I stand back, pointing my gun at his forehead. "This is for my brother, you fucking bastard."

I squeeze the trigger once more, my bullet hitting him square between his eyes. Blood pools behind his head, all the life draining from his face.

I push out a slow, shaky breath, taking a moment to collect myself. Then I turn around, about to continue my search when the door opens fully, Esme standing in front of me.

But she's not alone.

Silas Archer stands behind her.

And he's holding a knife to her throat.

CHAPTER THIRTY-SEVEN

Creed

"If I were you, I'd drop your weapon. Unless you want the princess' next breath to be her last."

I don't immediately comply, still too stunned by this turn of events. I didn't know who I expected to be behind all of this, but it wasn't Silas Archer. Seeing him here only increases my confusion. Makes me wonder what the hell is going on. Sure, his name briefly came up in my brother's investigation into Callie Sloane's disappearance after Jameson Gates suggested he may be involved, since he viewed Jameson's relationship with Callie as a threat to a potential marriage between Esme and Jameson.

But I tossed out that theory once I learned about the recording Jack Sloane found.

The recording he wanted to discuss with Gianna Vale.

"Now, Captain!" Silas barks, his gruff tone snapping me out of my thoughts. He tightens his grip on the knife, a few droplets of blood seeping down Esme's throat.

I hesitate for another moment as I search for a clear shot. But Silas knows exactly what he's doing. Knows I won't do anything that could bring any harm to Esme.

"Okay." I hold up my hands in surrender, slowly bending down to place the gun onto the floor.

"Kick it over."

I do as he requests, sending the gun skittering several feet away from him. If I can't use it, neither of us can.

"Any other accessories I should know about? I'd get rid of them now because if I find them later, it won't end well for your little princess here."

I lift my shirt so he can see I'm not hiding any other weapons anywhere on my body.

"Good."

He relaxes his grip on Esme, but still keeps the knife against her throat. Then he reaches into his back pocket and tosses a thick, black zip tie onto the floor in front of me.

"Put that on your wrists and kneel on the floor."

I grab it, eyes not leaving Esme's as I secure the plastic restraint to my wrists, using my teeth to tighten it.

Once I'm kneeling, he pushes Esme to her knees, as well. As much as I hate how roughly he's handling her, at least he no longer has a knife to her throat.

And I'll do everything in my power to keep it that way.

"This is about the video, isn't it?" I ask. "The one that Warren Clark shot? That Jack Sloane discovered?"

Silas steps away from Esme, shoving his knife into the inside pocket of his suit jacket as he moves toward me, slowly clapping.

"Bravo, Captain. You figured it out. It just took you ten years longer than your brother. But we all can't be the favorite. Can we?"

"What's on that video? What are you willing to kill people over?" I sneer, stomach churning.

"I was simply doing my job and protecting the monarchy."

"My uncle didn't die in an avalanche," Esme interjects frantically. "He was murdered. They all were. And that video proves it." She glances at Kane's body. "Proves he did it, along with Henry Gates. And Silas paid them to do it." She shoots daggers at him. "When he learned Warren Clark caught it all on video and that his son found it, he had Jack killed, but not before learning he'd made a copy."

"So that's what this is all about? Proof that you conspired to assassinate an entire branch of the royal family?"

"That's not even the worse part," Esme continues. "He did so under a direct order from my grandfather."

I blink repeatedly, her words like a punch to the gut. "Your...grandfather?"

"I'm sure you can see why I can't allow something like that to get out," Silas interrupts with a smirk. "So…" He stalks toward Esme. "Where is it?"

"Like I've already said," she retorts, discreetly scooting back against the wall. A hint of pride fills me when I notice her rub her restraint against the hard corner of the door-jamb, taking care not to draw too much attention to what she's doing. "I have absolutely no intention of telling you. And without me, you'll never find it."

"That *is* what you said." He strolls away from her, stopping in front of Kane's gun and picking it up, despite the blood on the handle. "But perhaps you haven't been sufficiently motivated."

He rushes toward me, pressing the barrel of the gun against my temple.

Adrenaline skyrockets through me, my heart pounding

a thunderous rhythm. It doesn't matter how many dangerous situations you've been in. Having a gun pressed against your head will always send fear spiraling through you.

"What's it going to be, princess? You give me what I need and you don't have to watch me blow a hole through your boyfriend's head."

Her eyes wide with terror, she parts her lips, uncertainty flickering in her expression.

"Don't do it, Esme," I implore, wordlessly encouraging her to keep trying to weaken her restraints enough to break free. "As long as you keep it to yourself, you're valuable to him."

"But—"

"No buts. No matter what he tries, don't give up the location. Promise me that."

"No, Creed." She shakes her head, tears pooling in her eyes before spilling down her cheeks. "I can't. I—"

"It's okay," I assure her, narrowing my gaze on her. Praying the connection between us is as strong as it's always been, and she can figure out what I'm trying to tell her.

For months, we spent nearly every morning together, running through dozens of different scenarios she might face if ever taken hostage.

While we've never trained this precise scenario, I'm confident she knows enough to figure out the best way to free herself.

"You tell him, and we're both dead." I swallow hard, working at the restraints around my wrists as discreetly as possible. "This way, only one of us has to die. Plus, I should have died dozens of times by now." I laugh through the lump building in my throat. "The way I see it, I've just been on borrowed time."

"Last chance, princess," Silas taunts, pressing the gun harder against my temple.

Regardless, I remain as calm as possible, keeping my eyes focused on Esme, praying to every higher power in existence that she knows what I need her to do.

"Five," he counts, focusing his full attention on me, since he obviously considers me the biggest threat.

But I've learned you should never underestimate Esme.

As he counts, I notice her working harder at her bindings, the grimace of determination on her face growing with every second. When he reaches the number two, the zip tie snaps, her wrists coming free.

But even though I trained her to use the opportunity to make her escape, she doesn't. I watch in horror as she jumps to her feet and advances toward Silas. Upon hearing the movement, he spins in her direction. The gun that was pointed at me is now aimed at her, his finger hovering on the trigger.

I launch myself off the ground, heart pounding wildly in my chest. With every ounce of strength I possess, I hurl myself at Silas. Despite having my wrists bound, I manage to knock the weapon from his grip with a resounding thud. I raise my arms over my head, about to bring them down to my sides in a decisive motion to break free from my restraints.

But before I can, a searing pain lodges in my stomach. It's sharp and biting, like nothing I've ever experienced before

Esme's screams fill the room, but all I can focus on is the knife protruding from my abdomen.

My vision blurs as I stumble backward and onto the floor, feeling lightheaded, the world spinning around me like a vicious carnival ride. Esme's too in shock by the sight of me that she freezes. Her momentary pause is all the time Silas needs to retrieve his gun. I expect him to aim it at me, but instead, he points it at Esme.

"Watch out!" I shout, the effort causing sharp pains to overwhelm me.

She spins toward him, and a gunshot rips through the space a moment later, the sound reverberating against the walls.

"*No!*" I bellow, panic racing through me. Time seems to stand still, the seconds stretching, neither Silas nor Esme immediately moving.

Then Silas teeters backwards, a crimson pattern blooming on his shirt.

I blink, disoriented, convinced my eyes are playing tricks on me. That I'm hallucinating from the loss of blood.

But as Silas collapses, my father appears in the doorway, leaning against the doorjamb for support.

"Dad?"

"I've always hated that arse."

I chuckle, then wince through the pain. My dad fixes his expression on me, hitching a breath when he sees the knife. Esme rushes toward me, my father close behind.

"Creed," she whimpers, her face twisted in fear. She hovers her hands over my body, obviously too scared to touch me. "Oh god. I'm so sorry."

"Don't be," I manage to say. "You did good. All those extra self-defense classes paid off."

"I choked again. I—"

"It's okay." I lean further against the back of the reading chair where I once went down on Esme. "I'll be okay."

I close my eyes, feeling almost weightless. I wonder if this is what it feels like to die. Wonder if, in the seconds before, all your troubles suddenly disappear, allowing you to go in peace.

"Hang on, son," my dad croaks out as the sirens draw near. "Help's almost here. Just hang on."

"I fulfilled my oath," I whisper, the strength draining from my body. "I protected her at all costs."

He chokes out a sob. "Yes, you did."

I flutter my eyes open, giving my dad a smile before shifting to meet Esme's tear-stained gaze. My mind races with everything I want to say to her. But I fear I'm out of time. So I stick with what's most important.

"I love you."

She vehemently shakes her head, gripping my hand with both of hers. "Don't you dare die on me, Creed Lawson. You're not allowed to die."

Using my last bit of strength, I raise my arm to cup her cheek. "Today." I drop my hand, no longer able to keep my eyes open. "Tomorrow."

"Always," Esme finishes as the darkness takes over, her lips on mine the last thing I remember.

CHAPTER THIRTY-EIGHT

Esme

I pace the length of the waiting room in the private wing of the hospital, my flats pounding a staccato beat on the polished floor. My hands feel like ice with the uncertainty filling me, despite the sweater I'm wearing. The thick, musky smell of sanitizer hangs heavy in the air, mixed with the sweet aroma of flowers.

I've tried everything to keep my brain occupied. Sitting. Reading one of the countless magazines the hospital keeps here to distract worried friends and family members that their loved one could die. Hell, I even spent some time in the children's room coloring with Marius and Harriet, who rushed to be with me the second they heard the news.

But nothing has been able to distract me from the fact that Creed's currently on the operating table, his life hanging in the balance.

All because he tried to protect me.

Despite the fact that Creed was briefly wanted for

murder, the waiting room is now filled with dozens of guard members, including the General of the Royal Guard himself, all of them here to support Creed's mother in her time of need.

Based on the anxiety and fear covering her face, she can use all the support she can get.

We all could after everything we learned tonight. No doubt the palace PR team is working overtime handling this clusterfuck.

Which is why I shouldn't still be here. Should be with my father as he navigates this period of uncertainty.

As he mourns the loss of his brother all over again.

But I can't pull myself away. Not until I know Creed's going to be okay.

Thankfully, the bullet that hit his father missed his heart by several inches, and he was out of surgery fairly quickly. The same can't be said for Archie, or Lieutenant Marcus Williams, who was manning the front gate this evening when Kane paid him a visit.

As tragic as it is that two men lost their lives in the line of duty, all I can think about is Creed, who's been in the operating room for hours now.

I try not to overthink it. The doctors warned us he was in critical condition and surgery would take quite some time to make sure they didn't miss any damage.

But with every minute that passes, my mind races with all the possible outcomes, each one worse than the one before.

Needing a break from the crushing weight of losing Creed, I spin on my heels and head toward a set of double doors.

"Where are you going, ma'am?" General Hudson asks, stepping toward me, a silver brow raised in concern.

"To the ladies' room. I won't be long."

"Do you want me to come with you?" Harriet asks, standing from her chair.

I shake my head. "I'll be fine."

She gives me a small smile, then rejoins Marius, resting her head on his shoulder, closing her eyes once more as they try to get some sleep. It means so much that they're still here, even after I told them to go home. They said as long as I stayed, they would, too. That's the type of friends they are. Always supporting me in my moment of need, no matter what.

Wrapping my arms around myself, I slip out of the waiting room, thankful for the brief reprieve.

While there's nowhere else I want to be right now, I hate feeling like I'm under a microscope, everyone in that room analyzing everything I say or do.

I just want to be alone to process what happened tonight.

Or, more accurately, last night.

I'm about to turn down the corridor toward the ladies' room, but slow my steps when my eyes fall on the closed doors of the chapel. I've never been one to pray, even when forced to attend services with my family on all the important holidays.

But if there were ever a time to start, this is it.

I open the heavy doors, a thick silence hovering in the air. A few rows of cushioned pews fill the dimly lit space, a cross set against stained glass on the far wall. I start toward one of the pews, but pause when I notice a table with tiers of candles in red votives, some lit, most not.

I quietly pad toward it and grab a long match, lifting it to one of the flames. Then I light a candle for my uncle. For my aunt. For each of my cousins. For my mum. For Adam. For Callie. For Jack. For Lieutenant Williams.

And for Archie.

With each candle I light, the tears falling from my eyes grow heavier, the anger over how many lives have been lost increasing. My heart twists with hatred, muscles tightening with rage and frustration. I want to scream. Want to shout. Want to do something to correct these wrongs. But nothing will bring any of these people back.

And I hate it. Hate that so many people have died, all because of my grandfather.

"Oh, sweetie," a soft voice says in the seconds before a pair of arms wrap around me in a comforting embrace.

I don't resist them, allowing them to hold me and comfort me in a way no one has in years.

"He'll be okay."

I pull my head up, meeting Creed's mother's eyes, her own awash with fear, worry, and a myriad of other emotions. But through it all, there's hope. And it's that hope that causes my heart to shatter even more.

"How do you know?" I choke out through the boulder in my throat. "How do you know I won't be back here in a few hours, lighting another candle?" I gesture at all the flames I just lit, the sheer number sickening and tragic.

She runs her hands down my arms. "I don't know." Her voice trembles, tears filling her eyes. Regardless, her resolve remains strong. "Only He or She does." She glances at the cross.

"How do you do it?" I ask, the words leaving me before I can stop them. "How have you stayed so put-together, watched your husband and son continue to risk their lives every day, even after losing Adam?"

She squeezes my arms. "Because I believe in what they're doing."

I look toward the candles, every one representing someone who lost their lives because of the monarchy, apart from my mum. "I'm not sure I do." I shift my gaze back to hers. "Not anymore. I—"

The sound of the door opening cuts through, and we both look toward it as a man in scrubs steps inside, a face mask dangling from one ear and a cap covering most of his salt-and-pepper hair.

"My apologies, Your Highness." He bows toward me, then looks at Mrs. Lawson. "Ma'am. My name is Dr. O'Neal. I'm the lead surgeon who operated on your son. I was told I could find you here. If you'd like to step outside, I can give you an update."

Mrs. Lawson squeezes my hand, and we follow the doctor out of the chapel.

"How is he?" she asks immediately.

The doctor looks my way, obviously hesitant to say anything in front of me since I'm not technically family.

"It's okay," Mrs. Lawson assures him, voice trembling slightly. "Whatever you're about to tell me, I plan on sharing with Her Highness anyway, so you may as well save me the trouble."

"Certainly, ma'am."

My pulse speeds up, the seconds seeming to tick by in a slow march. Dr. O'Neal licks his lips, delaying his news even more. I study every inch of him, looking for a clue as to the outcome of Creed's surgery.

Praying it's not what I fear it is.

"As you know, your son suffered a severe stab wound to his abdomen. These types of injuries can pose serious risks and complications, particularly in that area of the body. There are lots of parts. A lot of vital organs. The difference between life or death can be a matter of mere millimeters."

"And Creed?" I ask, voice strained. "Is he—"

"Luckily, Captain Lawson was in top physical shape.

Because of his athletic physique, the knife needed to cut through more muscle in order to do serious damage to any of his organs than is the case for most people . So he'll be fine."

The instant those words leave his mouth, both me and Mrs. Lawson exhale a long breath, our bodies sagging with relief.

"Thank, God." Mrs. Lawson looks up to the ceiling. Her words aren't just a normal reaction to receiving good news. She's actually thanking God, whoever He or She may be. I lift my eyes skyward, as well, sending up my own silent prayer of gratitude.

"He's really okay?" I press, needing his confirmation.

Dr. O'Neal nods. "He's really okay."

Mrs. Lawson wraps her arm around me as if I were her own child.

"We'll be keeping him here for the time being to monitor him. Make sure there aren't any side effects from the surgery or the stab wound. It could take quite some time until he has his strength back, but since he's in good shape, I expect him to make a full recovery."

I close my eyes, exhaling another deep breath of relief.

"Thank you so much, doctor," Mrs. Lawson says.

"Not at all, ma'am." He smiles.

"Is he able to have any visitors?"

"He's still pretty drugged up, so he'll be in and out of consciousness, but you're welcome to sit with him. Even if he may not remember much when he does wake up."

Mrs. Lawson turns toward me. "Why don't you go sit with him, dear?"

"Are you sure? I don't—"

"He'd love to see you. I want to stop by his father's room

first and tell him. And call Rory, too. I'll just be a few minutes behind you."

"Thank you."

"Of course." She wraps me in another hug, lingering for several long moments.

When she releases me, I join Dr. O'Neal, following him through the quiet corridors, stopping outside a door in the recovery unit. "Go ahead. If you have any questions, you can ask someone at the nurse's station to page me."

"Thanks again, doctor."

He bows his head. "Your Highness."

I watch as he retreats, then face the door, steeling myself to see Creed. I have no idea what kind of shape he'll be in after enduring hours of surgery. But at least he's alive.

My hand on the knob, I turn and step into the sterile hospital room, my eyes falling on his slumbering form.

This man has always seemed unbreakable. Invincible. Indestructible.

Seeing him in a hospital bed with wires attached to him guts me.

Reminds me just how close to dying he was.

How close to losing him I was.

How close to losing him I still could be, especially after the way I behaved. How I selfishly demanded he put me first over the oath he took.

When it was that oath that ended up saving my life.

Drawing in a deep breath, I make my way toward him and sit in the chair beside his bed, the rising sun casting a subtle glow in the room. It's a reminder that it's always darkest before dawn. Now that the sun is rising, everything will be okay.

As I take Creed's hand in mine, savoring in the warmth of his flesh, I know it will be.

"Always," I murmur, brushing a soft kiss to his knuckles.

His eyelids flutter, as if he's trying to open them, his lips parting slightly.

"Always," he repeats in a barely audible voice before the drugs pull him back under.

CHAPTER THIRTY-NINE

Esme

The sidewalks leading up to the palace swarm with reporters and photographers as General Hudson navigates the SUV past the front gates. He typically doesn't take on guard duty himself, but after last night's events, he wanted to allow everyone who needed time off to take it, considering we lost two guard members, and two more are currently in the hospital, having survived life-threatening injuries.

Unfortunately, I'm not allowed the same luxury, as much as I'd love nothing more than to crawl into my bed and sleep for the next week.

But I don't exactly have a bed to go home to. I don't have a *home* to go to, considering it's now a crime scene. Even once the police have concluded collecting all the evidence, I doubt I'll want to go back to that place, not after everything I endured there.

For now, I plan to stay with Anderson, although last night I slept at the hospital, refusing to leave Creed's side until my brother had to physically pull me away in order to get ready for today's press conference.

"Your Highness," Oliver, the head butler, greets as he opens my door, offering his hand to help me down from the car. "Your brother and father are in his office if you'd like to join them." He leads me into the foyer, the scene reminiscent of the last time I was here for a huge press conference when my father officially announced Anderson's engagement to Nora.

This is a completely different type of press conference, though. One that could result in the monarchy becoming a thing of the past.

Maybe that's okay.

Maybe we've all been holding onto antiquated customs and traditions for far too long.

"Actually, I'd like to visit the memorial gardens first since the press conference isn't slated to start for an hour."

Oliver slows his steps, flashing me an understanding look. "Of course, ma'am." He bypasses the grand staircase, escorting me toward a pair of double doors leading to the famous Lamberside Palace gardens.

Normally, there would be heaps of tourists milling around, taking photos of all the flowers and fountains, particularly at this time of year.

But as a result of last night's events, the palace is currently closed to all tourists, allowing me a chance to enjoy the grounds in peace.

"I'll come get you when it's time," Oliver tells me as I'm about to step off the rear verandah.

"Thank you, Oliver."

He nods. "Ma'am."

I close my eyes and tilt my head back, savoring in the feel of the sunshine warming my face, birds chirping a happy melody nearby. Twelve hours ago, I didn't think I'd ever feel the sun on my skin again.

But I'm alive.

Thanks to Creed.

I meander through the grounds, enjoying the peace and quiet as I make my way toward the reflecting pool at the far end of the garden, a memorial to my uncle, aunt, and cousins. Considering the palace is closed, I don't expect to see anyone here.

But as I approach, I spy a familiar figure sitting on a bench. Her attention is focused on the peaceful ripples in the water as tears stream down her face, her typically hardened expression filled with emotion. She barely resembles the severe woman I've known all my life.

Yesterday, I'd questioned if my grandmother knew what my grandfather had done. While we may have never gotten along all that well, I seriously doubted she'd be okay with any of his actions, even if it was to protect the monarchy, as Silas claimed.

As I watch her today, it's more than apparent this news is as much of a shock to her as it was to me.

Probably more so.

On timid feet, I move toward the bench and sit beside her. I don't say anything. I doubt there's a single word in any language I can say that will make any of this hurt less. So instead, I grab her hand, a lame attempt at offering her comfort.

But when she squeezes, I know it was exactly what she needs, especially as she drops my hand, only to wrap her arm around me and pull me against her.

"I'm sorry," my grandmother manages to say, her normally firm voice wavering.

She doesn't embellish further.

But I don't need her to. Those two words are all I've needed to hear from her.

I meet her tear-filled eyes. "Me, too."

She sucks in her bottom lip, shifting her gaze forward to a fresh set of memorial wreaths on display on either side of the pond.

"It's like losing them all over again." She shakes her head, obviously still struggling with the truth.

I am, too.

"It was one thing to learn they'd died in a tragic skiing accident that I couldn't do anything to prevent. It's another to learn they died in such…" She trails off. "Those poor babies." Her voice catches before her expression hardens. "I wish that bastard were still alive so I could kill him myself."

"Who? Silas?"

"No. Well, yes. There are quite a few things I'd love to do to that sniveling worm."

A laugh escapes my throat at her rather astute assessment of Silas Archer.

"I'm talking about Theodore."

It doesn't escape my notice that she doesn't refer to him as King Theodore, or my grandfather. In her eyes, he most likely lost that privilege.

He has in mine.

"When I learned everything he did, I thought the same thing," I tell her. "But I'd like to think the karma gods paid him a visit and he's burning in hell right now."

"Where he's forced to spend eternity eating canned tuna fish and listening to bagpipes, the two things he probably hated the most."

I burst out laughing. "And wearing sneakers that are perpetually covered in mud," I add, remembering all the times he scolded me for having muddy shoes when I was a small child.

"And there are no razors to be had, so he's forced to grow a big, bushy beard."

I throw my head back, my laughter increasing, my grandmother joining in.

I don't think I've ever heard her laugh before. It's oddly reassuring.

"I truly am sorry, Esme," my grandmother says once her laughter dies down, remorse covering the lines of her face. "I thought…" She pauses, pinching her lips together. "I don't even know what I thought. I guess I wasn't raised *to* think. Just to do what I was told. I never considered questioning anything. But I'm glad you did. Glad your mother raised you to think for yourself. To make your own decisions. To stand up for yourself and what's right, even in the face of danger." She grabs my hand, her eyes filled with admiration and respect. "I'm incredibly proud of you."

"Thanks…Grandma."

For years, that term of affection felt foreign on my lips. I always referred to her as the Queen Mother or my grandmother. Never Grandma. But now, it feels right.

"And what of Captain Lawson?"

"What about Captain Lawson?" I ask warily.

She shrugs. "Don't you think it's time you made your own decision about him, too?"

On a long sigh, I look forward, worrying my bottom lip. "Truthfully, I'm not sure where we stand." I glance her way. "Things are…complicated."

"They're only complicated if you make them that way. He loves you."

It's not a question. More of a statement.

"And you love him."

Again, it's not a question, so I simply nod.

"Then the rest are just details you need to work out."

My jaw drops, wondering who this woman sitting beside me is and what she did with my grandmother. "I thought you said there's no place for love in a monarchy."

She smiles sheepishly. "That's what I thought. Or, more accurately, what I was *trained* to think. Probably to convince me to go along with a marriage I wanted nothing to do with. But just because someone says something doesn't make it true. Your brother and Nora made me see that." She leans toward me, lowering her voice. "As have you and Captain Lawson."

"But—"

"But nothing. If this entire experience has taught me anything, it's that holding onto these antiquated rules can cause more damage than good. Your uncle lost his life because of it. My son…"

She trails off, her chin quivering once more. Closing her eyes, she draws in a deep breath to compose herself. When she returns her gaze to mine, it's full of determination.

"Fuck the rules."

I gasp, hearing my grandmother swear leaving me momentarily speechless.

"Your Majesty…" I feign indignation, covering my chest with my hand. "That kind of language isn't very becoming of a lady of your station."

"You want to know what I think of my station?" she responds, a hint of mischief in her eyes.

"What's that?"

"That it's utter bullshite."

I burst out laughing once more, my heart fuller than it has been in a while. Fuller than I thought possible after last night.

"Pardon the interruption."

We both dart our eyes behind us, Oliver standing there with a confused expression on his face. I doubt it's because I was laughing in a place that's normally somber. But because my grandmother was also laughing. Something she never does.

"The press conference will be starting soon."

"Of course." My grandmother starts to stand. I jump to my feet, helping her up and offering her my arm.

If Oliver finds our behavior odd, he doesn't mention it. If anything, I notice a hint of a smile on his face as he escorts us through the palace.

Just before we enter my father's office, my grandmother stops me.

"I'd like to do more of this."

"What?" I lean toward her, dropping my voice. "Swear?"

"No." She rolls her eyes. "Well, maybe." She winks. "But this." She gestures between us. "Spend time with you. Get to know you. Do you…" She hesitates, a hint of vulnerability in her expression. It's a strange look, considering I once thought nothing scared her. "Do you think we can do that?"

I give her a wide smile. "I'd love to."

As we step into my father's office and both Anderson and my father rush to hug me, my grandmother joining us, it feels like I have what I've wanted since I learned my uncle died all those years ago.

I finally have a real family again.

CHAPTER FORTY

Creed

My heavy eyelids flutter open, a bright light greeting me, temporarily blinding me. I absent-mindedly wonder if this is heaven. If someone upstairs deemed me a good enough human to deserve a spot up here. I've tried to live a decent life. I've made mistakes. Who hasn't? But I'm not a horrible person.

When my eyes fall on Esme curled up in a chair, peacefulness radiating from her gentle features, I'm convinced I must be in heaven.

At least my own personal heaven.

Maybe that's what heaven is. My heaven isn't the same as someone else's. It's different for everyone, some supreme being rewarding us for a life well spent with what makes us happiest.

There's no doubt in my mind that the sight of Esme in a pair of yoga pants, oversized t-shirt, her mussed-up hair on the top of her head in a messy bun makes me happy.

At the same time, I wonder if maybe this is hell.

The idea of never being able to touch Esme again, never feel her lips on mine, is a punishment worse than hell.

"Esme," I whisper weakly, my throat raw and voice strained.

She snaps her head my way, wide eyes meeting mine. In a heartbeat, she's on her feet, rushing to sit in a chair beside my bed. She grabs my hand, the warmth of her skin making me curse my luck even more.

This *must* be hell.

Any minute, Esme's going to disappear and I'll be tortured with a new memory. A new reminder of what I can no longer have.

"Hey, baby," she chokes out, producing a glass of water from somewhere and lifting a straw to my lips. I sip, the cool liquid putting out the fire in my mouth and throat.

"I'm sorry I died on you," I say, my vision still hazy.

Everything except for Esme. She's the beacon of light in my murky surroundings.

"Only you would apologize for dying." She shakes her head, her laughter like a beautiful melody I could listen to over and over again. She uses her t-shirt to wipe the tears from her cheeks. "You're not dead, Creed."

"I'm not?"

She smiles, an air of relief about her.

As she curves toward me, more and more of the cloud hanging over me seems to dissipate, things becoming clearer.

"If you were dead, would you feel this?" She moves closer, her lips a breath away, remaining just out of reach.

But I need to feel her. Need her kiss. Need to know she's real and not just some cruel joke I'll be forced to suffer for all eternity.

"Feel what?" I murmur.

"This."

She touches her lips to mine, and a current shoots through me, cutting through the last bit of fog, making me realize I am alive. That Silas didn't kill me.

That we both survived.

"See? You wouldn't have felt that if you were dead," she says with a smirk. "Now would you?"

"I can't be too sure. Maybe you should kiss me again." I waggle my brows. "Make sure I really *did* feel it."

A smile lights up her face, making her even more beautiful, something I didn't think possible. "Gladly."

She leans toward me again, pressing her mouth more firmly against mine. She swipes her tongue against the seam of my lips, and I open for her, sighing at the sweet taste of her. But she ends the kiss too soon, making me hungry for more.

I'll always be hungry for more of her.

"How about that one?" she asks, lips pinched into a flirtatious grin.

"I think I felt it. Maybe one more, just to be sure."

She laughs, a low throaty sound that sends a thrill through me. "Fiend."

"For you, always."

"Always," she repeats breathlessly, gradually lowering her lips back to mine.

Her kiss is slow, her mouth moving unhurriedly against mine. I bring my hand to her cheek, relishing in the feel of her skin.

"I'm alive," I murmur once she pulls away.

She squeezes her eyes shut. "You're alive."

Something in the way she says it makes me think it's just as much an affirmation for her as it is for me, a reminder that she didn't lose me, even after everything we endured.

Now that the fog from whatever drugs I'm on has cleared, everything comes rushing back. From learning Jameson had been killed, to Silas pointing his weapon at Esme and a shot going off, making me fear the worst, only to learn my father had managed to drag himself to our aid.

"My dad," I say frantically, eyes searching her for any clue as to what happened to him. We'd finally turned a corner. Finally reconciled after years of never getting along. I can't stomach the idea that he didn't make it. "Is he—"

"He's fine." Esme rests a soothing hand on my arm. "In fact, I should probably go tell him you're awake." She stands from her chair. "I'm sure he'll—"

I grab her wrist, stopping her from leaving. "Not yet. I…" I trail off, trying to collect my thoughts.

When I thought I was dying, there were so many things I wanted to tell her. But I knew I didn't have much time, so instead, I stuck with what I thought was most important. And that was telling her I loved her, despite my actions.

But this is my second chance.

I'm not going to fuck this one up.

I need to tell her everything I wanted to days ago.

"I should have kissed you at the party," I declare, my voice unwavering.

She returns to her chair, and I can see my reflection in her glassy green eyes.

How many tears has she cried for me since I almost died?

How long has she been sitting in this room, waiting for me to wake up?

How can I possibly earn her forgiveness?

I'm not sure I deserve it. Not sure I deserve *her*.

But I'm going to spend the rest of my life proving to her that I do.

"I shouldn't have put you in that position," she interjects

through the audible lump in her throat. "I knew how important retiring with honor was to you. I—"

"But I never should have done anything to make you doubt me. Make you doubt my love. I never should have put my career first. It's what my father did and made me resent him. What I swore I'd never do. I'm sorry it took almost dying for me to finally wake up and realize I was making the same mistake. That I was being a daft fool."

Nodding, she licks her lips, seeming to process what I can only describe as a lackluster apology. But it's all I have.

"You know what they say, don't you?"

"What's that?" I ask, hope brimming in my eyes.

She flashes a smile I feel deep in my soul. "Admitting you're a daft fool is the first step to recovery."

I laugh, a sharp pain throbbing in my side. I reach for it out of instinct, finding a bandage covering my lower left abdomen.

"Sorry." She grimaces. "I didn't mean to make you laugh."

"It's okay. The pain reminds me I'm alive," I say through gritted teeth, taking several deep breaths to work through the ache. Once it becomes much more tolerable, I meet her eyes. "But maybe we refrain from jokes for now. At least until my stitches are out."

"I can do that."

"Good." I reach for her, cupping her cheek once more, the atmosphere shifting from playful to serene. "From now on, I promise to kiss you anytime you want. I love you, Esme."

"And I love you." She skims her lips against the corner of my mouth, and I close my eyes, basking in her devotion. "Today." She moves to the other side. "Tomorrow."

"Always," I murmur, pulling her toward me just as the door swings open.

Esme quickly straightens as a nurse enters the room.

"I figured you were awake since your readout showed your heart rate increasing." She looks up from her tablet, noticing Esme beside me for the first time. "Unless there was something else making your heart rate go up a bit." She waggles her brows.

"I…" Esme begins.

"Don't worry," the nurse assures her with a wink. "Your secret's safe with me. Although, I will admit I've been rooting for the two of you ever since you took that bullet for her. It's better than the stuff in my romance novels."

"No need," I say, grabbing Esme's hand and meeting her eyes. "No more secrets."

Her face lights up. "No more secrets."

"No secrets," the nurse interjects. "Duly noted. Now, let's see how we're doing, Mr. Lawson. How's your pain?"

"I don't think I'll be running a marathon anytime soon, that's for sure. I'm not too proud to admit I'm pretty bloody sore. I wouldn't mind something to help."

She types a few things on her tablet, then meets my eyes. "Well, you've come to the right place. We've got the good stuff here. But first, I need to do a quick exam. Check your incision to make sure we're not getting infected."

"I'll give you some privacy." Esme stands. "I could use a shower anyway. I haven't had one since yesterday morning." She makes her way to the door.

"Hey, Esme?"

"Yes?" She meets my eyes.

"Where was it?"

She furrows her brow. "Where was what?"

"The recording. You made it sound like Silas would never find it."

"And he wouldn't. At least, I'm pretty sure he wouldn't."

"Why? Where did you put it?"

A blush blooms on her cheeks as she steals a brief glance at the nurse before meeting my gaze. "You remember that… gift you gave me before you went to the States with Anderson this last time?"

I nod, lips curling into a devious grin from the memory of all the fun we had with that little gift.

"There's a little compartment in it to store the charging cable. Which also happens to be enough space to hide a small flash drive."

I throw my head back and laugh again, not even caring about the pain that radiates through me. Who would have guessed that a sex toy would end up protecting the truth?

"You're right. Archer definitely wouldn't have known to look there. Hell, I doubt he would have known what it was."

Esme beams. "Probably not." She holds my gaze for another beat, then opens the door.

"Esme?" I call out once more.

She glances over her shoulder.

"Will you come back?"

She smiles, a peaceful expression washing over her face. "Always."

CHAPTER FORTY-ONE

Esme

"**A**re you sure you're up for this?" I ask Creed, checking my reflection in the mirror as I sit in front of the vanity in the primary suite of his townhouse. "It's only been three weeks. You can take some more time to heal."

He emerges from the bathroom, a towel wrapped low around his waist, his scar prominent against his previously unmarred skin.

But it's not nearly as bad as it was three weeks ago.

Every day, he gets a little better.

And every day, his scar heals a little more.

It'll never go away completely. He'll always have it as a permanent reminder that he almost died. But it will also serve as a permanent reminder that he survived.

"You heard what the doctor said," he reminds me.

"I did." I spin around in my chair as he approaches, droplets of water still visible on his skin, his dark hair damp from the shower. "He said you need to take it easy."

"He also said it's okay for me to resume some normal activities." He waggles his brows, yanking me to my feet. "I can think of a few activities I'd love to resume with you." He buries his head in the crook of my neck, his unshaven jawline scraping against my skin.

I whimper at the combination of his lips and teeth nipping and tasting me. What I wouldn't give to push him onto his bed and lose myself in him. Feel his body on every inch of mine.

But his doctor was quite clear on this matter.

"Remember your doctor's orders," I tease. "No strenuous abdominal workouts for at least two months. As he reminded you, sex is an abdominal workout."

He groans. "This is going to be the longest two months of my life." He pulls back, cupping my cheek. "I just want to be with you."

"You *are* with me."

He narrows his gaze. "You know what I mean."

"I do."

I can physically feel his frustration. I'm suffering through it myself. Sure, we've fooled around a little, especially in the past few days as his pain became more tolerable. But him using one of my toys on me or watching as I get myself off isn't the same. I miss that connection. Miss showing him how much I crave him.

"I'll tell you what." I give him a sultry smile. "I'll help you relieve some of this…pressure." My hand grazes the taut muscles along his chest before traveling down his body, coming to rest on the edge of his towel. I tug gently and his erection springs free. "But you have to promise me something."

He licks his lips, his Adam's apple bobbing up and down. "What's that?"

His breathing quickens as I slowly push him backward across the room, carefully lowering him onto the bed. Then I pull the sash from my robe, allowing it to fall to the floor before crawling beside him, the space between us radiating with electricity and anticipation.

"Don't," I begin, covering his mouth with mine before snaking down his body. "Move." I drag my lips down his chest and stomach, brushing a kiss to his scar. Then I straddle his legs, wrapping my hand around his erection. Our eyes meet as I dart out my tongue and circle the tip. "A muscle."

I part my lips, about to take him in my mouth.

But before I do, I look his way once more. "Do you promise?"

"Fuck yes, I do."

"Good." Then I wrap my mouth around him.

"I don't know for sure, but I think this is a first," Creed remarks an hour later as I re-apply my makeup in the back seat of the SUV, driven by my new CPO, Captain Charlie Porter. He was one of Archie's top guys, and the one he trusted most.

Like Archie was the one Adam trusted most.

I only hope I have better luck with Charlie. Something tells me I will, especially now that Silas and Kane Kingsley are dead. And Henry Gates is sitting in a prison cell, having been apprehended trying to flee the country.

At first, I hated the idea that he was still alive, considering all the lives he took, including his own son's, a truth that came out when the woman who pointed the finger at Creed came clean and said Henry Gates threatened to deport her and her family if she didn't cooperate. But the more I thought about it, the more I realized that death would have been too humane a punishment for Henry Gates. He deserves to rot in prison with none of the luxuries he grew accustomed to, all financed by the blood of his victims.

"What's that?" I rub my lips together to help spread my lipstick around more evenly.

Creed leans into me, his voice a sinful whisper as he says, "A member of the royal family being late for an official function because she was sucking cock."

I flash him a devious smile. "I didn't hear you complaining at the time. In fact, from the sound of things, you were quite enjoying it."

His pupils dilate. "Oh, I was, princess." He grabs my hand, lifting it to his lips. "I absolutely was." He presses a soft kiss to my knuckles.

I still find myself looking over my shoulder, worried about who might see us.

Worried Creed could lose everything if anyone learned the truth.

Not anymore, though. Creed's now free to be with me, having signed his discharge papers the day he was released from the hospital. In fact, it was the first thing he did, heading straight to the palace instead of his house.

Even though there's nothing preventing us from going public with our relationship, we haven't had a reason to, since Creed's spent the last few weeks resting at home. And I've been more than happy to play nurse.

I think Creed's been more than happy for me to play nurse, too.

Still, we haven't needed to think about the next step in our relationship.

Now that we're about to attend a public event together

— a ceremony honoring Archie, Creed, and his father for their actions in saving my life — it's something we need to think about.

Hell, it's probably something we should have thought about before we were only a few minutes away from the palace.

"I just want you to know that we don't have to do this," I tell him.

"I told you before. I feel fine. I'm getting stronger every day. I can stand for a few minutes."

I shake my head. "Not the ceremony." I lean closer, dropping my voice. "Us. Going public. You're still recuperating from your injuries. And your doctor recommended limiting stress. As you know by now, nothing about being with me is easy. Nothing about being with me ever *will* be easy." I grab his hand, linking his fingers with mine. "So if you want some time for it to just be us before letting in the rest of the world, I'm okay with that. All of this will be an adjustment. I don't want you to feel like you have to declare your intentions for the world to see, despite what my actions at Anderson's party may have led you to believe. I know you love me. That you want to be with me. That's enough for me. I—"

Before I can finish my thought, the SUV comes to a stop, and the door opens, one of the valets holding out his hand for me.

"We can wait," I tell Creed, then take the valet's hand, allowing him to help me out.

The second I emerge from the car, cameras flash, reporters and photographers fighting for my attention.

"Princess Esme! Just a word."

"Over here, Your Highness!"

"How are you feeling, Your Highness?"

"Hey, Esme!"

At the sound of the last voice, I freeze in my steps, slowly turning around to see Creed standing mere feet behind me. His dark eyes burn into mine with a searing intensity, stealing all the breath from my lungs.

"Yes?" I swallow hard, my pulse steadily increasing.

The determination in his gaze as he stalks toward me is electrifying, nothing about his movement showing even a hint of the pain that still plagues him.

"I'm ready now," he thunders, his declaration ringing in the air.

Before I have a chance to utter a single syllable, his lips are on mine, consuming and possessive. The sound of camera shutters becomes more incessant, the numerous flashes going off nearly blinding from the dozens of photographers capturing our kiss.

But he doesn't stop.

If anything, he kisses me harder. Deeper. Greedier.

Leaving no question in anyone's mind who we are to each other.

When he tears away, I take a few seconds to catch my breath, trying to put out the inferno raging inside me from this man's kiss.

"Creed, I—"

"I've been waiting twenty years to finally be able to kiss you whenever and wherever I want." He frames my face in his strong hands, not allowing me to escape whatever he's about to tell me. "Do you honestly think I was going to want to wait another bloody second?"

"I don't want you to think that I'm pressuring you to do something you're not ready for. I don't want you to think I only want to be with you in public. I don't. I—"

"Don't you remember what I told you in the hospital?"

"What's that?"

He curves toward me. "That I promise to always kiss you, no matter where we are."

"Well, then..." I purr, slipping an arm around his neck. "Why don't you kiss me again?"

"Gladly..." He moves his hand to my lower back, lips hovering over mine. "Princess."

Then he kisses me again.

The first kiss of the rest of our lives.

And it's just as incredible as he promised it would be.

CHAPTER FORTY-TWO

Creed

The soothing sound of ocean waves sweeping onto shore surrounds me as I stare at the starry sky, the moon shining brightly. It brings back memories of all the times I'd sit in the back yard with Adam and we'd look at the stars, making up our own constellations based on shapes we thought we saw.

Now, it's something I do with AJ whenever he spends the night at my place. I may not be his father, but I did help raise him. So this past year, AJ's been spending a few nights a month with me, which has allowed Rory a chance to have a social life.

And date.

Last time I spoke to her, which was just a few days ago, things with the new man in her life are going quite well, to the point they're considering moving in together.

In a new place with no connection to the past.

I think both Rory and AJ are looking forward to starting

this new chapter. I couldn't be happier for them, especially since this time last year, Rory thought Hayes Barlow was not only dead but had killed her fiancé. Now they're about to move in together.

It just shows how unpredictable life can be.

Once Hayes' name was officially cleared from any and all wrongdoing, we began spending time together. Probably because I was the only friend he had left. Or maybe I was the only friend he was interested in having, since I was the only one who believed him. And because of all the time I spent with him, Rory got to know the man he really is.

At first, they both tried to deny it. But as I learned from my relationship with Esme, you can only deny your feelings for so long until you reach your breaking point. And Rory and Hayes certainly reached theirs.

"You know, there's no need to sneak around at four in the morning anymore."

When I hear Esme's voice, I turn toward her, my heart expanding in my chest as my eyes fall on her. It doesn't matter that she's one of the most powerful and influential people in the entire country. She looks like the girl next door in her tiny shorts, loose t-shirt, and messy bun.

And it doesn't look like her power in this country will be taken away anytime soon.

Even after the truth about the disgraced King Theodore came out, the people of this country still supported the royal family, so much so that the referendum to turn the monarch into a ceremonial role failed miserably. I think most people liked the reminder that they're just like the rest of us with their own problems.

There once was a time when being relatable was frowned upon in the monarchy. Now, they've embraced it. Along with a completely new royal household to support a new way of doing things.

"What can I say?" I approach her, looping an arm around her waist and tugging her against me. "Old habits are hard to break."

She hoists herself onto her toes, lips brushing mine. "And you're one habit I have no intention of breaking anytime soon. Or ever."

"Me, neither." I move my mouth against hers, our tongues briefly tangling. "Come on. I've got a surprise for you." I grab her hand, pulling her away from the beach villa and toward the sandy path we used to walk together every morning all those summers ago so we could have a few private moments to ourselves.

Despite all the heartache we endured, they're some of my favorite memories. I've always loved Esme. But in those quiet moments when she didn't have to pretend to be someone she wasn't, I truly fell in love with her.

And now that we're free to be together, I fall in love with her a little more every day. She gives me a *reason* to fall in love with her a little more every day.

I love her generous spirit, as demonstrated by how much she strives to constantly give back to those in need.

I love her quick wit and sharp tongue, always keeping me on my toes.

And I love her relentless nature, as evidenced by how hard she worked to finally get her community restaurant off the ground.

What once was her dream has now become mine, too. I may not be as good of a chef as Esme, but I'm in that kitchen every day, even when she's not, coordinating all the volunteers that have shown up to either help or as payment for receiving a meal.

Initially, I wasn't sure what I wanted to do after I retired from the guard.

Now, I couldn't imagine doing anything else.

Plus, my doctor essentially forbade me from doing anything that required any sort of strenuous physical effort. I wouldn't want to, anyway. I put my life on the line every day for eighteen years. I've more than paid my dues.

Time to enjoy my pseudo-retirement.

I keep my fingers linked with Esme's as we stroll toward our secret spot, listening as she attempts to guess whatever her surprise is.

But I have a feeling she never will.

At least, I hope she won't.

"Can you at least give me a clue as to what it is?" she asks after several unsuccessful guesses.

"You do know we're only a few minutes away." I shoot back. "You'll find out soon enough."

"But you know how I get."

I chuckle. "That I do."

This past December was our first Christmas together. And I realized just how horrible Esme is around presents.

Maybe because she hadn't had a real Christmas in years, if ever. I was thrilled to finally give her one, complete with a tree we cut down and decorated together, and presents I wrapped by hand and placed under the tree, all for her.

At first, I had no idea what to get for a woman who could buy anything she wanted. Who has an entire vault of priceless jewels.

But Esme doesn't care about the price tag. Only the sentiment behind the gift.

It didn't stop her from shaking each present to try to figure out what was inside, though.

"You're worse than AJ was when he was a toddler."

"I know, but—"

As we round the bend and the elephant boneyard comes into view, she stops in her tracks, eyes going wide at the sight of dozens of tiny candles flickering in the pre-dawn night, a blanket already set up in our usual spot with a bottle of champagne chilling in a bucket.

"What is all of this? I thought we were just going to watch the sunrise."

"We are." I link my hand with hers, my pulse quickening with every step I take toward the blanket.

I've been in hundreds of dangerous situations. Yet I've never been more petrified than I am at this very moment.

Licking my lips, I face her, grabbing both her hands. "Do you know what today is?"

"Besides Sunday?"

"Yes. Besides Sunday."

She pinches her lips together in contemplation. "Is it the one-month anniversary of the first time I popped a zit in front of you?"

I shake my head, my chuckles echoing in the air. Being with Esme fully and openly has helped me see her in a completely different light. Has shown me sides of her I never knew existed. Because I wasn't allowed to know them before.

But now I'm able to see all the facets that make up this amazing, frustrating woman, and I love them all, even her imperfections.

Especially her imperfections.

"Not that, but you can feel free to pop your zits in front of me anytime."

"Good to know. Is it the anniversary of the first time we got an invitation addressed to both of us, like a real couple?"

"Another good guess, but not quite."

She takes a few moments, the wheels turning in her head.

Then she inhales a sharp breath. "I've got it. And this time I know I'm right. It's the six-month anniversary of when you made me your emergency contact on your passport."

"Again… No."

She huffs out a breath. "Well, I'm out of ideas here, so why don't you just tell me."

"Okay." I adjust my stance, meeting her gaze that's alight from the candles. "It's the one-year anniversary of the night you asked me to kiss you, and I turned you down."

"Oh." Her shoulders fall as she frowns. "I didn't… Well, it's not a day I like to celebrate."

"It's not a day I'd typically celebrate, either. Which is why I want to replace that memory with a better one. I don't always want to remember it as the day I almost lost you for good. That I chose my job over you." I squeeze her hands, my heart rate kicking up. "I want to remember it as the day that I chose you. And I hope to god, you choose me," I manage to say through the lump in my throat.

Before she can ask what I'm doing, I drop to one knee and reach into the pocket of my cargo shorts. When I pull out a tiny velvet box and flip it open, revealing a sparkling diamond ring, she gasps, hand flying to her mouth as tears well behind her eyelids.

"I don't have a lot to offer you, Esme. I don't come from a certain upbringing. Don't have a trust fund. Hell, I've never even gone to college. But despite all of that, despite the fact that we are as opposite as two people can be, there's no doubt in my mind that we belong together.

"For the longest time, I wasn't sure if I'd ever get married. Wasn't sure I deserved to be happy enough with someone to take that step. But I want that with you. I want to wake up next to you every morning. I want to fall asleep beside you every night. I want to celebrate ridiculous anniversaries, like farting and zit popping."

She laughs through her tears, swiping at her cheeks.

"And I want to spend every day of the rest of my life loving you. In private. And in public. No matter where we go, I want people to physically feel the love we share. Because I fucking love you, Esme Louisa Victoria Grace Wellingston. And I'd be honored if you would marry me. Let me love you today. Tomorrow. And always."

She blinks back her tears, struggling to get her emotions under control. After several seconds that feel like an eternity, she's finally composed enough to nod her head and squeak out, "Yes."

"Yes?" I repeat, taking the ring out of the box and bringing it up to her finger.

"Yes, Creed. I'll marry you. Today, tomorrow, and always."

I slide the ring on her finger, then jump to my feet, lips hovering over hers. "Always," I murmur.

She cups my cheek, the diamond on her ring sparkling in the moonlight. "Always."

Thank you for reading *Broken Crown!* I hope you enjoyed the conclusion to Esme and Creed's story.

Want one last taste of Creed and Esme? Then sign up for my mailing list to get a bonus chapter. Just click the link or scan the code below.

https://www.tkleighauthor.com/broken-crown-signup

If you'd like more of these characters, be sure to check out Nora and Anderson's story in Royal Games!

https://www.tkleighauthor.com/t-k-s-books/royal-games

Thank you so much for taking the time to read this book. If you enjoyed it, please let your friends know by leaving a review so more people can fall in love with Creed and Esme.

ROYAL GAMES

Since the day I was born, my life's been planned for me.
When you're heir apparent to the crown, you don't have
much choice about your future. I made my peace with that
years ago.

Or so I thought.

Until I learn I may not have as long of a future as I originally
believed.

So I do what most people do when forced to come to terms
with their own mortality. I take a road trip.

I'm not sure what I hope to find along the way.

I certainly didn't expect to find her.

I should walk away. We don't just live in two different coun-
tries. We come from two different worlds. Not to mention,
she doesn't even know who I am.

Or, more appropriately, *what* I am.

But I can't ignore this strange connection I feel toward her, as if I knew her in another life.

Until I realize I *did* know her in another life, one I hoped to leave in my past.

When she learns the truth of who I am and what I've done, will she be able to look beyond that and see the man beneath the crown? Or will I forever be punished for what I am?

Scan above or type the address into your web browser to grab your copy.

https://www.tkleighauthor.com/t-k-s-books/royal-games

ACKNOWLEDGMENTS

Thank you so much for following me on this journey with Creed and Esme. Writing a book, especially a trilogy like this is always a time-consuming endeavor, and it definitely takes a village. So I'd like to take a minute to thank my amazing village.

First and foremost, a huge thanks to my husband, Stan, and my daughter, Harper Leigh. I couldn't do this without their support.

To my wonderful PA, Melissa Crump — you're a rockstar, babe. Love you!

To my fantastic beta readers — Lin, Melissa, Sylvia, Stacy, and Vicky — thanks for always reading for me and offering feedback.

To my admin team — Melissa and Vicky. Thanks for keeping my reader group and page running. Love you ladies!

To my review team — Thank you for always not only reading my books but also taking the time to write reviews. Your support means the world to me.

To my reader group — Thanks for being my super-fans

and giving me a place to go when I need a break from writing.

And last but not least, a big thank you to YOU! My amazing readers. I'm so grateful for your support. Whether this was your first book or mine or your thirty-first, I'm truly grateful for your support.

Can't wait to share even more stories with you very soon.

Love & Peace,
~ T.K.

ABOUT THE AUTHOR

T.K. Leigh is a *USA Today* Bestselling author of romance ranging from fun and flirty to sexy and suspenseful.

Originally from New England, she now resides just outside of Raleigh with her husband, beautiful daughter, rescued special needs dog, and three cats. When she's not writing, she can be found training for her next marathon or chasing her daughter around the house.

facebook.com/tkleighauthor

instagram.com/tkleigh

tiktok.com/@tkleigh

bookbub.com/authors/t-k-leigh

pinterest.com/tkleighauthor